Shortlisted for the **Governor-General's Award for Fiction**, the **Ethel Wilson Fiction Prize** and the **Danuta Gleed Award for Best First Work of Fiction**.

"At once ruthlessly precise with her descriptions and generous to her characters, Fleming makes a bracing, truthful debut with these 13 stories." — *Publishers Weekly*

"When you find yourself reading slower and slower toward the end of a book because you don't want it to end, you know the book's a good one. Fleming's evenhanded, sharp-eyed and often hilarious narratives traverse the frenzied chaos of urban life with ease and precision ... In a well-constructed landscape of language and story, Fleming reminds us that, paradoxically, it's the differences we really share with one another." — Sheri-D Wilson in *The Georgia Straight*

"In vivid, complex, character-driven stories, Fleming explores the underside of the Canadian Dream and peels back layers of deceit ... Fleming jumps into the skin of each character and pulls the reader into their world." — *Vancouver Sun*

"I laughed; I cried. It's a cliché but it's true. No angst here. Just a clear-eyed view of life from women and men, young and old, gay and straight ... Fleming has a voice of her own, much like two other writers of the same generation, British Columbia's Eden Robinson and Toronto's André Alexis." — Victoria *Times-Colonist*

"*Pool-Hopping* is witty and chock o'block with TV generation references, but never at the expense of a nuanced narrative. The stories resonate for anyone who's suffered through Brownies, punk bands or mean-assed sleepovers. But they're also laced with stark expressions of humanity, care, and pain." — *Loop Magazine*

"All 13 stories in this first collection testify to Fleming's faith in the power of narrative. Although there is no lack of physical action — suicide, physical and sexual assault, car crashes — it is the act of storytelling which is the stronger force ... [It] functions as a weapon of retaliation and as a balm for the wounded." — *Malahat Review*is

Pool-Hopping

and Other Stories

o o o

ANNE FLEMING

Polestar Book Publishers acknowledges the ongoing support of The Canada Council, the British Columbia Ministry of Small Business, Tourism and Culture, and the Department of Canadian Heritage.

Cover design by Val Speidel.
Cover photograph by T. Vine/Tony Stone Images
Printed and bound in Canada.

The following stories have previously been published in slightly different form: "Conkers" in *This Magazine*; "The Glare of Something Bigger" in *Event*; "Pool-Hopping" in *The New Quarterly*; "Clap" (now called "You Would Know What To Do") in *Prairie Fire*; "The Middle of Infinity" in *Vital Signs* (Oberon Press, 1997) and "The Defining Moments of My Life" in *Prism International*.

Library of Congress: 98-88272

Canadian Cataloguing in Publication Data
    Fleming, Anne, 1964-
    Pool-hopping
    ISBN 1-896095-18-6
    I. Title.
    PS8561.L44Y68 1998   C813'.54   C98-910616-0
    PR9199.3.F562Y68 1998

POLESTAR BOOK PUBLISHERS
P.O. Box 5238, Station B
Victoria, British Columbia
Canada   V8R 6N4
http://mypage.direct.ca/p/polestar/

In the United States:
Polestar Book Publishers
P.O. Box 468
Custer, WA
USA   98240-0468

Thanks to Zsuzsi Gartner, Murray Logan, Peter Eastwood, Shannon Stewart, Anna Nobile, Linda Svendsen, Pat Fleming and Cindy Holmes for acute and varied commentary on the stories. Thanks also to The Banff Centre for the Arts Writing Studio, the Creative Writing Department at UBC and Polestar Book Publishers for their support.

Pool-Hopping

and Other Stories

For my mother, Patricia Fleming.

The Defining Moments of My Life

A Chronology in Two Parts

Part One: The Defining Moments of My Life as Envisioned by My Mother When Pregnant With Me

1.

I am, like David Copperfield and most other people real and imagined, born. This event occasions my mother enough pain and struggle to be worthy of the word "labour," but not so much that she begins to believe my entry into the world will be her exit.

During these difficult but ultimately meaningful five or six hours — eight at the outside — her husband frets with worry in the waiting room, absently ripping the petals off the flowers he bought in the first giddy half-hour, and whose stems he snapped soon thereafter from too much anxious clenching.

He is not disappointed in the least to learn his first child is a girl.

2.

I am an attractive baby, even as a newborn, with enormous eyes and long lashes. All the nurses love me on first sight. I breastfeed easily and happily.

3.

Eight weeks later, my christening takes place in St. Clement's Anglican Church. I wear the slightly yellow but still gorgeous lace gown that my mother's grandmother tatted by hand for her first child's christening and that has seen eight christenings since. My father holds me proudly by the baptismal font. After handing me to the priest, he coughs in a weak attempt to mask his deep emotion and rubs his strangely watery eye with his knuckles. My mother takes his hand. She, too, bites back tears. Afterwards they have a fabulous luncheon at which no one gets drunk and everyone coos appreciatively at me and my mother.

We are pretty as a picture. She does not leak breast milk onto her best dress, the blue silk. I smile.

4.

I am an easy baby, gurgling happily in my crib. Each stage described in the baby books I enter into promptly and exactly. At X days, my eyes focus past ten inches and I display an interest in the mobile above my crib. At Y months, I roll over. At Z, I begin to crawl.

All this while, my mother is utterly absorbed in me, and so, when he hurries home each night from his job with the great future, is my father.

5.

At two, I chatter away animatedly and am almost completely toilet trained. My father gets a promotion. When they learn the happy news that my mother is again pregnant, they put a down payment on a house in Moore Park. We are nicely ensconced there by the time my mother gives birth, even less painfully than to me, to my little brother, on whom we all dote, me included, in my clumsy toddling way.

6.

I have a happy childhood, which consists of:
a) An easy adjustment to school after making shy and clinging

to my mother's skirts when she delivered me on the first day;

b) A cute and unshakeable conviction at age six that I will marry Timmy Mills, the adorable blue-eyed first-born of my mother's best friend, Peg;

c) Well-attended birthday parties, creative Hallowe'en costumes sewn by my mother, fun family Christmases at which no one passes out or kicks the dog, and many other seasonal festivities;

d) Skating lessons, swimming lessons, piano lessons, ballet, tap, and lessons at anything else I happen to be good at;

e) Sunday school; and perhaps

f) One sorrow: the death, in old age, of my grandfather. My grandmother lives till she is at least ninety, or whenever my mother can conceive of losing her.

7.

I get my period. Of course my mother has lovingly explained my entrance into womanhood before the sacred event. I embrace my womanhood with bashful pleasure, feeling closer than ever to the woman who brought me into the world. I turn to her with the difficult questions in my life, like how to let a boy know you like him without going too far, and how to get blood stains out of underwear.

8.

a) I continue to be attractive, as my brother also turns out to be. We are popular and have lots of friends. Mother makes us a nutritious lunch each day.

b) I go on my first date.

c) I have my first boyfriend.

9.

I get the lead in the high school play, preferably *West Side Story*.

~~10.~~
~~I have my first abortion.~~

Sorry. 10.
I am valedictorian and give a moving speech, thanking my parents for their support.

11.
I go to university on a scholarship I don't need.

12, 13, 14.
I have a brilliant career as well as a brilliant marriage, and several children as adorable as I was.

And so on.

o o o

Part Two: The Defining Moments of My Life as Seen by Me

1.
I am not, if you go by Shakespeare's way of thinking, born. I am untimely ripped from my mother's womb via C-section. (I always did think that was a bit of a plot cheat — one may be untimely ripped, but one is still of woman born.) Before the decision to open my mother up, labour is a monstrously painful and long process, and I hear about it often, every time I am deemed an ungrateful child.

2.
I am a startlingly ugly baby, with a big swath of coarse black hair down the middle of my head and onto my low brow, and a bumpy red rash over my entire face. The effect is not unlike that of a black-haired pig we see some years later at the Royal Winter Fair scratching its flaky skin against the door of the stall.

The hair falls out, the rash goes away, and I am still none too pretty. I cry almost constantly. It drives my mother to distraction and causes my father to yell at my mother to shut me up, he needs his sleep, whereupon he storms out of the house in a rage swearing he'll sleep in his office, which he may or may not do. This is what he does when my brother, though not biologically related, takes after me in the vocal cord department.

3.
One of my earliest memories — I will call it my first — is of a geranium on the kitchen table. Just that. The geranium — red and green on the pale grey table, lit up by a small patch of sunlight — and the sound of traffic outside. Apparently I pulled all the petals off this geranium, in fact off any flowers I came in contact with, but I don't remember that. I remember it whole, in the sunlight.

4.
My other early memory is of playing with the nap of the beige carpet under the ironing board as my mother works above me. The iron hisses across spritzed shirts. The air smells of seared starch. And then there are spots on the carpet under the place where my mother is no longer standing. Putting my finger in the biggest spot, inches across, I lick it to make sure it is what I think it is. Yes. I am a wound-sucker; I know that metallic taste and I love it. It's the taste of me, my cut finger or knee or lip. The same taste coming from someone else makes me feel funny.

5.
My adopted brother arrives. He has black hair and brown skin and hollers all the time. I can't believe I ever hollered that much or that loudly, though I am told repeatedly it is true.

6.
I have a childhood in which:
a) I hate my clothes. My mother makes them or gets them passed down from her sister's daughters. I lobby for hand-me-downs from my boy cousins, to no avail. The clothes are cute skirt-and-top outfits or cute patterned pant-and-top outfits.
   One weekend at my cousins' I steal Jeff's red-and-yellow

striped shirt. I'd take his blue corduroys too, but I'm afraid my greed would reveal me. I start carrying the shirt with me in a plastic bag and change wherever I can, in friends' garages or in the bushes in the park.

Seeing myself in a mirror at school, I realize the shirt doesn't do much to change the overall effect. I am still wearing a brown skirt with gingham appliqué mushrooms.

I continue to wear the shirt anyway until a close call with my mother wanting to know what's in the bag forces me to stow it in my hiding spot in the park. The next day I discover it half-burnt, sodden, and unrecoverable. I cry.

b) Timmy Mills calls me and my brother ugly. This follows on my mother telling me gleefully and regularly — every time we see an infant, in fact, cute or ugly — that I was an ugly baby.

She has told me I look cute in various outfits. More accurately, she has said that outfits look cute on me. "It's a pretty little outfit, isn't it?" she will say. "You look sweet in it." She has not said that I am pretty. Not that I want to be. Handsome suits me better. But for the first time I notice my mother makes a distinction between me and my clothes. She herself is pretty, as my father is handsome. I have heard my mother say to her friends, joking, "We get by on our looks." I look like my father, and the effect is not pretty.

My brother is only five, and too little for me to have thought much about his looks. Sometimes, when people ask, I say our father is a Cree Indian and that we spend summers on the trapline. You don't look Indian, they say, and sometimes I say, *You better sleep lightly cause you never know when an Indian is sneaking up on you, and you never know what we'll do either, because we're dangerous.*

"Yeah," my brother will say.

c) I realize words can have unexpected consequences.

My brother Danny, though almost four years younger, is a good companion. He is game for almost anything. He can keep up, he never whines or complains or tells on me and my friends when we smoke in the park and light fires, burning mitts and hats lost under the snow in winter, or other articles of clothing that we find. (I am on the lookout for boys' shirts, but mostly we find underwear and socks and wonder how their owners came to leave such things behind.)

But he has nightmares, my brother. Our father says he is too old to sleep with his parents, so when he wakes up in terror he comes to me, the person who put the seed of fear in him in the first place.

He dreams his real father has come to kill him in his bed.

7.

I get my period when I am ten. Not expecting this for a couple of years at least, Mom has not yet given me her Soon You Will Be a Woman speech, but I know what's going on. I don't think I'm bleeding to death with some mysterious disease. I know what menstruation is. I have read my friend Elaine's copy of *Are You There God? It's Me, Margaret.*

There's an unofficial club of girls who have read this book. They whisper and giggle and make like they have a superior knowledge of the world. A friend of my mother who has a daughter a couple of years older than me says she doesn't care what the school board thinks, this book is a true representation of girlhood and should be on the curriculum. She has started a petition.

I do not like the book. If it is a true representation of girlhood, then I am not a true girl. All of Margaret's friends look forward to getting their periods and are happy when it arrives. There is talk of small amounts of rusty-brown blood in the underwear.

The blood in my underwear has never been rusty brown, not even on the very first day. It is brilliant red. There is lots of it. I am always getting up in the middle of the night to find I've bled through my nightie onto the sheets again and have to scrub them out with cold water. I learn to sleep a light, uncomfortable sleep on my side.

I stain things: car seats, couches, swings. At school I work on ways to casually lean over so I can check between my legs for blood. I perfect a light probing gesture down the back of my pants to check for wetness as I get up, but several times I notice people notice.

My mother is not a big help. After giving me her modified, My God, You're a Woman Too Early talk, she provides me with a box of pads and the instruction never to use hot water on a blood stain. She seems to blame my inability to manage my period on my general inadequacy at being female rather than on a startlingly heavy flow. Not that she says anything; it's just these looks she gives. She claims to have a heavy flow herself, so I assume that she must be right, that there is some innate girl thing, some tidiness and cleanliness gene that I simply don't have.

It's not until I'm fourteen that I figure out that I can stick a second pad to the back of my underwear at night to catch the flow. Finally I can lie on my back and get a few nights' rest, but it's no help during the day.

I determine to use tampons. I open a box of Kotex snuck from my mother's bathroom. They look like white bullets on sticks. I crouch over the toilet and try to insert one. It feels like a white bullet on a stick. I push. I swear. Push. Wince. Pull it out. Dump. Flush. Pull another tampon from the package. Reread the instructions, noting the approximate angle of insertion. Try the foot-on-the-bathtub method. Adopt a speedier plunge. Am pleased with the success of this. Put my foot down. Try to walk around the bathroom.

I finish the whole box and hope Mom is not having her period. The next day I go to the drug store and buy a box each of Kotex, O.B. and Tampax. It costs my entire allowance. I manage to insert a Tampax.

It lasts three-quarters of an hour.

8.

The same friend of my mother who championed *Are You There God? It's Me, Margaret*, gives my mother *The Diary of Anaïs Nin* for her fortieth birthday. She has inscribed it: "Here's to spotted G's." I read it after my mother is finished. It is not as racy as I expect, but there are bits I read over and over. With my door closed and my hand between my legs.

9.

At seventeen, I win a part in *West Side Story*. I am the tomboy, always trying to get into the gang and always getting ridiculed and kicked around instead. My character's name, interestingly, is "Anybody's."

My mother is appalled. She knows I could not possibly be Maria, but she thought maybe a chorus girl, maybe even Bernardo's girlfriend, or Riff's. Anybody but Anybody's.

The girl who plays Maria, who I've always thought was a flirty snot, turns out to be okay. Her name is Sara, and while she waits for her scenes she drinks coffee and does the *New York Times* crossword puzzle, which I've never heard of before. The first time I meet her she asks me for an eight-letter word for crazy. "Um," I say. She is a year older than me. She's sitting with Colin Vogl, who I know from track. He does javelin. He is Officer Krupke in the show. I keep saying "Um," because I can see she is in the process of writing me off and I don't want to be written off. I can't think of a single word for crazy except mad, which of course is five letters short.

"Cracked," says Colin.

"That's only seven," she says after a pause.

"Demented," I say, my mind suddenly unleashed. "Deranged, insane, nuts, cuckoo, off your rocker, loopy, lunatic, unhinged, bats."

"Unhinged," she says. "Thank you."

We begin to give each other vocabulary tests we get out of *Reader's Digest*. We score well. When we don't do the crossword, we smoke drugs in the parking lot, me, Sara and Colin, who supplies the weed. Getting high is not the point of this exercise, at least not for me, because I don't, not at first. The point is Sara and Colin and me. Maria, Officer Krupke and Anybody's. Or, as we soon become to each other, Santa Maria (being a Christian icon cracks Sara up because she's Jewish —

the irony is not lost on us that so was the original Mary), just plain Krupke, and Buddy. Me.

10! 10! Let's Sing A Song About 10.
I get high for the first time. Sara and Krupke and I lie in the middle of the football field after smoking up behind the dumpsters, and for the first time I really feel it. The clouds are stupendous. "I love you guys," we all say. Other times we say it like fakey-fakey actor types, "Oh, I just love all of you guys," blowing kisses, but this time we say it like we mean it. We sit up and put our backs together, leaning in a circle. Sara holds my hand. "I feel pretty," Krupke hums. Sara and I take his hands. We get up and skip around in a mockery of an interpretive dance circle, singing the song. I realize that Krupke is gay.

11.
Timmy Mills is paralyzed after plowing his mother's car into a telephone pole on the big hill on Mount Pleasant south of St. Clair.

12.
My brother gets busted for shoplifting a water pistol at the variety store. I used to steal Dubble Bubble from there by bending down and putting them in my socks. The one time I got caught, the guy put me in the bathroom for five min-utes, saying he was going to call my parents, but then let me go after I blubbered like an idiot and swore I'd never steal again. On my brother he calls the cops.

My father picks my brother up by the shoulders and shakes him. Danny scrunches up his eyes and kicks as hard as he can. He gets Dad in the hip and the thigh and when he almost hits the groin, Dad slams him into the wall and lets go. Danny howls.

My father has previously thrown plates full of food, dented the fridge with his fist, torn the door off its hinges, and smashed my mother's antique dining room chair, but he has never hit my mother or me. Or my brother. "Don't you ever hit him again," my mother says and then tells him to get out. I am amazed that he does. He comes back sometime while we are asleep because he's there the next morning. When he apologizes to us at breakfast, we don't look at him.

13.

I cut my hair for the performance of the play, though the Home Ec teacher doing costumes has said, "Just tuck it up under a cap, dear. No need to go too far."

My parents freak. "You look like a boy," my mother says.

"I'm supposed to look like a boy," I say.

"You're supposed to look like a girl trying to look like a boy."

"A facsimile," my father agrees, "not the thing itself."

"What can you do?" I say, shrugging. "What's cut is cut."

"Are you being flip with me?"

"I'm just saying what is."

My father paces a few steps away and adopts a considering tone. "She's just saying what is. She's just — saying — what — is. Does she actually know what is?" He paces back, looking at the floor, finger to his chin. "Does she? No, I don't think so. Should I tell her? Is she old enough to know what is? Or should I tell her if she takes this play too seriously, she won't be taking it at all? That her career in drama is hanging by a thread?"

He looks me up and down to see if I am quivering or not, to see if he's got me. He has. He says, "Get out of my sight. You look obscene."

"Talk about a career in drama," Sara says of my father when I tell her about this the next day.

My brother comes and sits on my bed while I cry and plays with his Rubik's cube. "I like it," he says. "I think you look good."

13.5

My father steps up his scrutiny of my appearance, leaving for work only after he has seen what I'm wearing each morning.

Of course I am careful to look like a girl. I wear earrings and bangle bracelets and high-waisted pleated pants. I even wear blouses, though it pains me emotionally and the shoulders are too tight.

He does not come to the play itself, which is fine with me. My mother comes with my brother and Peg Mills, who hasn't gone out much since Tim's accident. Mom is teary-eyed afterwards — it is, after all, her favourite musical and the one she starred in when she was in high school. She hugs me. She hugs Sara. "You were great," she says. "You were all just terrific. Oh, does it take me back, though!" She hums a bar from "I Feel Pretty" and takes a couple of waltz steps. "Oh!" she says, wiping tears from her eyes.

After the opening night pop-and-chips party in the drama room, a bunch of us go to the Morrissey on Yonge Street, a bar famous for not asking for ID. The strategy is to mix up the younger-looking people with the older-looking ones. I wait nervously in line with Sara, who has fake ID, and Krupke, who's looked old enough to drink since he was fourteen. Except that I start debating the relative merits of successive Dr. Who's (I'm a Tom Baker fan, myself) with Winston Yeung, and Sara, who played her part like a star, is now being mobbed like a star, so by the time they get to the door I have fallen far behind them. The bouncer lets them in. He lets Winston in. He lets everyone in. Except me and the boy who plays Baby John. Baby Bob, we call him.

"Nice try, boys," he says, laughing. "Come back when your beard starts to grow."

Sara and Krupke don't see what's happening. Baby Bob and I turn away without looking at one another, sensing that each other's eyes are too full to bear being seen. We put our hands in our pockets and head up the street toward the subway. I walk slowly, hoping that Sara and Krupke will come after me.

"He thought you were a guy, eh?" says Baby Bob. I shrug. "That's so weird. You don't look like a guy to me." Oh no, I think.

Baby Bob drapes his arm across my shoulders. I twist away from him so it falls off and pick up my pace. I immediately sense that I've hurt him more than if I'd just said, "Don't, Bob." Other girls, the ones with the girl genes, would have known that ahead of time. Thankfully we take different routes at the subway station.

On the way home I take my childhood shortcut through schoolgrounds and backyards, darting like Anybody's from shadow to shadow.

13.67

There is a long line-up for the bathroom at the closing night party, and Sara comes in with me. "It won't make the wait any shorter," I say. I close my eyes while peeing, and the room spins a bit. It has just hit me that evening that I only have another month of Sara and Krupke — three at the most — before they go away to university. Next year they won't be here. Next year they will forget about me, their little high school friend.

No, no, they have said between tokes. Never, they have said.

Sara idly flashes the light on and off in the bathroom, then leaves it off. Streetlight comes in through the frosted glass. She pees, saying, "Help me up," when she's done, though she doesn't need it.

She hangs onto my arms. She looks into my eyes. My stomach is full of happy bumblebees tumbling all over one another. She kisses me. This is exactly what I've wanted since the first day I met her, though knowing it is news to me. I kiss her back.

People start pounding on the door. "Let's get out of here," Sara says, pulling up her underwear.

Though tempted, we don't ditch Krupke. He is now as maudlin as I was earlier, only about the jock who takes him for "rides" after school but won't otherwise talk to him. We climb the fence into the cemetery and spend the rest of the night communing with the dead and dodging security. A couple of times Krupke turns to find us holding hands, whereupon we take his as well.

13.99
My mother is in the kitchen waiting for me when I get home.
I expect an earful. More than an earful. I get it, but a different kind than the one I was expecting. It turns out I am not
the only one who did not come home last night.

"Good!" says my brother when he hears the news. "I hope
he never comes home."

14.
My father returns the next afternoon and sleeps for two days
before checking himself into rehab at Homewood.

15.
Sara and I skip school and go to Toronto Island. We stop for
crusty rolls and shaved salami from Poko's Deli. In the line-
up we stand close enough that our clothes touch. It is unbelievable. The bees inside me zoom around in wild abandon.
We stop again for kiwis and a bag of Oreos at Dominion. In
this line-up, I read *The National Enquirer* over her shoulder.
Her hair is against my cheek, the front of my left shoulder is
against her back. I have never been so aware of a few square
inches of skin. If you gave me a pen today, I could draw you
an exact outline.

Because it's the middle of the day, we are able to find an
unpopulated section of beach near Hanlon's Point. We eat our
lunch. We talk. Sara, who is never shy about anything as far
as I can tell, is suddenly shy. We lie in the sun with our sides
touching. She turns over on her stomach and puts her arm
across me. I stroke her hand. I lift it to my mouth and kiss it.
I kiss each knuckle, each nail, the pad of each finger, the palm.
I want to kiss the whole rest of her, but I don't know where to
start; I don't know how this is done. Luckily, she does.

She has her hand up my shirt when movement down the
beach makes us hurl ourselves apart. A Doberman trots up to
us, a friendly one who licks our hands. We laugh at ourselves.
Just a dog. We sit up, waiting for its owner. Our hands touch
where we support ourselves on the sand.

The owner appears. "Gorgeous day, eh?" he says and looks out over the water. "Sure would be nice to be sailing." I make the mistake of agreeing.

He tells us he used to have a sailboat but had to sell it when he got divorced. Sara runs her hand over mine. He tells us what kind of boat it was, and what kind he wants for his next boat. Sara's fingers make the hairs on the back of my hand stand up. He tells us he got the dog 'cause he was lonely. Her fingers run over my wrist, up my forearm. Cinnamon is the dog's name. Cinnamon Girl, from the Neil Young song.

"Go away, go away, go away," Sara starts chanting without moving her lips.

"Well," he nods to Cinnamon, "my girl's waiting on me. You have a nice day now."

"You too."

"Ha," says Sara when they're out of sight. She rolls on top of me. Her weight is splendid. Her tongue is as liquidy-thick and inevitable as molten lava and almost as hot. Her hands are acrobats. This is it, I think. This is it.

15^{∞}

I have my first non-self-induced orgasm, there on the beach at Hanlon's Point, sometime around 2:30 on a perfect day in June.

$15^{\infty+1}$

We get to know Toronto's parks by night, all the wonderful, dark, out-of-the-way pockets where two bodies will fit together.

(n-2)

Sara goes to Trent. We write a lot of letters. "My bodacious beautiful Buddy Budski," Sara writes. "When are you coming to visit?"

I did it. I TOLD my roommate about us. I was very nervous but pretty sure she'd be cool about it, and she was. Her parents — the ones who called her

Rainbow, natch — have lots of gay and lesbian friends, in fact, her two godmothers are lovers. Whoa. I told her about your godmother, the Anglican nun who sends you crucifix jewellery every birthday. What's her name again? Anyway, slight contrast. So I'm liking her a lot — Rain, that is, not Aunt God — and she says it's no problem, she'd be happy to find a place to crash whenever you come to visit. "YOU-MUST-COME, YOU-MUST-COME" (said like the Daleks on Dr. Who, "EX-TERM-EE-NATE, EX-TERM-EE-NATE"). I'm sorry you are so bored and lonely. Of course, if you came here and visited me, you wouldn't be, n'est-ce pas? Mais non. Pas solitaire. Tout ensemble encore. So come, okay? Next weekend? Oh, except I forgot, you have some family do then, don't you. So the one after. I have to go to my appallingly simplistic Canadian Geography course now with the patronizing prof. I think I should drop it. Except it's a prerequisite for things I do want to take. Argh.

Love you more than Barney loves Fred. No, I mean Lucy loves Ethel. I mean just a heck of a lot. Your Santa Maria ("Oy, these blue robes, they weigh a girl down!").

(P.S. A "nullipara" is: A. an empty subset in Venn mathematics; B. a meaningless comment; C. a woman who has never borne a child; or D. a ciliated micro-organism.)

I am not able to go to Trent until the end of October. Hallowe'en. This is because my father wants weekends to be "family time" now, so he can think he's making reparations for the damage he's done and is turning us into a loving and supportive family who will help each other (i.e. him) through this difficult time and all other difficult times to come.

I would like for Sara and myself to spend our first weekend together since the summer closeted in her room, reading, talking, doing crossword puzzles, kissing, touching. Sex would be nice, too, but it's Sara's touch I've been missing more than anything. Just her hand running through my hair or across my back.

But there's this Hallowe'en party she and Rainbow don't want to miss, it's going to be great, they're going as Starsky and Hutch. As lovers. "I mean, the subtext was always there, wasn't it?" Rainbow says.

Sure, but what am I supposed to go as? The car? The bad guy?

"You could be the girlfriend we're not interested in," Rain says. When I don't laugh she says, "Kidding. It's so nice to meet you finally. I feel like I know you."

Rainbow came with Sara to meet me at the bus station and has not left us alone since. I don't know yet whether I like her or not. If I hadn't met her through Sara, I almost certainly would. Whether she likes me, I can't really tell.

All fall I have been writing to Sara about how worried I am about my brother because he doesn't want to do anything anymore, how he hardly talks at all, even to me. He eats. He sleeps. He listens to music in his room.

I've been writing to Sara about my father and how in some ways he's worse now, if only because he's around more. He comes home after work and hovers over us, watching everything we do. He tells us how we're not doing it right, whatever it is, math, chopping the beans, cleaning the bathroom. He tells my brother he can give him extra help in school since my brother seems to need it, which of course he doesn't and only confirms what my brother suspects, that my father thinks he is stupid because he's an Indian.

I have written about how hard all this is on my mother and how she seems to take it out on me.

Sara should know I'm not in the mood for a party with a bunch of yahoos I don't know drinking their faces off.

"Can't we go as Pete, Linc and Julie?" I ask. Rainbow has blonde hair not unlike Peggy Lipton's.

"Where would we get an Afro wig in the next two hours?" Rain says.

I lie back on Sara's bed. I think I might cry. Hallowe'en is like New Year's Eve. You have to either get right into it or ignore it, and I have never been able to do either.

"Let me look in my Tickle Trunk," Rain says. Maybe I do like her. She stands on a chair and rummages through the top shelf in her cupboard. "Cowboy hat. You could be Stan the Man from Alberta." She tosses the hat down. "Pig nose. You want to be Miss Piggy? A little mascara, flouncy dress?"

Sara laughs.

"Okay, maybe not. Little old lady? World War One flying ace? Colonel Klink?"

The party is at another residence in a big hall. We go late-ish, after drinking beer in our room with Marcus, another costumeless friend of Sara and Rain. Marcus wears the cowboy hat. "Marcus. Cowboy. They're just two words I never thought I'd hear in the same sentence," he says. He practises introducing himself on the way over. "Hi, I'm Marcus. I'm a cowboy. Yup, Cowboy Marcus, that's my name."

He asks me how I'm going to introduce myself. "I'm not," I say, turning up my jacket collar. "I'm too cool to introduce myself."

Sara has dressed me as James Dean, starting with a tensor bandage wrapped around my chest so my breasts don't show, then an undershirt to hide the bandage, and then a white T-shirt. Jeans. A red bandana. A bomber jacket. She has gelled back my hair and got me to bite my lips to redden them. I look in the mirror. I like what I see. It's not James Dean, but I like it. It's Bud.

Starsky and Hutch are all over each other all night. Predict-ably, I guess. That's what they said they were going to do. I doubt it occurs to anyone but me that they aren't just two straight girls having some fun at the expense of fags and a seventies TV show. I think even they think they are just play-ing. They get a good reaction.

And then a drunk boy dressed as Hitler says, "Starsky?

Starsky? Vat kind uff a name iss Starsky?" and I think that Sara is going to rip his face off or at least knee him in the balls. I start forward, but Rain has already got him spun around and is remarkably smoothly, as if she'd done this before, handcuffing him with the toy cuffs she bought. (She tells me later she and her sister spent countless afternoons practising this. They didn't have a TV, so they acted out their favourite shows instead.) Sara rips the paper swastika off Hitler-boy's sleeve.

"Hey, hey, hey," he says. "It was only a joke."

"You're an asshole, Matt," a big guy dressed as Julius Caesar says.

"Yeah, yeah, okay, I'm an asshole," he says. "Sorry."

"Go home, Matt."

"Okay, okay," he says and wanders off, still handcuffed.

I put my hand on Sara's back and ask her if she wants to go. "No, I don't want to go, I'm not going to let some sophomoric prick ruin my night."

But then she cries. I hold her, glad it's me and not Rain, thinking it's significant it's me and not Rain, that I still have the right to be the one to hold her when she cries.

Back in the room Rain gets out her guitar and we sing songs; we sing "Will the Circle Be Unbroken" in three-part harmony, and it feels like it used to feel with Sara and Krupke, like we all love each other and it will always stay that way. We pull the beds together and sleep with Sara in the middle.

(n-1)

On the bus on the way home I look out the window at all the bare trees in the wind out there on November 1. I see a big-framed skinny dog trotting down the shoulder like he had a purpose. I think I'd like to be a dog going somewhere in the rain. I remember the lonely guy on the beach, calling his dog Cinnamon Girl, how pathetic I thought it was — *I could be happy the rest of my life with a Cinnamon Girl* — how Sara and I made fun of him afterwards. How I kinda liked him.

Anomaly

On the first Sunday after Labour Day, Mr. Riggs divvied up the roast strings, crisp with fat, between his two daughters.

"No one can accuse Lawrence Park Church of giving up on its young people. They want guitars instead of organs? They want jeans instead of grey flannels?" A slender pink roll of beef fell away from his knife. "By all means! By all means!" He repositioned the bone-handled carving fork with a neat jab. "Let them mob the altar in their peasant get-ups. Let them hammer out freedom…"

"Woo-oo," his son said into his napkin. Mr. Riggs gave no sign of hearing.

"Let them hammer out justice." Another pink slice nestled into the pile heaping up on the platter. Glynnis, salivating, was glad she had the roast strings to suck on. She wondered when her father was going to stop.

"Let them hammer out the love between their brothers and their sisters."

"Aw-awl over this land," said James. Their father eyed him sternly for a moment, then went on.

"One Sunday a month. What can it hurt?" He swung a broad smile around the table to each of his children. He gave them an even broader wink. His aren't-I-a-fun-with-it-kind-of-Dad wink. His isn't-your-mother-an-old-stick-in-the-mud wink.

He waited for them to smile back. Glynnis concentrated on the roast strings. James played with the fall harvest centre-piece. It was Carol, eager to please, who popped him a wet-lipped grin. He slipped her another piece of crisp fat.

What their mother had said to bring on tonight's mono-logue was that she hardly felt like she'd been to church at all. It was a neutral statement, not a judgment. If it did stray to the critical, it was only to say, This will take some getting used to, this love and flowers and Jesus on a first-name basis.

For Glynnis, the opposite was true. She had felt more than ever like she was in church, watching the teenagers up there singing, beating their tambourines, tossing their long hair. She was more aware of the hand-me-downs she wore — a stiff baby-blue frock and white leotards with the crotch halfway down her thighs and shiny shoes with buckles that dug into her feet.

"Next week can we wear jeans?" she asked.

"You don't have jeans," her mother said.

"We could go to Thrifty's."

"One more time and that radio goes."

"It's *my* radio," said Carol.

"Pants, then."

"If your mother wants you to look decent at church, you'll look decent at church," their father said. "This drop-in cen-tre for the young teens, this 'Odd Spot,'" he went on. "Now, there's a solid idea. Off the streets. Away from drugs. You give them a place to fool around and work off their energy, give them a young guy to get them talking, and you give them a chance to go right in the world, to grow up to be the men they were meant to be."

Men? Glynnis thought.

Glynnis loved the Odd Spot. She loved how the youth worker talked over her head about Vietnam and Quebec and com-munism when nobody showed up to the rap sessions, and taught her to do back flips off the stage onto the gym mat.

She liked to be able to say at school, "Oh, yeah, the other day at the Odd Spot…" She liked the way other seven year olds admired the casual authority with which she spoke about this hangout for thirteen and fourteen year olds.

So it was with longing that she passed the ground floor rooms of the Odd Spot on her way into the first Brownie session the following week. Her throat was dry. It was a hot September afternoon, as hot as June but not so humid, and she was dying for a Lola. She had her weekly dues — her Fairy Gold — in her brand-new little Brownie purse. If it weren't for two things, she would be sucking on that pyramid of frozen syrup right this minute. The main thing was that getting in trouble with Brown Owl was no regular matter of getting in trouble, but doubled at least, or quadrupled, because of who Brown Owl was: Mrs. Riggs herself. Pretending to go to the washroom and ducking into the Odd Spot instead to buy a Lola with the Fairy Gold her mother had given her moments ago — a plan she was half-formulating on the way in — would not wash. It would take too long, and besides, Glynnis was on her best behaviour.

Today was Glynnis' first day as a Brownie. A year ago, on Carol's first day, Glynnis had been consumed with envy. For as long as she'd been coming to Brownies with her mother — as long as she could remember — Glynnis had wanted her own uniform, two neat rows of badges sewn down the arm, a white scarf with orange maple leaves knotted neatly at her throat. She'd been convinced that if only her mother would advocate on her behalf, the Girl Guide Organization of Canada would give her a test proving what exceptional Brownie material they were letting slip by for lack of a single year of life and would grant her special advance-Brownie status. Today, in Carol's old uniform, cinched in where it was loose with her new Brownie belt, Glynnis didn't much care.

Nonetheless, Glynnis was acting particularly helpful. This was not because she aspired to the heights of virtue, but because she knew she would get in big trouble later in the day and hoped to soften the blow with advance good behaviour.

She knew it would have little or no effect, and in fact might have the reverse effect of proving that she knew she'd been bad and was trying to shirk her just punishment, but she couldn't help herself.

Lawrence Park Church had two gyms, a smaller one upstairs and the large one down. The downstairs gym had a kitchen attached to it, a large modern kitchen to service the father-son and mother-daughter banquets held each year, and all the church dinners and pancake breakfasts. Going from the kitchen to the upstairs gym was a dumbwaiter. They must have been optimistic, those post-war church architects, anticipating churchgoing crowds of a size to fill both gyms. During the sixties and into the early seventies they were not far off. With the Odd Spot and the youth group, Scouts and Cubs, Guides and Brownies, the UCW and the bible group, the place was in use every afternoon and evening. Tuesday afternoons it was Cubs downstairs, and Brownies up.

The church saw enough use that the gym floors were refinished every second summer. This year, the upright piano had been shuffled about in the process so that it blocked the cupboard under the stage where the Brownie equipment — the mirror pond and electric campfire and cardboard toadstools — was kept. Mrs. Riggs, Glynnis and Carol set to pushing it out of the way.

The piano was on castors that, when they deigned to roll at all, crunched, groaned and squeaked in succession. One spot in their revolution — the groan — was particularly sticky and required a good heave each time they came to it. Where Carol halfheartedly leaned against the piano as if pushing a shopping cart, Glynnis threw her weight into it like a Roman slave in a quarry Christianly heaving a chunk of granite off her sworn enemy. Who happened, today, to take the form of Carol's teacher, Mrs. Harris.

"Come on, girls, one more good shove," said Mrs. Riggs. Crippled, but grateful for her life, Mrs. Harris would realize how wrong she'd been about Glynnis. She'd kiss her feet, gratitude oozing from every pore. Except the thought of Mrs.

Harris actually kissing her feet, that thick face with its pursy lips bent over her nether appendages, was not a pretty one. Glynnis fell back for a moment to regather her strength, then pushed again from the bottom of her toes.

The castors crunched and started to groan. She felt that sudden euphoria that comes with knowing you're using the whole strength of your body and using it well. Just as she was swelling into the heart of this euphoria, feeling with each step the line of her body go from bent leg, coiled spring, to full extension, spring uncoiled, the far castors snapped off and the piano lurched suddenly away, then screeched to a halt as the remaining metal stubs dug into the newly refinished floor. The hammers crashed in great ringing discord against the strings, and Glynnis slammed into the piano face-first. She biffed it with the heel of her hand. Stupid piano. Stringing her along, letting her push her guts out, when the whole time it sat there waiting for the right moment to prove it could move perfectly well on its own. After hitting it she felt better, and she noticed that the after-hum of the piano strings made a satisfyingly ethereal sound. If she hadn't been on her best behaviour, she would've made a peace sign with her fingers and said, "Ooo, psych-a-*del*-ic!"

o o o

What Glynnis was going to get in trouble for was something she did not think was wrong.

She had been planning, for show and tell that day, to take the Beefeater doll her mother had brought back from England that summer, to talk about the Beefeaters and the Tower of London and executions and the princes in the tower. But the night before show and tell, Camper Barbie had knocked the Beefeater's head off playing kung fu fighting.

It had been a glitch, headlessness, but it seemed to be a rectifiable one. All she needed was a paper clip to fish out the elastic inside the body and snap it over the hook that stuck out of the lower end of the head.

"Glynn-is!" Her mother called her to set the table.

She rummaged in the drawers of the desk she shared with Carol. Carol's drawers were neat and tidy, which made it easy to see there were no paper clips. Glynnis' drawer was crammed to the top.

"I'm not asking you again," called her mother.

"I'm coming," Glynnis yelled.

Glynnis turned the drawer over on her bed and spread out the contents like Hallowe'en candy. So many things she'd forgotten she had. A broken watch found in the park. One Labatt's IPA beer cap amid a whole box of Blue and Export caps. A set of Snoopy pencils. A crochet hook? She didn't know where it came from, but it would certainly do the trick.

Carol marched into the room. She had two walks — a bobbing, long-strided one when she was happy or she felt in charge, and a slouching shuffle when she felt sad or put-upon. Today it was the bob. "Mom says if you're not downstairs in less than a minute, your TV privileges are suspended for a week." She turned smartly on her heel and bobbed two steps, swinging her arms, before bobbing right onto the Beefeater's head, smashing it into plastic shards.

Carol. "Clumsy Carol," as their father had taken to calling her lately. That week she'd already broken a good china tea-cup, a lamp and the towel rack in the bathroom. Now it was the Beefeater's head.

"I'm telling," Glynnis said.

"Go ahead. It's your fault for leaving it on the floor, any-way."

"Fine." Glynnis started for the door. "Mom!" She pitched her voice loud enough to sound like she meant it, but not loud enough for her mother to hear.

Carol caved in. "Don't! Please, Glynn? Pretty please? I'll... I'll...give you my allowance."

At dinner, Mrs. Riggs asked if Glynnis was ready for show and tell.

"Of course," Glynnis said. She was annoyed at the tone in

her mother's voice that implied she expected her not to be, and at the look that followed, implying she did not believe her when she said she was. Glynnis didn't have to rehearse everything the way Carol did. If she knew what she was talking about, she could make it up on the spot, which she did now.

"This is a Beefeater doll." Glynnis held up the imaginary doll. "The Beefeaters were guards at the Tower of London that was a prison. They're called Beefeaters because they ate beef when not everybody had enough money to eat it. The Tower of London is where Henry the Eighth's wives were kept before they were beheaded, about which there is a song that goes, 'With 'er 'ead tucked underneath 'er arm she walked the bloody tower.' It's also where the princes in the tower were kept, who were heirs to the throne, but they were put there by Richard the Third who was their uncle and who people think killed them."

"Well!" her mother said, beaming. "I *am* impressed."

There was not much to be impressed about, but Glynnis accepted the praise anyway. History was her brother's hobby, British history in particular. He could recite kings and queens for days. When they were younger they'd pretended he was Richard the Third and Carol and Glynnis the princes. They had also pretended that he was Henry the Eighth and they were his wives. Glynnis had loved being the feisty Anne Boleyn laying her head on the chopping block. Dying could be just fine if you knew ahead of time you'd get to carry your head around in your hands and haunt people.

After dinner, Glynnis wanted to put Camper Barbie's head on the Beefeater, but Barbie was Carol's and Carol wouldn't let her since it would involve cutting off Barbie's hair to make the Beefeater hat fit over top of it. They tried stuffing her hair under the hat, but it wouldn't stay on and it looked stupid with an elastic holding it in place.

And then it occurred to Glynnis — what she could take instead.

"Carol," Glynnis said to her class the next morning, pointing her sister out with a wave of outstretched palms like the ladies on *The Price is Right* showing off a fridge, "is a genetic anomaly. She is an albino."

Glynnis liked both these words. Anomaly. Albino. Albino she knew already. "Anomaly" came from the talk their father had given them the week before, trying to convince Carol she was neither adopted nor a foundling. Their father's talk ran to red- and white-eyed fruit flies, and the girls did not entirely understand it. Glynnis wished that she were the albino. She wanted something that special to recommend her.

"Anomaly" was not in the *Random House Children's Dictionary*, which was the classroom's main reference work, so Glynnis had to explain it. Except now that she was put on the spot, with the whole class waiting and the teacher smiling at her, she was at a loss.

"It means…" She couldn't say "special." Special was not quite it. She couldn't say "weird" either, because Carol was sensitive.

"It means like…" She knew what it meant. It was a scientific word, a scientific weirdness, which was not the same as regular weirdness. "You know, like…"

And then she had to wonder if she did know what it meant, since the test of knowing was being able to say, and she couldn't. She hated when this happened to her. How do you describe in *other* words what a word already says all by itself?

"An irregular occurrence?" suggested the teacher gently.

"Yeah," she said.

A snicker came from the back of the class, and she hurried on to explain what pigmentation was, and how Carol had none, which made her skin and eyes extremely sensitive — in fact, she was legally blind. The class was rapt again. Glynnis went on about how a lot of mammals had albinos — rabbits and rats and mice — and how albino pigs had no sense of smell because it was the pigment in their nasal receptors that made them work. This had also been part of their father's talk.

Carol stood by, with a small smile now, her eyes blinking behind the bulbous lenses of her pink plastic glasses. Being slightly on the pudgy side, and having an air of squishiness about her, Carol resembled nothing so much as the Pillsbury Dough Boy — albeit with bottle-bottom glasses. Their brother had been the first to notice this, and Carol had been flattered enough that she had perfected the Dough Boy's giggle. As her finale for the morning, Glynnis poked her sister's stomach and out came that bashful titter. Carol was a hit.

But when Glynnis caught up with her on the way home that afternoon, Carol was crying. She cried a lot these days. Before Glynnis could even ask what was wrong, Carol swung her Loblaws bag at her.

"Everybody hates me, and it's all your fault," she said. Her lower lip looked extra-pink turned out like that, and her glasses started to fog up from her tears.

Glynnis got an ugly feeling in the pit of her stomach. "Is not," she said.

"Is too. Everybody knows you used me, and they all think it's terrible. You were just using me for your stupid baby show and tell."

"No I wasn't."

"Yes you were. Even my teacher thinks so, and she's going to phone Mom and tell her what you did."

She would, too. Mrs. Harris had hated Glynnis ever since she'd caught her pulling down Kevin Money's pants to prove he didn't wear underwear. Mrs. Harris had pegged Glynnis then and forever as a bully.

Carol and Glynnis had to go straight home to change before going to the church to set up for Brownies before everyone else arrived. Glynnis dragged her feet. Maybe Mrs. Harris had already phoned. But Mrs. Riggs was in brisk good spirits and did not even scold them for being late.

o o o

"Rowena, honey, are you all right? I heard a terrific noise coming up the stairs, it was like an elephant with hayfever. Oh my god, the piano? Well, what were you doing, pushing it all by yourself? At least no one was hurt. My luck I'd have been lying on top, singing 'Am I Blue.' I'd have toppled right off and spilt my martini." This was Mrs. MacDonald, the unlikely best friend of Glynnis' mother, and the mother of Glynnis' best friend, Sandy. Also the mother of Carol's former best friend, Alison, who Mrs. MacDonald pushed forward now. "Alison? Don't you have something for Carol?"

Alison MacDonald had short curly blonde hair and a chipped front tooth from falling off their garage last year. The MacDonald kids were known for being bad. Sandy was the exception. One older brother had been arrested for possession of marijuana. Another had been sent to private school in an attempt to straighten him out. The oldest girl had run away from home at sixteen and had lived with a man in his thirties for almost a year before she came home.

Glynnis missed Alison coming over to play with Carol. Alison always wanted to *do* stuff. "Let's go climb the willows and spit on people in the park," she'd say. Or, "Let's go to the ravine and pretend we're lost and we have to live off the land." Glynnis and Carol were not supposed to go to the ravine at all, day or night. Alison had brought adventure into their lives.

Now Alison handed Carol an envelope without looking at her. "Here," she said. "It's an invitation to my sleepover."

"She forgot to give it to her at school today. What will you forget next? Your feet? Your teeth? Your fingernails?"

"Maw-awm." Alison shrugged her mother away from her.

"They're all attached," said Sandy, laughing. "She can't forget them."

Alison sighed impatiently.

"All right, all right, I'm going. Good luck, Rowena. I don't know how you do it, all these girls. You're a saint."

"Pshaw," said Mrs. Riggs. She had a seemingly endless store of expressions nobody else used.

A pink look of pleasure had spread across Carol's face when Alison gave her the invitation, even though Alison had clearly not forgotten to give it to her but was being forced to by her mother. Glynnis looked away.

That night, without being asked, Glynnis set the table, cleared it, chopped the beans, washed the lettuce and pared the carrots. After dinner, she got right to work on her project on caves, down in the basement, thumbing the 1930 encyclopedia set they were allowed to cut things from. Stalactites hung from the ceiling, stalagmites came up from the ground. "That's the spirit," Mrs. Riggs said, meaning the Baden-Powell spirit.

By nine o'clock, up in the kitchen eating the snack she was allowed because Mrs. Riggs was in a good mood, Glynnis started to think she was home-free, that her good deeds had paid off a cosmic dividend and Mrs. Harris had decided not to call after all. Precisely at that moment the phone rang.

Glynnis was marched straight upstairs to Mrs. Riggs' bathroom, where she was smacked five times with the back of a hairbrush. Then she was held in a vice-grip on both shoulders facing her mother.

"You," Mrs. Riggs said, "are a deceitful little show-off."

Glynnis turned hot all over. Her palms sweated, her neck itched, her eyes stung as if she had gotten insect repellent in them.

"I'm embarassed and ashamed. Now I want you to tell me what it is that you did wrong."

It was like walking through a maze of prickle bushes blindfolded, this enforced confession. You edged up one avenue, hands out like a sleepwalker, wincing at the dead ends, sidestepping and trying again. You ended up saying things you didn't believe. Glynnis still did not feel she'd done anything

particularly bad, but now she had to guess all of what her
mother would think was bad about it, and tell her. And then
her mother would think that she'd known all along it was bad
and that she was malicious as well as deceitful and selfish. She
also had to look at her mother through all of this, look her in
the eyes. That was what the hands on the shoulders were for,
to keep her from turning away. But Glynnis found when she
looked into her mother's eyes she could not say anything at
all. She started to shake and cry. Her mother let go and waited
for her to finish crying. "I can wait all night if I need to," she
said.

"I should have told you...I...I...broke the Beefeater's
head."

"And?"

"I shouldn't have taken Carol to show and tell."

"Why?"

"I don't know."

"Yes, you do."

"Kevin Money took his sister."

"She was an infant, it will not affect her life. Now, why?"

"It's not my fault Carol has no friends."

"Glynnis Riggs, stop this right now and tell me the truth."

"But she..." Glynnis was still sniffling, and she felt a sob
surge up her throat. She tightened her jaw muscles and nar-
rowed her eyes, trying to keep it down. She tried to swallow
it, but it was too big to swallow. It washed out of her like a
wave hitting the shore.

"All right, then, if you can't control yourself, I'll leave you
alone to think of your sister and what you've done to her. You
can come downstairs when you're ready to tell me why it was
wrong."

Her mother left, closing the door behind her. Glynnis felt
the unfairness in her muscles and the guilt in her glands, below her ears, behind her jaw. She sat on the floor and wrapped
her arms around her knees.

Unfair: Carol hadn't minded at first. *Carol* broke the
Beefeater. Glynnis had not told on Carol. Carol should

learn to be proud of being different. Carol *had* been proud, up there, doing the Pillsbury Dough Boy. *Glynnis'* teacher never said anything about it. *Glynnis'* teacher never said it was mean or that she was using Carol. She wrapped her knees tight, squeezed her feet together, and rocked forward and back.

Guilt: She shouldn't have been playing kung fu with the Beefeater. Or Camper Barbie. She shouldn't have told her mother she was taking the Beefeater when she wasn't. She'd lied.

She unfurled herself slowly and pulled at the fringes of the red oval bathmat, braiding them. Time passed, she had no idea how much. Her mother's voice outside the door said, "Glynnis, I'm waiting." Her wet innards were hardening like limestone into stalactites.

At Brownies her mother said to new girls who stared or giggled at Carol, *Carol is an ordinary girl like you. I won't have her stared at...* Glynnis could feel it starting to come, what she would say. When she could repeat it again and again in her head, she went downstairs.

Her mother sat at her desk looking over pattern books. "I should not have taken Carol for show and tell because she is not a sideshow attraction, she is an ordinary girl like anybody else."

"And?"

"I shouldn't have lied."

"And?"

More. There was more.

"Did it make you feel important showing off your sister?"

"I shouldn't have used my sister to make myself feel important." Glynnis felt like she was going to cry again. She concentrated on her calcified innards.

"That's better. See? You did know, if only you'd thought about it. It's very important to me that when you are punished, you understand why you are being punished. It does no good to slap a child and not tell him why."

This had happened to Mrs. Riggs as a child, she'd often told

Glynnis, slaps with no explanations, and she'd sworn she'd never do that to her own children. She took Glynnis' face in her hands, then chucked her on the nose with an index finger.

Carol was already in bed, listening to the CFTR Top Ten countdown on her clock radio. "Did you tell her I broke it?" she asked.

Glynnis got into her pyjamas without looking at her sister. "What do you think?"

"She's going to kill me."

"I told her I did it."

"You did?"

"'Course I did." Glynnis went to brush her teeth.

"Thank-you, thank-you, thank-you," said Carol.

When Glynnis got back from the bathroom, Carol was up on the bed singing, "You put the lime in the coconut and shake it all up." They had done this every night for a week, danced to this song on their beds, jumping back and forth. Glynnis got into bed. Carol jumped over to it. "You put the lime in the coconut and call de doctor," she shouted. Glynnis answered by turning to the wall.

"Carol, in bed, right now," their mother said, coming in to kiss them goodnight. A car door slammed in the driveway. Their father was home and would be wanting their mother's company at dinner. Mrs. Riggs turned the radio off and gave Carol a kiss. She had to pull back the blankets from over Glynnis' head to kiss her, and Glynnis pulled them back up again right away. Mrs. Riggs turned out the big light, leaving them with the bedside light.

"Hello, hello," called their father. "Nobody interested in greeting the old man?"

"Hi, Dad," Carol yelled. "Hi, Dad," said their brother from his desk. Glynnis said nothing.

"Glynnis?" Carol said finally. "Aren't you going to read?" Because of her eyesight, Carol could only read very large print and Glynnis was in the middle of reading her *My Friend Flicka*.

"No."

"Please?"

"No."

Carol begged. Glynnis was resolute. Finally Carol turned off her light. Glynnis could hear her sniffling in the dark.

"I hate you," she said.

"I hate you more," said Glynnis.

"Do not."

"Do too." It always made them laugh in the end, Do not-Do too, they couldn't help it. It was so stupid, and besides, somebody always got mixed up and said the wrong one eventually, so the other could say, "Aha! See? I was right, you just said 'Do too.'" By then they would almost have forgotten what it was they were arguing about.

Mrs. Riggs favoured sensible gifts for girls. Not Barbie dolls (the ones Carol had were gifts from her Aunt Helen) or anything advertised on TV, not boy-gifts like trucks or Tonka toys or Hot Wheels, but craft kits or skipping ropes or Doris Day records. Today, for Alison, Carol had a make-your-own model birch-bark canoe kit, and Glynnis had a Girl Guide whistle.

Strictly speaking, Glynnis had been invited as a companion for Sandy, not as a guest of Alison, but Mrs. Riggs had thought it polite for her to take a gift also. There had been some doubt, given that Glynnis was still in disgrace from the show and tell incident, that she would be allowed to go at all, but Mrs. Riggs had at last given her assent.

The MacDonalds' house, just one street over, was much like their own, a large, sturdy, brick square set down in a comfortable margin of green. It felt strange to go to the front door, glossy green and formal, with its stone porch. The side door, scratched up and ordinary, was the proper entrance, where they could chuck their boots and coats down the stair to the right before coming in. The MacDonalds' house was brighter and messier than their own, and it was easy to be there.

They played games in the garden and ate hot dogs and cake. Carol dropped the egg off her spoon more than anybody else, and even Alison couldn't make up for it. Glynnis' team won, and in the next race she found herself on Alison's team. Carol cried three times and was cheered up twice by Mrs. MacDonald and once by Sandy before it came time for the presents. Alison tossed aside the kit with barely a glance. The whistle merited a couple of exploratory blasts before it too was set aside. She got two pairs of toe socks, a frisbee and an Elton John album. They played more games, and then they got into their pyjamas and brushed their teeth.

Glynnis and Sandy were supposed to sleep in the den and let the others have the run of Alison and Sandy's room, but they snuck upstairs because Alison was planning a séance. More specifically, a levitation. They planned to levitate Carol. She was the heaviest, and the difference between her regular state and her levitated state would, therefore, be the more marked.

How levitation worked was this: the girls arranged themselves around Carol's body as she lay on the floor on her back, Alison at her head. The lights had to be low or off. Each of the girls would put two fingers of each hand under the portion of Carol's body that was in front of them. "Ready? One, two, three, lift," Alison said. The girls strained and heaved and could hardly lift Carol off the ground.

"She is dead," Alison began, and the next girl intoned the phrase in turn, "She is dead," then the next, all the way around the circle. *She is dead. She is dead. She is dead.*

"Clouds come close to the earth," said Alison. *Clouds come close to the earth. Clouds come close to the earth.*

"Spirits, seeking their own." *Spirits, seeking their own.*
"The fog swirls round her head." *The fog. The fog. The fog.*
"The fog *is* her head." *The fog is. The fog is. The fog is.*
"The fog is her body." *Her body. Her body.*
"She is lost to the mist." *Lost to the mist.*
Morning dawns. The mist rises. The fog lifts. The new day begins.
"She is light as a feather, now RISE!"

And they lifted her as easily as a cardboard box. They got to their feet and lifted her higher, above their heads. Eighty pounds above their heads, like it was nothing. Carol giggled, and suddenly she became heavy again. Glynnis thought she saw Alison and her new best friend, Bridget, pull their hands away altogether before Carol crashed to the floor, but she wasn't sure.

"You dropped her," Sandy said.

"She laughed. You break the spell when you laugh," said Alison.

"She's dead. Dead people don't laugh," Bridget said.

"I felt like I was dead," Carol said. "It was weird, it was like…"

But Alison and Bridget and the others ignored her. "You guys know the ghost of the bloody fingers?" asked Alison.

"Tell it! Tell it!" the others said.

"Everybody knows that one," Carol said.

"Did you hear anything?" Bridget asked. "I thought I just heard the body say something."

"How could it?" Alison asked. "It's dead."

"She's dead," Glynnis said, her skin quivering with suppressed laughter.

She's dead. She's dead. She's dead, the others repeated.

"You guys," Carol said.

"Do you think it'll start to smell?" Bridget asked.

"You know, you're right, it probably will." Alison sniffed the air. She was so good at being serious it was funny. Glynnis laughed harder.

"I think it's starting to already," said someone else.

"It is, it *is*."

"We'll have to bury it tomorrow."

"Come on, you guys."

"Why not tonight?"

"You know, that's a good question. Why *not* tonight?"

Glynnis was splitting her side. Even her own laughter seemed funny to her. She didn't know if she'd ever stop. It was starting to hurt.

Sandy poked her. "It's not funny anymore," she said.

"Poor Carol."

"Poor Carol."

"She had her whole life ahead of her."

"Not a very promising life, but still."

"I didn't really like her, did you?"

"Of course not, but it's sad anyway."

"You guys, I'm alive." She jumped up and down and waved in front of Alison's face. "See? I'm alive."

Glynnis stopped laughing. She had no pride, Carol; it was embarrassing.

"So sad."

"Leave her alone," Sandy said to Alison.

How weak Carol was here, how easy to hurt. At home it had always gone the other way — James hurt Carol hurt Glynnis — never the other way around, at least not in any lasting way. But here it had turned around for a night, and Glynnis had loved it.

All night Glynnis had been having the time of her life while Carol had the misery of hers, and that had made Glynnis' night even better. Alison *liked* her, Alison wanted *her* on her team, Alison wanted to make *her* laugh. Alison despised Carol, she could see that too, and it had made her happy. It had made her giddy until now, when Sandy tried to stop it, and she knew her friend was right.

"Yeah. Leave her alone," Glynnis said.

"Leave her alone? Of course we'll leave her alone. She's dead."

"You know what I mean. Come on, Carol, sleep downstairs with us."

"I don't need *you*," Carol said with total condescension. As long as no one came to Carol's defence, she could pretend the rest of them were teasing her the way they'd tease any of their number. Now that someone had — someone younger, someone's *little sister* — she couldn't pretend anymore.

"Isn't it past your bedtime?" she went on. "Little kids need their sleep."

There was an awkward pause, then Alison said, "Good night, John-boy," sealing their fate. They went downstairs.

"CAROL IS A FART," wrote Glynnis on Sandy's back with her finger. "ALISON IS A POO BALL," Sandy wrote back, but Glynnis didn't believe that for a minute.

Nobody wanted to be a Fairy. Fairies were gay, like cat-eye glasses, pointy sneakers and flowered wicker bicycle baskets. (Carol had one on her girl's bike, a white basket with pink and purple flowers on it. Alison had a banana bike with a metal basket. Glynnis didn't have a bike.)

This was how Brownies was divided up, into sixes: Fairies, Pixies, Elves, Gnomes and Sprites. Each six had a little song they had to sing at the beginning of each meeting, holding hands and skipping in a circle. The Sprites' went, "Here we come, the spritely Sprites, brave and helpful like the knights." And the Gnomes': "Who are we? The laughing Gnomes, helping others in our homes." Elves helped others, not themselves, and so on.

Some people had to be Fairies, that was just the way things were, and since you had no choice in the matter, you could not really be held accountable. Unless you were gay to begin with, being a Fairy wouldn't count against you. You had to make a show of not wanting to be a Fairy anyway, of which Glynnis had done a passable job, though she'd actually wanted nothing more. Alison MacDonald was a Fairy.

That first night of Brownies, Glynnis had hung on her mother's every word as she read out the names. Sandy was made an Elf. Another friend was made a Pixie. This boded well. Her mother would not put her in the same group as friends she saw every day, thinking it important to expose her to a wider range of people. She didn't know anyone in the Fairies except for Alison, and this boded well, too.

"Glynnis Riggs?" her mother had read out. It sounded funny, the whole name, because she usually only said it that way when Glynnis was in trouble. "Fairies."

Glynnis had slouched over to join the Fairies, feigning disappointment, but feeling, in fact, gay. "Oo-oo," she said when she got there. "I'm a Fairy." She flopped her wrist for effect. Mrs. Riggs looked up from her list, her sharp blue eyes especially piercing between the black of her reading glasses and the dark brown of her thick eyebrows. Alison laughed behind her hand.

When it came their turn to sing, Alison and Glynnis had skipped up a storm. "We're the Fairies, glad and GAY," they sang, swinging their arms high. "Helping others every day."

It became a thing, acting gay.

"Yoo-hoo," Alison took to saying. "Fairies over here." And Glynnis would skip over, "What is it, darling, what is it?" They acted like a combination of Alison's mother and Felix Unger on *The Odd Couple*.

Mrs. Riggs did not catch on for several weeks, but when she did, she gave them a talking to. "Gay is a perfectly good word," she started. "And Fairies are older than the hills." It seemed to pain her that Glynnis found being a Fairy laughable.

She explained that "Brownies" itself was another word for Fairies, that every country had a traditional belief in them, the Irish had "the little people," the English had "the Brownies," and so on. "Brownies," this time she meant the institution, "leads you into the world of imagination. Or it would, if you would let it." This did not strike Glynnis as being true. Brownies was about knots and semaphore, Morse code and first aid, sewing and knitting and being good as gold. Imagination, she and Alison had. Brownies had a round mirror, flagstone-shaped construction paper and cardboard mushrooms. Brownies had props. It did not have imagination.

Mrs. Riggs grew more severe as she ended her talk. "I don't think you realize how you look when you prance around like that. You look ridiculous. You sound ridiculous. You are ridiculous. Every *bit* as ridiculous as the people you are mimicking. Homosexuals are sick, sick people, they are *not* funny, and neither are you," she said.

Homosexuals? thought Glynnis.

"Glad she's not my mother," Alison said after she'd walked away, and Glynnis got an itchy feeling in her throat, as if she might cry. She did not want to cry, and this turned the itch into a fury that she felt on the skin of her arms and neck like a sunburn, tight and hot. She wanted to hit her mother, to whack her sturdy panty-hosed calves with a hairbrush.

"Yoo-hoo, Fai-ries," Carol called out to them, because of course now that Alison and Glynnis did it, everyone did. Mrs. Riggs was too late — the tradition had taken root and would not be easily stamped out. "Come and practise semaphore with the Pixies."

"Shut up, Carol." Glynnis and Alison said it exactly together.

That night in bed, Carol said to Glynnis, "She'll get bored of you next week, you know. She does this to everyone."

Glynnis didn't say anything because she knew it might be true.

The Cub Scouts that ran at the same time as Mrs. Riggs' Brownies were led by one of the younger fathers in the neighbourhood and his bachelor brother. They were lax, these two, and didn't care much what the boys did so long as they could light a fire, tie a couple of knots, play hard and not be sucks. Cubs consisted, as far as the Brownies could see, of making an astonishing amount of noise while playing floor hockey. Glynnis and Alison were not the only ones who would have preferred to be Cubs. Mrs. Riggs had an ongoing battle with Brian and Dover Smith. More than once she'd left the Brownies in the large fluttery hands of her young assistant, Tawny Owl, to bawl them out.

One week the Cubs threw beanbags at Brownies from behind the stage curtain. As soon as Mrs. Riggs' neat brown figure huffed out of the room — Glynnis noticed she walked a little like Carol when happy, that bob — Glynnis leaned over to Alison and asked if she wanted to go play foozeball.

"Foozeball?" Alison asked. "What's that?"

"You don't know what foozeball is? Come on." And she took

her to the games room in the Odd Spot. No teens were around. They rarely were.

"Oh, this game," Alison said. "I didn't know what it was called. I've always called it Soccer Guys on Sticks." She spun the defence line like an expert.

It was 7-4 for Alison when Tawny Owl found them. "Here they are," she sang out (and she was one to sing out). "Boy, are you two ever in trouble. We've been looking all over for you. Didn't you think we'd miss you? Come on. Boop-boop!" Boop-boop meant hurry up. It was an expression she'd picked up from Brown Owl.

The fifth whack of the hairbrush that night stung as much as ever, but the confession was easier to come up with. "I shouldn't have snuck out of the Brownie room to play foozeball because nobody knew where we were and everyone was worried about us." It still made her want to turn away when her mother took her by the shoulders. What she was looking for was contrition, which Glynnis wasn't sure she felt. Ruefulness she felt, and dread, and a very small feeling, a comma in the middle of her stomach that might be contrition. She looked her mother in the eyes, and the comma, the sense of having done something wrong, grew bigger, though in her head she was still thinking it was *their* fault for being worried when there was no need to be. She and Alison were fine. Of course they were. What was there to worry about? And why did they always say, We're not angry, we were *worried*, when it was clear they were angry? But the comma swelled to the size of her chest, and she clenched her jaw not to cry. Her mother let her go.

Carol had been listening to her parents downstairs. "Alison's a bad influence on you," she said when she came to bed. "You shouldn't be allowed to see her. You're too easily led."

"I'm the one who said we should go play foozeball."

"You only did that to impress her."

"Did not."

"Did too."

"Did not."

"Did too." There was a giggle in Carol's voice, as if she was hoping Glynnis would start to laugh soon.

"Go stuff it, Carol," Glynnis said.

Carol jumped out of her bed and onto Glynnis'. Glynnis tried to kick her away, but Carol grabbed her feet and sat on them. Then she worked her way up so she was sitting on Glynnis' stomach, pinning her hands above her head while Glynnis struggled. She let a piece of drool hang over Glynnis' face, then sucked it back up. "Say you're Alison MacDonald's little monkey."

"You're Alison MacDonald's little monkey," Glynnis said.

Carol gripped her wrists tighter and drooled again. She sucked it up. "Say it."

Glynnis stopped struggling for a second before gathering all her strength into her hips. She bucked Carol off her, head-first into the wall. Carol started crying and kicking in a pink-faced fury until their father flung the door open, with a deeper fury than Carol's could ever be.

They didn't read that night either. The next day Carol taped a line down the middle of the room, just like she'd seen on *The Brady Bunch*.

The Riggs and the MacDonalds had a party in common to go to on Friday night. Alison and Sandy's older sister, Mary, made popcorn and let the four of them watch *The Wizard of Oz* while she and her best friend smoked hand-rolled cigarettes in the back yard.

Alison and Sandy had seen the movie before, though Sandy only remembered the wicked witch and the flying monkeys and kept covering her eyes when the woods grew dark and scary. Carol was scared too. Every time Sandy drew her legs up on the couch, Carol did the same. They watched through their fingers. Alison and Glynnis remained scornful, though it was a stretch for Glynnis during the scene with the poppy fields doping the adventurers into sleep. She didn't like the thought of plants exerting that much power over a person, of being in thrall to something that strong, of sleeping when you desperately needed to be awake. But Glynnis didn't let on and Carol and Sandy did.

During the commercials Alison pretended to be the Wicked Witch of the West and Glynnis her evil flying-monkey minion.

"Quit it, you guys," Sandy kept saying. "I mean it." She appealed to Glynnis specifically. "Come on, Glynn."

"Eeee-eee," Glynnis replied, swooping down on her from the top of the couch until Sandy finally said she didn't like Glynnis anymore and she thought she should go home.

"You can't send her home," Alison said.

"She's my friend and I can send her home."

"Okay, so now she's my friend, and I can invite her back."

"What's going on down there?" Mary called from the top of the stairs, without really seeming to care. "You're both staying till your parents come to get you."

Later, when Glynnis' parents were saying goodbye to the MacDonalds in the front hall (which took forever, as always), Alison said to Glynnis, "Too bad you're not your sister's age. Then you could really be my friend." Carol heard this and went outside. Glynnis found herself smiling at Alison, then felt terrible and hurried out to sit on the steps with her sister. She wanted Carol to say something or punch her arm, but Carol hugged her knees against the chill and was quiet.

Monday and Tuesday at school, Sandy wouldn't talk to Glynnis or play with her at recess, and neither would their other friends. Sandy had got to them first. Alison, of course, rarely did more than say hi at school. Glynnis had never expected anything different. On Monday, Glynnis played on the monkey bars with the boys. She noticed Carol by the tree-well at the girls' end, playing with a girl from Brownies with cat-eye glasses. Last fall Carol had been part of a group that skipped rope every day at recess. This year it was just her and the other girl, playing their little games. It was sad, and in a way it wasn't fair.

Of course in another way it was totally fair. Carol was a suck and a liar and a cheater. She was all these things because she needed to be. She couldn't win fairly, so she cheated. She was clumsy and awkward, so she lied. She was an albino with bad vision and sensitive skin and chubby legs, so she was a suck.

She *was* ordinary. And because she was ordinary, she didn't know how to milk her difference. For a minute, in the classroom, seeing her do her Pillsbury Dough Boy, Glynnis had thought Carol had got it, had understood the way out. She hadn't. She probably never would. She was doomed.

Glynnis thought maybe she should play with Carol and the girl with the glasses, whose name, she had found out yesterday, was Daintry.

"Hey, what're you doing?" she asked.

Carol blinked suspiciously and didn't answer, but Daintry said they were playing house, did she want to play?

"House?" asked Glynnis. She noticed Alison MacDonald and Bridget swinging themselves under the chain-link fence back into the schoolyard not twenty feet from where she was. "House?" she asked again, louder. "Are you kidding?" She walked over to the monkey bars.

Later that afternoon at Brownies, the Cubs shot spitballs at them from the dumbwaiter. Mrs. Riggs bobbed out again, not before whispering some sort of admonishment to Tawny Owl.

"All right, everybody," Tawny Owl said, clapping her hands. "Let's…" No one was paying attention to her. Two girls were at the piano — now propped up on bricks at the broken end — showing another girl how to play a simple one-finger duet that most girls already seemed to know.

Another group was over at the window, misting up the cold October panes with their breath so they could draw happy faces and make impressions of feet with the heels of their fists.

Others were playing jacks, some were tying knots, some were even practising semaphore.

"Let's what?" said Daintry.

"Let's you and I play Paper, Scissors, Rock," Tawny Owl said.

Alison started a game of frozen tag. No one would unfreeze Carol. She was still frozen when the game petered out, and Alison and Glynnis jumped from behind her, pretending to be Flying Monkeys. She shrieked and ran behind the piano, and then she tried to be a Flying Monkey herself. Alison promptly became the Wicked Witch and chastised her for not bringing back Dorothy. She pointed at Sandy. "There she is! Get her!"

"I'm not Dorothy," said Sandy. "I'm Toto."

"And your little dog, too," said Alison, bearing down on Sandy, who ran away barking.

"There's Dorothy," Carol shouted, going after Glynnis.

"I'm not Dorothy," Glynnis said, thinking fast, but not fast enough. "I'm somebody else."

"You are too Dorothy," Carol said. It was not playful, Carol's voice.

"Am not." She ran up to the piano and slid underneath it so her legs stuck out the front.

"Hey, Alison," she yelled. "Hey, Alison, who am I?"

Carol ran after her. "You're Dorothy, and I'm taking you to the Wicked Witch of the West." Carol tried to drag Glynnis out by her shoulders.

"No, I'm not." Glynnis hooked her feet on the front of the piano so Carol couldn't pull her out. She felt the piano shift a few millimetres on the bricks. Carol's knees were behind Glynnis' head while she tugged. Glynnis pulled her head forward, then bashed it back against Carol's knees. Carol yelped and jumped away. "Alison!" Glynnis slid back under the piano and called again. "Alison! Who am I?"

"I don't know, who are you?" Alison asked.

"The Wicked Witch of the East. Get it? The Wicked Witch of the East."

Alison laughed. Glynnis could hear her on the other side of the piano. She started to laugh too. She was just pulling herself out from under when a chubby brown leg swung past her.

"No you're not, you're Dorothy because I say so!" Glynnis had never heard Carol's voice like that. It sounded broken, like a dream she'd once had about a Chatty Cathy doll that went berserk. She watched her sister's foot kick the bricks.

The piano gave the same crash as before, dissonant and ethereal, but this time it was accompanied by a high wail that Glynnis only later recognized as her own.

Glynnis spent seven weeks in the hospital. Her right femur had been crushed and was reconstructed with a metal bar and pins. The first week she was delirious with pain and painkillers. She could not imagine what she would say to Carol, or what Carol would say to her. Her mother had told her that Carol was miserable with sorrow and that Glynnis must forgive her, but Glynnis didn't know what that meant. She didn't remember feeling anything but pain ever in her life, though she knew she had, she knew she had felt emotions in her body once, that they had even felt acute, but she couldn't remember what it was like to feel them.

In the second week, Mrs. Riggs led Carol into the room by her shoulders. Glynnis had thought Carol would look different somehow, more colourful, or leaner, but she looked just the same: a lank-haired pink girl in a skirt that pinched a line of fat in her waist, with little eyes turned bulbous by her glasses. She twisted once under Mrs. Riggs' hands but kept moving forward when her mother let her go a few steps from the bed.

"I'm sorry," she said rigidly. She swallowed. "I'm sorry." Then she dissolved, screwing up her eyes and saying it over and over like there was nothing else to her. Glynnis' own eyes felt hard. She didn't say anything, she didn't blink. There was an empty cave inside her so cold it burned. It was not her leg.

"I'm sorry, I'm sorry, I'm sorry," Carol said.

Mrs. Riggs came forward and took Carol's shoulders again, but gently. Glynnis could see she was about to be told to say something to her sister. She didn't want their mother's words between them.

"I know," she said. "I know."

Nelson

When there was a big wind, Jean always won. A regular wind and the outcome, though less certain, still tipped in her favour. A light wind and she was doomed.

She considered not racing on those dismal bright July days when the birch leaves drooped in the heat, showing none of their silvery undersides. Those days when air became visible and the cicadas droned high and long and sharp, when sweat flooded out of Jean's billion pores making streamlets and rivers, torrents of thin, sticky body-water running down uncomfortable places. Those days when she could not get cool no matter how many plans she laid to put her body in contact with the water — capsize maneuvers with the Intermediates, or landings with the Juniors, standing waist deep to catch their bows. She considered faking illness or running the Committee Boat or taking her half-day. But Jean had her pride, her pride that compelled her to race when she knew she'd lose. When everyone knew she would lose, and when everyone knew why but pretended they didn't. This pretence was the reason she could never back out, even if she genuinely was sick, for Jean had a handicap that would never allow her to be the Achilles, the petulant star. On the contrary, because of this handicap it was mandatory that Jean be the best sport imaginable.

"Good race, Nelson," people like her friend Alison Peck would say, using her last name as everyone did.

Though they were the same age and equally good sailors, Peck had this year been named Head of Sailing, leaving Jean the paltry post of Assistant Head. "Listen, it's in name only," Peck had sworn after they'd found out. "In reality? Co-heads. You and me. Co-heads." It was this kind of thing that had kept them friends through their many years of competition. But a note of cynicism crept into Jean's thinking this year. Yes, they'd stayed friends through difficult situations, but neither of them had won definitively before. Plus, Jean noticed, Peck had never taken her co-heads idea to the director. Jean knew the director would never have gone for it — "Ultimately, Jean, I don't feel confident in your ability to demonstrate responsible behaviour in a wide variety of situations," she'd said in their interview — but Peck didn't know that. Or did she?

"Good race, Nelson," people like Margie Trebbick and Goldie Cook, two of the other sailing instructors, would say.

"Good race, Nelson," the senior campers would say.

And though Jean would roll her eyes amusingly and never make excuses, sometimes she wanted to slug them because she did not want to be a good sport, and of course that's what they really meant, "You're such a good sport, Nelson." As if she ought to be grateful for their consideration, grateful that no one laughed anymore except the little kids, the ones who still found fat people funny. People here knew her better than anywhere else, and still they did not know this.

Except Cathy McVitty. Mac would say, "Well that sucks, eh?"

Pride made her sail, yes. But also, you never did know when a wind would come up. It could be the most somnolent day, you could be becalmed forever, tracking a creeping course between the buoys, and then thwack, it'd hit the sail, a big beautiful wind that came so fast it still smelled of the prairies. And then. And then it'd really be a race.

This particular windless race day was worse than most. This windless day she would not have campers for her crew, girls she knew, girls who knew her. Today Nelson Smith would be her crew. Nelson and Nelson, deadweights in a tub.

The race was the culmination of a strategy the director had come up with to make the maintenance men feel more a part of the camp, a sort of amateur psychology thing, the underlying intent of which was to keep them from bringing their buddies in the off-season, drinking their faces off and lighting fires. The idea was to pair them up with a staff member who would give them lessons. Canoeing lessons, sailing, tennis, riding, kayaking, even pottery if they wanted, stained glass, lapidary, copper enamelling. To make things seem like a fair exchange, the men taught carpentry, canoe repair, roofing and small machine repair.

The maintenance men were boys mostly, local boys who needed work for the summer. Nelson Smith was the exception. Nelson Smith was twenty-three — local, but not a boy. Normally that would have made Jean more comfortable with him.

In the winter, Jean went to a private girls' school. Summers she came here, a private girls' camp. She didn't run into boys her own age much (though that would change in the fall when she went to university). The times she did, she tried to be cool, to alter her persona not at all. She hated seeing the effect boys had on other girls, seeing the girls grow more exuberant or more demure, seeing them flatter and fawn and say things they didn't mean. So she tried to be exactly herself. At the time she would think she was doing a creditable job of it, but afterwards she was never certain she hadn't been just like the other girls — too quiet or too loud, a marshmallow or a weiner.

The problem, Jean realized, was the spectre of some sort of relationship hovering there in the air, whispering, *Will this be the one? Will this be the one?* And then, *Will this one think* Jean *thinks he's the one?* She had seen panic in the eyes of boys whom she knew liked her as a person when they realized if they hung out with her too much, people might get the wrong idea. She had seen the second thought hit them, escalating their panic — my god, *she* might get the wrong idea. What they were not perceptive enough or brave enough to see was that she had trained herself not to get ideas. Ever.

With men, the possiblity of a relationship was not present, not to Jean's eyes. Oh, certainly she'd had men leer at her and pinch her bum on the subway, but she knew that was something different. With men — teachers, neighbours, store clerks, family friends — Jean could be herself, without second thought, without effort, the way she was with girls and women. Nelson, though…

Until race day, Jean had never seen Nelson in shorts. The first lesson, he and Dwayne — his younger, self-appointed sidekick — had worn jeans. Jeans. When they should've known they had to wade out thigh deep to where the boats were moored and that jeans and wading were like peanut butter and mayonnaise; they were two things that just didn't go together.

She sat on the porch of the sailing hut and watched them coming down the path in their jeans and T-shirts and ball caps and moustaches, seeming so foreign all of a sudden she felt certain that when they spoke it would be in a different language.

"Is this the right place for sailing?" Nelson said. English. Amazing.

Up close they seemed even more foreign. She could see the stray hairs sticking out the top of Nelson's Hard Rock Café T-shirt, and the peeling patches of skin on Dwayne's nose and forehead. She could see Dwayne's moustache for its straggly little self; she could see the individual pieces of stubble that made up Nelson's five o'clock shadow.

Maintenance men were things you saw in the distance, she realized. They kept themselves apart from the life of the camp, avoiding centres of activity. If they had to repair the docks, they did it at lunch when everyone was in the dining hall; if they had to repair a bunk or a cabin door, they did it during activity periods. Jean liked it that way. She suspected they did too.

And now, at four in the afternoon when they'd normally be doing what? — she had no idea, fixing stuff, watching TV, going off to Diving Rock for a swim — and when she'd normally be repairing sails or doing lesson plans or sneaking out for a sail on her own or hanging out in the staff lounge, here they were, in the flesh, three feet away from her, waiting to learn how to sail. How had Peck got out of this? Oh yeah, a senior staff meeting. Co-heads of sailing. Right.

Nelson sat with his arms crossed and his chair tipped back while she went over the parts of the boat. *Bow, stern, gunwales, hull, rudder, tiller, mast, boom, boom-vang, transom*...How did this get to be something she actually cared about, knowing the parts of the boat? They were bored stiff, they thought this was all stupid, they thought sailing and tennis and riding were for children and rich people. They had better things to do. *Port, starboard, windward, leeward, luff, leech, clew*...She did care about it, she loved it, what was wrong with that?

"Why don't they just call things what they are?" Dwayne asked with a raised lip in objection to one rope being called a sheet and another a painter.

Jean was stumped. The language of sailing was inevitable to her, not separate from the whole of her vocabulary. It simply was, the way beef was beef and not cow meat.

"History, Dwayne," said Nelson.

"Huh?" said Dwayne.

Nelson shook his head and looked back at Jean, waiting for her to go on.

He continued like that when they got out on the water — after dragging his wet jeans into the boat like a heavy net behind him — not awkward, not eager, but not like Dwayne either, who gawked at the Seniors sailboarding in their bathing suits and ignored Jean unless he didn't have a choice or could see down her shirt.

While Jean showed them the different sets of the sail, all they had to do was uncleat and let out, or cleat and haul in, the jib sheet when they went about. She had to keep interrupting Dwayne to remind him of his job, but Nelson kept an eye on the wind and on the cut of the sails and on everything Jean did while he listened to Dwayne prattle on about the truck he was going to buy and the tires he was going to get for it and the four-wheeling he was going to do.

They'd been out about ten minutes when that great afternoon wind came up and heeled the boat over. Dwayne was on the leeside getting closer and closer to the water and looking nervous.

"Time to hike, Nelson," she said. Hiking was the best thing: the body as lever. Jean loved how shifting her weight even a small amount made such a measurable difference. And when the wind was her equal and she had to put her muscles into it, working that body-lever out the side of the boat, she exulted.

"Here, hook your feet under the hiking straps. Now sit up on the gunwale and lean out. More. More. More. Arch your back. That's it! You go far enough, you can dip your head in the water." Nelson's weight brought the boat almost level again. "Bring yourself in when the wind lets up a bit. In, out, in, out, it's a constant adjustment. You're always watching the wind." He glanced behind him at the wind, a happy intense look on his face. She gave him a good long tack and then went about, pushing the tiller away from her and ducking under the boom as the boat turned into the wind and onto its new tack. Jean heard the jib that Dwayne was supposed to be hauling in flapping loosely in the wind. He was staring down her shirt again.

"Dwayne! What are you supposed to be doing?"

"Yeah, right, the jib," Dwayne said, cleating it.

"Your turn to hike, Dwayne," Jean said. "Come on. Lean out, lean way out. That's it."

She waited until Dwayne got over his discomfort at having most of his body out of the boat, then turned sharply upwind, just enough to dunk his head in the water.

"Fuck, what the fuck?"

"Did you get wet? I'm sorry. My hand slipped."

He put a hand up to his head. "Fuck, my fuckin' hat."

"Hat overboard," said Nelson with a small grin.

They retrieved Dwayne's hat on the third pass. He scowled the rest of the lesson.

"Hey, Nelson," Mac said at dinner. "How'd it go?"

"You mean the Dukes of Hazzard Go Sailing? Great, if you
like having your tits stared at all afternoon." She told them
the story about dunking Dwayne and how they brought half
the lake into the boat on their jeans. "He's a piece of work,
that Dwayne."

"How about Nelson?"

"Nelson Smith, hmm. Are there unsuspected depths? I don't
know. I wouldn't count on it."

The second lesson, it was just Nelson. Dwayne was taking
pottery with Corey "Do You Like My New Halter Top" Pea-
cock. Jean almost missed him. At least he talked. Nelson was
like a stone. Usually Jean liked to draw quiet people out, to
ask them questions about themselves, and usually they responded. With many, she didn't even have to try — her bulk
seemed to provide them, falsely or not, with the safety they
needed to unload their cares, to talk about things they'd never
told a soul. With Nelson it was different. With Nelson, well
— Jean had a secret about Nelson that was at the root of her
discomfort.

"You from the city, too?" he said after a long silence. Meaning Toronto, of course, like the rest of the staff, not like himself. Jean answered that she was.

"Like it?" he asked.

Jean shrugged. Actually, she didn't like her life in the city
much, but was that the city, or was it her life? Being up north,
on the other hand, she loved. When she thought of running
away, that's what she wanted to run to — the lakes, the woods,
the small towns. Sometimes on the way up they'd stop at a
roadside diner and she would picture herself in one of those
polyester outfits, leaning her breasts over the counter to joke
with the plaid-shirted men who whistled at her when they
came in and showed her their new tattoos. She'd wear lipstick
and make cracks about skinny men climbing mountains. She'd
chew gum and read magazines. She'd drive a pickup truck.

She'd marry…Well, she'd probably end up marrying somebody like Dwayne or Nelson. That was a problem. She'd be bored inside a week.

"My sister's there," said Nelson. "She married a guy from Oakville, but now they're in Scarborough."

Whoa, thought Jean, pro*found*.

But he was a natural at sailing. He had an instinctual sense of how to set the sails, how much to let the boat heel over, how to make a smooth about. He even did a perfect controlled jibe on his second try. After a certain period of silence passed (apart from calls of "ready about" and "hard-a-lee"), it grew comfortable, and Jean enjoyed herself. They made a good team. And he didn't look down her shirt.

Race day he wore shorts. It was the main thing she noticed as he came down the path to the sailing beach — that she could see his legs. His legs that were skinny and white white white. She felt a sudden rush of affection for him. She wanted to show him her own white belly, but there was a bathing suit underneath her shorts and T-shirt, and besides, he would think she was crazy or worse.

Jean had seen a moose once when she was on a canoe trip, a cow that stood in the shallow water putting her massive head down and coming up with streaming mouthfuls of weeds and water. Jean had been so close that she could hear that sound, almost like suction, when a large object is removed from water and the water below tries to stick to it and the water around rushes in. That was the way she had felt when she'd climbed into the sailboat ahead of Nelson and Dwayne that day they wore jeans. The moose had run gracefully away into the undergrowth. Jean did not have that option.

She and Nelson had each made their changes. He'd changed from jeans to green work pants to shorts. She now let Nelson get in first, and on race day, there they were ahead of her, those white skinny legs like a heron's.

Jean and Nelson dawdled at the start line with the seven other boats. Most of them had one staff member with two or three campers. Margie Trebbick had Dwayne, and Jean had Nelson. He wanted to skipper this race; normally Jean wouldn't have let someone with so little experience take the tiller in competition, but she figured in this wind it wouldn't matter.

"Hey, Nelson." They both turned their heads. "This is the life, eh?" Dwayne was lying back on one of the seats, dragging his hand in the water. He splashed Margie in her white bikini. Margie didn't shriek; she would have splashed herself anyway to get a better tan.

Last year, Jean had shared a cabin with Margie. She'd never known anyone who slept naked before, and she admired the way Margie would hop out of bed in the morning, look out the window and light a smoke before even thinking about putting on clothes. She wasn't all that thin, either; she just had confidence. Jean liked her. In the boat with Dwayne, though, Margie's confidence was annoying, even smug, like she knew something Jean didn't and pitied her for not knowing, for not ever being able to know.

"We go slow enough, we can waste the whole afternoon," Dwayne said.

"You go ahead and go slow, Dwayne," Nelson said.

"Shouldn't be a problem," Margie said. She sucked her finger and stuck it in the air to prove her point. "How 'bout we race for last place, eh, Nelson?" she said to Jean.

"You go ahead," Nelson said again, and Jean became aware of her throat and how much she was swallowing. Nelson was watching the sails, watching their position relative to the start line, watching the lake for patches of ripples amidst the glassy bob of its surface. Peck stood up in the Committee Boat and raised a yellow square of cloth. "Is that the thirty second flag?" Nelson asked Jean.

"You got it," said Jean with contrived cheer.

"Guess we won't need to tack again before the start," he said. Was he stupid or blind or what? He actually thought they might be in contention.

The secret Jean had about Nelson was not that she had a crush on him, though since seeing his legs she couldn't be so sure. No, the secret Jean had was that Nelson's was the mental image she had used all winter to masturbate to. It had seemed safe enough at the time. She'd ruled out using boys of her acquaintance — it made her feel too awkward seeing them afterwards. Her practice instead was to imagine opening her legs to men she barely knew. Nelson qualified — he'd been at the camp for almost as long as she had, but she'd rarely said more than "How you doing?" to him. She hadn't thought that would ever change.

"How you doing," she asked partway through the first leg.

"Fine," he said. He smiled. She noticed his chipped tooth beneath his thick moustache. It hadn't featured in her visions of him either, along with his skinny legs.

"Hockey?" she said.

"Pardon me?" he said.

"Your tooth."

"Brother," he said, smiling again.

They were Adidas track shorts that he wore, grey with blue stripes, not too tight, not too baggy, but short, so that the bulge contained by the liner sometimes peeked through. It was all so different than she'd imagined, his body — so ordinary and real, so incapable, it seemed, of taking on her own. She felt idiotic for ever having thought of it, their two bodies together. Slapstick. She wanted to apologize to him for everything, for not having the creativity to imagine those legs, for not caring who he really was and not wanting to find out.

"How you doing," she asked, not five minutes after she'd asked the last time.

"Okay," he said. Then, after a pause, "Something I should be doing different?"

"No, no, you're doing fine."

Jean didn't want silence again. In each silence she started thinking she owed Nelson an explanation. She started rehearsing it in her head. Something nice and low-key, like, *You know, Nelson? You kinda seem like you want to win. But you know what? The problem is physics. You seem to understand physics. The more weight in the boat, the more hull in the water. The more hull in the water, the greater the friction. The greater the friction, the less the speed. You know what I'm saying, Nelson?*

"Ready about," Nelson said. She nodded. "Hard-a-lee," he said and pushed the tiller away. They ducked under the boom.

"You know what, Nelson?" Jean said. "You're good at this…"

He beamed. She looked away, about to continue, but he said, "Must be in the genes."

Jean immediately thought of his wet GWGs of the first day. He went on, "My grandfather worked the Great Lakes. Steam ships mostly. But sailboats too. He started a business when he was older, bought a sloop, took out tours on Georgian Bay. Took me along a couple times, showed me the ropes. I was like Dwayne, eh? 'Why's it called a sheet 'stead of a rope? Why's it called gunwale?' And he'd always say, 'History, son.' And he'd tell me where it came from. Like 'sheet,' that's from 'sheet-line,' because the line was attached to the sheet, the sail-sheet. And gunwale, that's kind of obvious, gun-wall, right? I loved it. Then he lost the boat."

"It sank?" Jean asked.

"No, the bank. He lost it to the friggin' bank. And that was it. Never sailed since."

"You or him?"

"Neither. He passed away soon after. Stroke."

"That's too bad."

"Yeah." He squinted and looked at the sails and the wind.

Jean didn't feel this was like other confidences from people she'd just met who dumped on her. Nelson wasn't lonely or a bore or a whiner or a blamer. She thought it meant he liked her. She thought it was the kind of confidence you tell people you like being with.

When the boats were spread out, all on their different tacks towards the buoy, it was hard to tell who was ahead of whom. But when they rounded the buoy, as they did, one by one, it was abundantly clear Jean and Nelson were dead last. Even

Dwayne and Margie — who, true to Dwayne's word, weren't even trying — cleared the marker before they did.

"Maybe you should take over," Nelson said as he watched them.

"I don't think that'll help."

"It's okay, I don't mind," he said.

"No, you're doing great."

"Yeah, but look where we are."

Jean's throat felt like a stiff tube inside her neck. Just when she was starting to feel as if things would turn out all right, here he was thinking it was his fault they were losing. They'd been out for over forty minutes. There was a faint pink sheen starting on Nelson's thighs.

"We're not going to win no matter who's at the helm," she said. "We're not even going to be close."

"What about that?" He nodded his head toward the bank of clouds creeping over the western sky.

"Won't hit us in time." She looked at him. He looked at the sails, at her, then back at the sails. He looked at the clouds. She took another breath.

"It's a matter of physics, Nelson." She said the last part deliberately, with a pause between each word: "I — slow — us — down."

He grinned. "Ain't over till the fat lady sings."

Automatic tears and anger flooded her face, like the kind that whooshed through her when she cracked her head full force on a table after picking up a fork. Scrawny little asshole.

"You want me to sing? Fine, I'll sing." She stood up. "*God save our gracious queen, long live our noble queen, god save our queen...*" She could have stopped there. Instead she launched into a crescendo. "*...Bum-bum-bum-bum, Send her victorious, happy and glorious, long to reign over us, god save our queen.* There. It's over." She would have sung the second verse too, the one she'd learned in grade five, make him really suffer, but she couldn't remember all the words.

He looked away and muttered that it was just a joke. The horn sounded from the Committee Boat as the winner crossed

the finish line. It *was* over. They'd be a good half hour behind
the other boats by the time they tacked up to the last buoy
and ran down to the finish. The wind was slackening. The
horn sounded again for the second boat.

"Take us in," she said.

"What for?"

"The race is over, Nelson."

"No it's not."

"You wanted me to sing, I sang."

"It was a joke."

"Right."

"You're the one who brought it up in the first place."

"Brought what up?"

"Your, you know, size."

"Take us in."

"Look, I'm sorry."

"Take us in."

"No."

"No?!"

"I'm finishing this race."

"Fine. You're on your own, buddy." Jean lifted herself up
on the gunwale, swung her legs around and slipped into the
water. She could feel the boat bob up behind her, but she didn't
look back.

"Jean," Nelson called after her. "Jean!"

She swam to shore. The boats started to come in.

Mac ran up. "What the hell, Nelson? I saw you swimming
in. What'd he do, attack you or what?"

Jean shook her head. "Nothing like that," she said in a
monotone. Nelson was still doggedly tacking. Dwayne and
Margie crossed the finish line.

"Should he…" Mac hesitated. "Should he be out there by
himself?"

Jean didn't answer immediately. She watched the bank
of clouds start to whip up a squall at the end of the lake.
It'd smack him. He'd see. "No," she said quietly. "He
shouldn't."

"I guess the Committee Boat can help him if he gets in trouble."

"Yes."

He'd started his downwind run, winging the sails on either side of the boat, jib to starboard, mainsail to port, the better to catch the wind, which was right behind him. An advance gust filled the limp sails like a bagpipe's bladder. He started a smooth scoot down the lake.

Then the real wind hit. A mallet on every square inch of sail, and most of the square inches were out the port side. The boat rocked hard to the left, dipping the sail in the water, rocked back once, then tipped cleanly to horizontal. There was grace, Jean thought, in its fall. Few things fell so gracefully. Not people or bicycles or books or plates. Trees might if they didn't have that crash and bounce at the end.

The boat, in a swift comic dénouement, turned turtle.

Only when she saw the Committee Boat moving on its way towards him did she realize she wanted to get there first.

God Save the Queen, for christ's sake. Fat, touchy and ridiculous too. Petty, to top it all off, waiting to see him get smacked by the wind. She raced to the canoe dock where the Zodiac was tied up, yelling at Mac to come with her.

Peck, her CIT and Nelson had righted the boat by the time the Zodiac reached it and were bringing down the sails. Peck was on board with Nelson.

"Hey," she called out when she saw Jean. "It's okay, we got it under control here."

That made it worse, that Peck was acting calm and understanding instead of outraged. Had the director told Peck what she'd told Jean about her reasons for their respective appointments? Was this the opportunity Peck had been waiting for so she didn't have to feel guilty anymore about being promoted over her friend?

"We're just going to furl the sails and tow her in," Peck said. "Really. It's fine."

Jean left the Zodiac with Mac anyway and swam to the

swamped boat with an extra bailer. Nelson started the hand-pump while Peck furled the sails.

"You all right?" she asked Nelson. He nodded. His pink thighs had goose bumps. "I'll help you bail." Cold rain started to fall. The lake water was warm. Jean bailed. Nelson pumped. Thunder rumbled in the distance.

Nelson rode back in the Committe Boat, while Jean and Mac towed the sailboat with the Zodiac. Jean wanted to be sitting next to him, silently, the two of them shivering together in their thin skins. Nobody else knew what their afternoon had been.

On shore, the director was hunched in the rain. Everyone else had gone in to eat. "My cabin, after dinner," she said to Jean, then strode away up the path.

"Yikes," said Mac.

It started to rain harder, driving Mac and the others just coming up the beach to their dry cabins. Jean stayed, watching the rain. Nelson paused as he passed her.

"Comin' down, innit?"

Jean didn't answer. Here was her chance to say sorry, but what was the point? There was too much to explain, and she doubted he cared anyway. I am the biggest idiot, she thought. The biggest, hugest, most idiotic, stupid idiot. Sobs lurked in her throat ready to burst out; she couldn't say anything now even if she wanted to.

Lightning struck the radio tower across the lake. One-thousand, two-thousand, three-thousand, four-thousand, five. Thunder.

"Good thing we're not out there," he said.

But Jean wished they were. She wished she'd laughed when she'd sung. The woman in polyester would have laughed. That's who he'd thought she was, a fat woman so secure she'd laugh at the jokes, genuinely, not hiding anything. He was being nice, but he didn't like her, not anymore.

He took his indifference up the path, leaving her in the rain.

Solar Plexus

At seventeen, Craig Broughton looked forty. His hair was the hair of the balding — lank and thin, starting well back of his forehead, with a line of lean, combed-back fuzz running the middle course of his pate. His forehead was pale and often wrinkled in thought, his chin was soft and pudgy, his fingers stubby, his glasses dug ridges into his puffy cheeks.

Craig Broughton, at seventeen, removed the mirror from the upstairs bathroom. His sister, to whom he did not speak and who did not speak to him, put it up again. He took it down. She put it up. He broke it. Their parents didn't believe in interfering in the relationship between brother and sister. If they fought, they fought; it was up to them to make it up. They did not imagine that they never would.

Inside Craig's pudgy soft face was the soul of a burning lover. That was what Craig didn't see when he looked in the mirror. And if he couldn't see it, knowing it was there, who would, not knowing? His long pale lashes, his nondescript eyes, the blackheads on his nose. None of it said who he was, and yet he was he. His body was his. His body was him. He had not always believed so.

From twelve to fourteen, Craig had been convinced he had a vocation for the priesthood. The family was not Catholic, but he had been serious; they had not known how serious he was. When his mother offered that he might want to keep his options open, he rebuked her with fiercely pious stares (he was not the beatific type). "Goodness! Look at him, Pete. I'm afraid he's going to start flagellating any minute." Unbearable, this mockery, but bear it he must. He went to his room to pray. Also to masturbate.

Which led him in the end to think that celibacy was not his thing after all. He started to wonder if sex could be his thing. He read D.H. Lawrence and science fiction free-love daddy-o Robert Heinlein along with whatever glossy mags he smuggled home (looking older than one's years had its advantages). Finally he read Henry Miller and knew he'd found what he was looking for. A man who would take women from behind or two at a time, a man who would get his cock sucked under the table at restaurants, a man who would call them cunts and they would come dripping, running, coming, coming. Unh.

His burning lover's soul had a particular object in mind — a girl he had had a single class with the year before. They had sat next to one another. He had made her laugh on several occasions. Once, when he noticed a classmate's finger-drumming was irritating her, he'd asked the offending student to knock it off and had thus earned a precious smile.

Fiona Theosakis was not particularly pretty or particularly popular. Or ugly or unpopular. Her smile, when it graced her face, was lovely, her eyes sorrowful. She did her homework diligently. Craig suspected her home life of severity. What form this severity took, he didn't know. An autocratic alcoholic father, say, and a wan workworn mother, maybe a snotty-nosed toddling brother left in her care.

She had a small group of friends, a tight knot of girls who went places together — the washroom, the corner store, the cafeteria. In Grade Twelve, however, Fiona was unlucky enough to have a different lunch from her friends.

Craig was not stupid. He didn't try to approach her in the cafeteria, a place he loathed in any case. (He would have preferred to hold the cafeteria in high disdain rather than loathing, but he could not keep his emotion at such a remove.) He ate in the hall, reading, leaning up, it just so happened, against her locker, which was in an alcove. "Sorry, am I in your way?" he said when she stood above him. Quick smile, slide over. Back to the book. The next day he sat a few lockers over, not to be obvious. The third day she asked what he was reading. "Nietzsche," he said. "What's it about?" she asked. He hummed for a minute. "The death of god and the birth of man," he said. "Ok*ay*," she said skeptically and walked off with her books.

But the next day she said, "Your name's Craig, right? I'm Fiona." Two weeks later she ate her lunch in the alcove too. She believed in god, although sometimes she wasn't sure. Her father was dying of lung cancer, and where was god in all of that? Offering a just reward for smoking his whole life, for contaminating the holy temple of his body?

When she found out a few days later that Craig smoked — Gitanes, of course — she said, "Don't. Don't smoke. It will kill you." He could have kissed her feet, right there, the way she said it, though he wouldn't stop smoking.

Craig was careful not to let his adoration show. He would be a friend, a confidant. One day she would cry for her father, cry and cry, and she would accept his shoulder, his kisses, his gentle stroking of hair. Then she would turn wild with grief, needing to feel alive, alive, every nerve alive, and they would ravish each other. This would happen in a park or woodland, on a warm fall evening.

Fiona left school every day by the southwest doors, walking the three blocks to the subway, sometimes on her own, more often with one or two of her friends. Each afternoon, Craig sat on his motorcycle at the mouth of the teachers' parking lot, waiting to see if she'd be alone and if he'd have courage. Each night he pictured their meeting, the graceful unfolding of fate: he pulling up smoothly beside her on his motorcycle, she turning to him instinctively, hair swirling like the softest skirt, hand wordlessly accepting the wordlessly proffered helmet.

The next time she was alone — about a week and a half after he'd started watching her — he did have the courage and gently eased out of the parking lot about a block behind her. But there was nowhere to pull up. Every parking space was taken. There was a bus stop she was just passing; he had to pull in there and yell or lose her.

"Fiona!" His voice sounded squeaky and muffled, even to him. She kept walking.

Lifting his visor, he yelled again. "Hey, Fiona!"

She turned. Oh, god, her hair, the swirl of it, it was exactly as he'd imagined. But she gazed blankly at the street with the wary, embarrassed look of a person unsure she'd heard right, and turned away.

Again he called her name. Another perfect swirl. Another unrecognizing scan of the street. He waved, fumbling with the strap on his helmet with one hand while ripping off his glasses with the other. Everything blurred, including her uncertain look. By the time he'd got his helmet off and glasses back on, she was coming towards him, smiling.

He was gelatinous all of a sudden, boneless. Somehow he managed to talk anyway. She wasn't going home, she was going to the hospital. She'd love a ride. She loved motorcycles, her uncle had one. She'd love a ride.

He handed her his spare helmet and she swung her hair — swoosh, swoosh — over her shoulders before putting it on. She straddled the motorcycle. His bones grew back into the hollows they'd left when they disappeared.

He took her to the hospital often after that. Not every day, not even every day she was alone. But often. He waited outside the hospital for long stretches before riding off. Sometimes he saw his reflection in store windows as he rode by. With the helmet and black jacket he looked like he *could* be someone's fierce tender lover.

Once he waited across the street until she came out again, her mother leaning on her arm in a flowered rain hood and cheap plastic boots, her younger sister lagging behind with a yo-yo. They got on the streetcar and went east.

For a week in late October, she did not come to school. For another week her friends skipped their lunchtime classes, a warm concerned knot around her again. When he said hi in the halls, they asked who he was, and she said nothing until he was out of earshot.

Friday afternoon the following week she found him at his locker. "Take me for a ride," she said. "I want to go fast." So he took her up Highway 48 to Lake Simcoe. She was shivering when they stopped. He gave her his jacket. They went down to the water and she started to cry, just as he'd imagined it, but when he put his arm around her, she pulled away and walked quickly along the beach. She sat down with the jacket around her knees. He followed and sat next to her. She shook. Her chin chattered up and down. He tried his arm around her again, lightly, then tighter. She felt thin and strong. All her muscles were tense.

He kissed her hair. Comfortingly, he thought, though surely she sensed the passion curled up in it. With each kiss he smelled her hair, some ordinary shampoo forever destined to mean her and her alone. His nose, his sight, his sense of touch, everything seemed sharper than ever, time seemed slower; it sat there on the beach like driftwood growing white. He tried a kiss on her cheek, half turned away. It turned no further. She swung the jacket from her knees to her shoulders.

He put his hand on her chin, to draw it to him. She let him. Her eyes were the fullest he'd seen. The only ones he'd seen this close up. "Don't," she said. He didn't think she meant it, but how could he know?

Henry Miller would know. Henry Miller could see through all the subterfuge of the words before sex. Henry didn't have to assess; he just knew from how much he wanted her that she must want him too. Craig put his lips to hers, moved his hand inside the jacket to her breast, the briefest flicker of tongue, tiny taste of bliss, the heavy, unbelievable roundness of her breast against his fingers. And then a crack like an anvil across his chest and he lay back, winded. Jesus.

"Don't," she said again, voice tense, on her feet, fists at the ready. "I'll walk home if I have to."

He sucked at the air, furious but too stunned to do anything about it. Who'd have thought an elbow could hurt so much.

She marched toward the road, clearly prepared to be true to her word. He wanted to chase after and tackle her, to punch her stomach, to knee her groin, to beat her and pound her and carry her away. His breath back, he panted. He wanted to hurt her any way he could, and he lay there knowing that until he was stiff and cold and it was gone.

Conkers

Chestnuts were biffing the sidewalk again. Not for roasting, these, but for stringing on threads and whacking other chestnuts on threads, a flurry of chestnuts exploding in October air.

To anyone else this might conjure up a nice rural scene — two boys in checked wool jackets, maybe, playing conkers, this chestnuts-on-threads game, by a split-rail fence under a fiery maple. But to Theresa conkers had always meant the comfortable haze of a downtown bar.

First it was her father's bar in Waterloo, when she was ten and her mother's business school classes went until six every night. Violins in one hand, grocery bags full of chestnuts in the other, she and her sister would race to the bar after school and eat chicken fingers and french fries while the hard heel of their father's hand pushed a needle and thread through the perfect woody brown knobs, turning chestnuts into conkers.

Then it was the dark basement on King Street that accepted their fake ID in high school.

Now it was with Fred in the Toronto bar that mixed young and hip in the back room with old and drunk in the front. Theresa would have preferred to play in the front, but she knew the back would spill out with them, and she didn't want to see the fear and envy in the eyes of the grey men with their thin, slicked-back hair.

Theresa and Fred matched. Skinny, both of them, and dressed in black. Theresa also favoured longjohns and second-hand cheerleading skirts. Both had stubble heads, a result of their weekly Ritual Shaving of the Heads, when they would slap Gregorian chants on the turntable, lather up and put an old Gillette with a new blade to work. Theresa loved having her head shaved, the rasp and pull of the blade over her scalp, the sharpness of it and the tingling afterwards. Sometimes she thought she loved the feel of Fred's hands on her head better than anywhere else on her body. Of course when he moved them somewhere else she had to reconsider. Fred's hands were long and thin, like the rest of him. When he was high he claimed his fingertips had eyes and that was why playing the bass came so easily to him and why it was so painful.

Theresa had seen Fred once before she actually met him, through the window of the practice room she'd booked at the university. He was using up her time, but the sight of him — tall, skinny, bald and unaware, bowing like that, with his whole body — it was something she couldn't interrupt. She ran her hand over her own bald head as she found her way out of the building.

And then he had shown up in her small ensemble group. Theresa liked to think she had outgrown her childish roman-ticism, but she couldn't help feeling that two bald people in one string quintet had to be fate. She moved in with him at the end of first year.

So many coincidences, not just the hair. Their fathers, for example. When Theresa was twelve, a drunk driver (could have been one of his customers, Theresa would never know) tried to pass her father when he was making a left turn on his way home from the bar. The car bent into a vee, and Theresa's father died of internal injuries at the hospital.

Fred's father, a lawyer, had had an accident too, one that left him worse than dead. Or so Fred claimed, and Theresa came to believe him. Fred's father's car hit a bridge piling going eighty kilometres an hour at one-thirty in the morning. No other cars were involved. After he came out of the coma he acted like his head was still full of glass, like his cortex was chopped into sections that worked on their own but didn't connect. He tried to go to work every day for a year. Fred's mother — and, later, Fred or his brother — had to chase him down and bring him back.

Late into the nights they told each other their stories, walking the streets after the bars closed, taking up the next watch in dessert shops, ending up in school playgrounds when the sun rose. There was not a chance she would have told anyone this, but Theresa thought of that first summer with Fred as a sequence from a movie, the kind that shows a newly in-love couple doing stupid and romantic things, like winning each other stuffed animals from the ring toss at the carnival, or falling into fountains with their clothes on. Or playing conkers in a smoky bar. Only thing was, Theresa could never decide on the music: Sex Pistols? Or *L'après-midi d'un faun*?

The day Fred spreadeagled himself over the bathtub to kiss her, Theresa thought she knew exactly what it meant: he'd won the undergrad composition contest. See? she wanted to say. See, you big bonehead? He'd been so wrapped up in his misunderstood rebel genius thing that he wouldn't even have submitted his concerto if she hadn't threatened to do it herself. She slapped her wet hands on his cheeks and kissed him back.

"So?" she said.

"I am a happy man," he said, dragging her out of the bathtub and towelling her off.

"And that is because?"

He hugged himself and rocked from side to side. It looked like glee. "Ooh, just let me keep it to myself a little longer."

They walked down the street to Café la Gaffe where Fred ate little and talked a lot, not about his concerto or what the judges had said or how he'd spend the money or who he'd like to see as soloists in the performance, but about Meech Lake, of all things, and then Machiavelli and Aztec civilization, ty-

ing them all together in that unique Fred way. He was buzz-
ing. He was on. It was driving Theresa nuts.

"Okay, just tell me," she said as he uncharacteristically insisted on paying for both their dinners.

He grinned enigmatically. "Tell you at The Horseshoe," he
said.

"Aw, come on, Fred," she said. She didn't want to go to The
Horseshoe. She had an eight-thirty class the next morning.
She was getting tired of this. Maybe he was just playing with
her head.

"Suspense. Isn't it great?"

Forgotten Rebels were playing, not a band Theresa had a
lot of time for. As far as she was concerned, they'd already had
their fifteen minutes. She danced to the one song she liked,
the one about Elvis that went "The big fat goof is dead, dead,
dead," then let Fred dance by himself to the rest. When the
band took a break, he brought three beers to the table, two
for himself and one for her.

"You want to know why we're celebrating? You want to
know why?" Fred was getting drunk. He had a streak of evil
when he was drunk that Theresa found exciting, particularly
when she was drunk herself. She liked it because it gave her
rein to be the same, to call him names, bite his nipples, wear
her cowboy boots to bed.

"Two things," he said. "Number One, Dad got out of the
house again, but this time he didn't just ride the subway, he
jumped in front of it. Instant death. Which'll give me a certain pleasure taking the TTC in the future, now that I think
of it. Number Two, I quit school."

Theresa's one hand flew to her mouth. Her other grabbed
Fred's wrist. "Oh my god, Fred. Oh my god."

"Isn't it fucking great?" Fred pulled his hand away and
downed half his glass of beer. "The brain-damaged goof is
dead, dead, dead!" he yelled, sucking back the rest of it.

Theresa had never considered leaving Fred until that night at The Horseshoe. She had this picture in her head of the two of them ten or fifteen years down the road, coming home from symphony rehearsals to their affectionate and musical children, who clamoured to hear again how Mom and Dad had met because they were both bald. Which was something else she wouldn't have told anyone, Fred least of all. And it was this, that she couldn't tell him these things, as much as or more than what he'd done that night, that made her think about leaving him.

He'd been a crazy man, and the grief, that he insisted was not grief, could only account for part of it. "It was anarchistic ecstasy," he said afterwards, "the first breath of freedom."

The band came on again. Fred cheered from the pit of his stomach and bounded up to dance. Thrash, actually. Theresa watched him, the incredible energy he had, the pain that was surely twisting his intestines the way her own had twisted the night her mother woke her and her sister to go to the hospital where their father was already dead. She had not been able to empty her bowels for two weeks after that. It was different for Fred, she knew — there had to be some release for him after all the years of rounding his father up in taxis — but this celebration was pretend.

Theresa watched him intensely, minutely, as if her gaze itself had healing power, as if all he needed was to be watched. He slammed his body up and down, sideways in the crowd, his eyes half-closed, his mouth grinning. Another guy knocked him into a table, almost tipping its contents onto the laps of the people sitting at it. Fred grabbed a teetering beer bottle and hurled it at the stage. Out of her seat immediately, Theresa didn't see what or who the bottle hit, she only saw Fred, ducking, and another bottle breaking against the wall behind him. She and the bouncer got to him at the same time.

On the way home he stepped on a dead cat that lay in the gutter. It was stiff, and one end tipped up under his step. "Miaow," he said, and did it again. He almost fell over laughing.

It was the grief that made her stay. The grief, she understood.

Fred cultivated a moroseness after he quit school that Theresa didn't think would last. He watched TV during the day and worked at a diner nights, a place that liked its staff to look strange and act aloof, part of a conspiracy to turn Toronto into New York that seemed to be taking over the city. Fred went out after work with other strange and aloof people who Theresa knew only by name.

One afternoon Theresa came home from a session her quintet had just done at a public school and found Fred on the couch as usual, watching TV. She talked to him as she hung up her jacket and got a coke from the fridge. She'd given up asking how he was. She reported on her day out of habit, or maybe because she couldn't stand not to talk at all.

"So we play for them, polite applause and everything, then they play for us, and you know what they played? I couldn't believe it. I'd totally forgotten. Had to be the first piece I ever did in orchestra." She came into the living room and lifted up his feet so she could sit on the couch too.

"I'm on the edge of my seat, Theresa," Fred said.

Theresa whacked him on the leg with the back of her hand. "Pizzicato Polka," she said.

"Pizzicato Polka!" Fred said, sitting up. "Holy good god, I played that too. I can't remember how it goes. Play it for me."

"That is so bad," he said when she'd finished. "Wait, play it again." Fred's electric bass was leaning against the wall in the corner of the room. He tuned it up. They played it the whole way through, and then again, improvising. Fred called in sick to work. Theresa ordered pizza and the two of them sat in the kitchen writing a new arrangement of Pizzicato Polka for a five-piece rock band, complete with lyrics and screaming guitar solo.

"Damn," said Fred. "We're just going to have to start our own band, or we'll never see our mantelpiece performed. What do you think? 'Tone-Deaf Nine Year Olds'? 'Poke Yer Eye Out'? 'Small Cretins'?"

Theresa hadn't laughed so hard in ages.

When We've Got Big Hair got a four-"N" review in *Now*, the booking manager at the bar moved them from Tuesdays all the way up to Fridays, an unprecedented leap. The bar was packed when they played now, and Theresa started to understand why the woman who played guitar in Fifth Column turned her back to the audience, like Jim Morrison. There was a rumour going around that some record company execs might even show up for one of the band's gigs. Pop culture commentary on pop culture was big at the time, and on top of "Pizzicato Punkster," the band did "The Mr. Slate Laid Me Off Blues," a country blues number that featured Fred doing the most mournful "yaba-daba-doo" he could wrap his teeth around.

It felt weird to Theresa, how crowded the bar was. She'd loved the Tuesday night gig they'd started with. There was something about standing on the tiny stage in a dark, partly filled room, something about the tinniness of small applause behind one loud thumb-and-forefinger whistle, that she found beautiful and sad. It made her want to grow her hair. But each week there were more people, more applause, more whistles. And each week there was Fred with the razor in his long thin hands.

All fall they played conkers between sets. It was something Theresa could concentrate on, something that felt solid and real and good, something that connected her to the world outside the bar. She was stony-faced now when she played with We've Got Big Hair. The reviewers loved her expressionlessness, the aura of New York about it, but Theresa hadn't realized she was doing it until she read the reviews. She didn't feel self-conscious like this when she gave classical recitals — quite the opposite. At recitals she loved the feeling of being watched, even of being stared at. She loved the whispers behind people's hands as she filed onto the stage. And the times that she played well, she forgot she even had a face that might be squinting, squishing its eyebrows together, lifting its lips from its teeth.

Those afternoons at the Duke, her father had told stories.

Sudbury stories, family stories, about moose hunting with his
father; about his foul-mouthed, pipe-smoking great-aunt and
his prim, churchgoing grandmother; about his favourite sister who ran away to Toronto with the parish priest. Theresa
had liked that story best, though she'd had a hard time relating fat Tante Louise and easygoing Oncle Marc with the characters in the story.

She wondered in high school, when her friends began to
hate their parents, their fathers, if she would have grown
impatient with him, if she would have thought he, like the
stories he told, was an embarrassing Northern Ontario
stereotype? Probably. But even in grade thirteen she could not
pass the bar he had worked in without finding her violin case
suddenly clunking against her knees as if she were eleven again.
She wanted to go in and breathe the smoke, hear his voice joke
with the men at the bar while she dipped her fries in ketchup
and he strung chestnuts.

Now conkers was becoming a spectacle, a part of the show.
Fred wrote a song, one of the ones Theresa didn't like, that he
insisted on playing at the end of each set. It was called
"Bonkers for Conkers." Fred told her that she'd lost her sense
of humour when she objected to it. She worried he might be
right.

"It's a novelty tune, what's the big deal?" Fred said.

"That's just it, they're all novelty tunes," said Theresa. "Why
can't we do something serious? Besides, it means something
to me."

Fred laughed. "You know how stupid that just sounded? Christ,
Theresa, it's a game. Okay, so you played it with your dad and
now he's dead. Well, I'm real sorry for you, but it's still just a game.
Other people played it too. And it's a funny song."

"It's not just the father thing, it's, it's — Oh, forget it."

"What? It's what?"

It's you and me, Theresa wanted to say. It's you and me
falling in love and thinking we'd stay that way. But that
sounded too much like a line from a bad movie. Theresa's bad
movie, that Fred would cut to ribbons if he ever saw it.

"Forget it, Fred," she said.

"Fine," said Fred. "Consider it forgotten."

And now Fred was explaining the game on stage to a bunch of people looking for oddity they could call their own. Theresa suspected he imagined himself on some international stage, talking about this relatively obscure game as though it were a Canadian national pastime or something. Fred had a way of making little things big. He was even calling for challengers from the audience. Theresa thought briefly about playing the wrong chords, deliberately, in half-time, but she didn't know if she could do it, even if she tried.

People crowded around the band's table as Fred talked Theresa into a demo game. He held out his first chestnut. It swayed from the thread between his fingers so he stilled it gently with his left hand. Theresa used to like that Fred played the game with great ceremony, with chess-like concentration. Now it seemed phony. She countered with off-handedness, slouching in her seat as she held the thread in her left hand and pulled back on the chestnut with her right, making like she was flinging peas from a spoon. She made a hit, but Fred's chestnut swung from its thread, unbroken.

"You've lost your touch, girlie," he said, grinning.

Fuck you, she thought as Fred interminably, melodramatically, set his sights on her chestnut.

After his conker bounced harmlessly off her own, he stilled it again and waited for her next shot. If I win this round, Theresa thought, I'll forgive him. No. If I win this round, I'll walk out of this bar right now and never come back. If I win this round … Theresa's chestnut smacked Fred's smartly. She heard the satisfying "chop" when it broke and watched as one of the pieces sailed to the next table, right into someone's beer. The crowd laughed, and the beer splashed onto the lap of a man busy exploring the ear of the woman next to him with his lips.

"Who the fuck threw something in my drink?" he said, looking around.

"Hey, at arenas and ball parks it's a privilege to have a piece of the game come your way," said Fred.

"What? Look, Baldy — "

"Ooo, 'Baldy,' that's creative," said Fred.

"Don't be an idiot, Fred," said Theresa. She did not want to laugh.

A man with a ponytail tried to placate the other guy. "Steve, Steve, take a downer. It was an accident. Look, I'll buy you another beer."

"Weird place, Stew," Steve said to the man with the ponytail and put his arm back around the woman beside him. Stew looked at Theresa and shrugged. He's trying to show his friends how cool he is by bringing them here, Theresa thought, looking away. He gets a kick out of their thinking his tastes are offbeat.

Fred's next shot missed completely, swinging around in an arc and hitting him on the chin. It wasn't fair that he laughed more genuinely than she did.

By proper sports etiquette, Theresa as the winner should have taken on challengers until she gave up her seat to someone else. But Theresa wasn't big on etiquette of any sort. It had been Fred's idea to ask for challengers; Fred could play them.

Theresa moved to an empty seat on the other side of the table and looked around for someone else to play with, someone she knew. Margot, the drummer, was head-to-head with her lover at another table. They could equally have been fighting or cooing. Either way, Theresa didn't want to interrupt. There was no sign of the keyboardist, Ricky, but she hadn't expected there would be. Ricky had a trick of disappearing at awkward times and making everyone nervous, but he always reappeared exactly when he needed to. None of Theresa's own friends were at the bar. She kept her two musical lives separate — the people at school didn't know she was in a band, and the people in the band didn't know she loved school. And Fred's friends didn't do anything. They didn't talk, they didn't play conkers, they didn't clap between numbers, they just sat, a silent cluster of cool.

Theresa spun her victorious chestnut around her index finger one way and then the other, watching Fred dispose of a short tubby man with a monk's haircut. Fred drank half a glass of beer between each round. He'd be drunk by the end of the night, not that anyone but Theresa would notice.

Ponytail guy — Stew — sat down across from her. Damn. She should have put her feet up on the seat. He'd been watching her, she realized now, while she'd been watching Fred. He signalled the waitress and ordered a beer.

"Theresa?" the waitress asked. Theresa didn't usually drink when she was performing. If she just nodded, she'd get a soda water. "Scotch. With ice." She hated the expression "on the rocks." She thought it was hokey drinking lingo that her generation should have dropped.

Stew said, "I was going to ask your name, but the waitress just said it for me."

"She did, didn't she." Theresa looked at her watch. Fifteen minutes before they went on again. Fred would make a good rock star, she thought as she watched him. He had a certain combination of belligerence and approachability that would appeal to people, and he had that raw sweet smile.

"Used to play that as a kid," Stew said, motioning across the table to Fred.

"Yeah," said Theresa.

"No. I mean *I* used to play as a kid."

"Oh," said Theresa.

"I was pretty good, too."

"So why aren't you lining up like everyone else?"

"Don't feel like it," he said. He smiled. "I'm Stew," he said. His smile had something behind it that made Theresa think of an old man she'd given up her seat to on the subway once. She'd smiled at him and instead of smiling back, he'd said, "Fuckin' kids."

"I gathered," Theresa said. She watched Fred take down a laughing woman with genuinely big hair.

The waitress came back and rested her tray of drinks on the table. She set two glasses of draught in front of Fred, who didn't look up, one in front of Stew and the scotch in front of Theresa.

"Let me get that for you," Stew said.

"Why?" said Theresa.

Stew seemed taken aback. "Just trying to be friendly —"

"It's on the house," the waitress said as she took Stew's money.

"Got an attitude to go with the hair, don't you?" said Stew. When Theresa didn't answer, he got up and left, mumbling something that she couldn't hear. Fred saw Theresa watching him and raised his glass. She raised hers in return, a reflex, then got up and leaned across the table.

"Would you ever buy a woman a drink? Not a friend or anything. A woman you just met in a bar," she asked.

"I might if she asked me to. Why? You want me to buy you a drink, bay-bee?" Fred saw the drink in her hand was thick and golden, not clear and bubbly. Before she could pull it away, he took it and put it to his nose. "No, I can see you have one already. Holy good god, the professional musician, drinking at a gig. Scotch, no less. Your standards are dropping, Theresa, you better watch it. You might end up like — like me."

"Don't bet on it," said Theresa and took back her drink, wishing she could think of better comebacks. She downed the rest of her drink and looked at her watch again. Ten minutes to the second set.

While she was in the washroom, Theresa thought again about leaving. Now. Not saying a word, just packing up her guitar and leaving. Fred could plead at her heels, not that he would, and she wouldn't say a word. She'd be a big powerful wall of silence. He might always win with words, but the big victory would be her wordless back swinging out the door.

The washroom the band used upstairs was only for them and the staff, and the door was propped open, so Theresa didn't think anything of walking out while she was still pulling down her skirt. As a result, she almost walked right into Stew.

"Jesus," she said.

"No, Stew, remember?" he said. He blocked the corridor.

"Do you mind?" Theresa motioned for him to move out of the way. "You're not supposed to be up here."

Stew didn't move. "I know," he said, "I followed you. I wanted to see you alone."

"I'm almost late for the next set," she said.

There was a space under his arm between his body and the wall that she might be able to get through. If he moved to block her, she'd knee him in the balls. But he surprised her — he let her go past. She broke into a little trot. Stew caught her right wrist from behind. He swung her back by it, grabbed the other wrist, held them both behind her back. She stomped on his toe with the heel of her boot. He didn't let go.

Stew pushed Theresa back into the bathroom. He shoved her up against the wall, her face against the cool plaster. Theresa yelled. He took her wrists into one hand, took her left ear with the other, pulled her face from the wall, then bashed it back against it. She stopped yelling. He let go of her ear.

Theresa felt her skirt being lifted, her longjohns being pulled down and then her underwear. She yelped with the pain as he stuck his fingers in her vagina. She tried kicking again, but he kept his body out of her reach.

"Bastard. You bastard," she said.

"Bitch. Cold bitch," he said.

"Next," she heard him say when he left.

Theresa sat on the toilet and cried. Fred came into the bathroom. He must have passed Stew in the hall. The stall door was open, but he didn't look at her as he used the urinal. Theresa could not speak. She took big shaking breaths to supply her lungs with air.

"Can't be that bad, Theresa," he said. "Come on, Theresa. We're supposed to be on stage. Besides, you like it rough."

He buttoned his jeans and left without looking at her. Her tongue, that had felt too large for her mouth, suddenly shrank to its regular size. She stopped crying. She washed her face in the sink, dried it with brown paper towels. A bruise was coming up on her right cheek.

Theresa played the first three songs of the next set with her back to the audience. She looked at the floor. The absence of her voice for the backing vocals felt like a wound. She liked it that way.

"Turn around! Turn around!" people yelled from the audience between each song.

Finally, Theresa turned around. The audience clapped and hooted. Fred looked at her as she stood up to the microphone.

"I want to — " Theresa cleared her throat. "I want to tell you what just happened to me. It happened in the bathroom, and it was not pretty. Maybe Fred can write a song about it someday."

A few people in the audience laughed. Fred stepped back from his own mike. He hung his head. She wanted to think it was in shame, but she doubted it.

"Yeah, maybe Fred can write a song about it, something like 'Wilma Got Raped in the Bathroom While I Watched.' I know it's not a very catchy title, but Fred's the word king. He'll come up with something."

The room was quieter than Theresa had ever heard it before, even on those half-empty Tuesdays. She didn't feel like she was talking loudly, but her own voice came blaring back at her through the monitors, a disembodied thing. It took her a long time to figure out what it reminded her of, but when the thought did come, it sang like a good vibrato: her speech to this falsely silent crowd was like voice-over. When she finished, the natural hiss and clink and murmur of the barroom would gradually come up, the band would start to play, the credits would roll.

The Middle of Infinity

I've been in jail before. In my mother's womb. Not that the womb was a jail, far from it. No, my mother was in jail, and I was in her. Ergo, I was in jail.

If you think of infinity, how even the tiniest number can still be divided in two, then divided in two again, you can almost imagine being alive forever. At the birth end of things anyway. At the death end, a second is more stubbornly a second — divide it all you want, you can't draw it out any longer.

So there I was, in jail. A parasite. Bobbing in amniotic fluid, oblivious to the trials of my host, my life. My mother.

My mother was not despondent to be in jail, not ashamed. My mother was exultant, not the less because it was in jail that I first made use of my new limbs. I had legs, I had arms. Flippers no more. I kicked. "I belong here, I really belong here," my mother said to her cellmate, Ruth, who wondered if she was delirious. "For the first time, I feel like I belong on earth. Feel this," she said to Ruth, who did. They were younger than I am now. It is not fair that generations cannot all live simultaneously. Except then they wouldn't be generations, would they? I was there, but I did not know her.

My mother, like so many other people, has another parasite of her own making inside her, parasite, strictly speaking, not being the right term, but it is something that feeds off her and replicates and will not die until she does, nor will it exit her of its own accord. My mother has cancer.

Cancer is a word, I've noticed, that TV movies say everyone wants to avoid. TV movies are full of cancer patients railing at their loved ones, "Say it! Say it, dammit! I have cancer. Cancer." (The sign, incidentally, that I was born under.) Their voices break on the last iteration, ca-a-a-ncer, and they dissolve into their unwept tears and their loved ones' arms. I have not found this to be true in real life. In real life, once the word cancer is out, you hear nothing but. It is what I said to my mother, dumbly, when she told me.

"I have cancer," she said.

"Cancer."

She looked at me with concern across the kitchen table. "I have cancer of the uterus."

"Cancer of the uterus," I said.

"I will have to have a hysterectomy."

"Hysterectomy."

"Yup," she said, looking down at her belly. "Hoof the whole football out." She patted the bulge falling down from her waist, the bulge that was evidence her uterus had seen some use. Me, for example, hoofed out under the sign of cancer.

"Uterine cancer," she said, getting up to clear off the table, never one to sit still for long. In jail she paced and stretched and sat down and got up, and after the kick she took Ruth (a stranger, though in jail for the same reason) around the waist and polkaed. Ruth became my godmother, not that my mother believed in god. If I had been born ten years later, she might have been my goddess mother, but I was born when I was, in the middle of infinity.

Ruth had cancer too. And died. Finito.

This time in jail I am cognizant of my presence here. It's disappointing, really. There are so many of us they have housed us outside the main compound in a building that puts me in mind, for some reason, of the portable at my public school.

Except that the Grade Three portable had a certain cachet about it, a certain freedom and status in being separate from the main building that this one lacks. Here we are not dangerous enough to merit real detention, only the show of it (a Rottweiler named Fluffy is our principal keeper), and now that we have exhausted the detention stories brought on by our surroundings, we've fallen into a sort of wan camaraderie.

This suits me well enough. I am tired of slogans and optimism and militancy. I do not congratulate myself on my courage and conviction like the others, and for good reason. I am not here, in the first place, because I believe in civil disobedience or anything noble at all. I am here for the love of a man. My mother would not be pleased. Because of Dean (the man) she thinks I am back in the activist fold, and because my mother taught me the language, Dean thinks I've been in a hiatus phase before returning to the fold.

Oo, the kick of guilt when she wrapped me in one of her sisters-in-the-struggle hugs after hearing what I planned to do. So easy to let her be proud, to let her believe the struggle for world peace and justice and sustainable development will carry on through the generations, through me. I know that if it's mother love or true love I shouldn't have to go along with them, I should be able to say, "Look, I'm apathetic, okay? I have a comfy life, and I'm not much inclined to put anything out to make it better for others." And they would say, "I love you no matter what, Adrianna," which they might, but then they would add, "I just can't *be* with you." So I practise my charade. I respect what they're doing, I really do. I just don't think it's going to make a big difference in the end. The people with money and guns will do what they want and everyone else will pay until the whole world blows up or burns out or whatever. (Mental note: go to the rifle range in Burnaby and give the durn things a try.)

o o o

She goes to the hospital alone. No suitcase, but a knapsack, books and flannel jammies. Her mother, Mrs. Upstanding Anglican, used to make her dress up to go to the doctor. Even went so far once as to cut her only and hard-won pair of jeans away from a broken ankle so as to present her in a dress at the Emergency Room. I used to think my mother exaggerated these tales of righteous horror. Grannies, according to my sources (those being books, TV commercials, maybe the odd child), were kindly, even doting creatures, bakers of cookies, knitters of ugly well-meant slippers. A breed quite unlike mothers, grannies — tame, charming, doughy. The festering bitterness my mother felt for her mother, my granny, was surely as ill-founded as it was enduring. Of course, a summer with the Matron herself — Divorce Summer — put me to rights.

Now, presenting herself to doctors and hospitals, my mother goes to the other extreme. In Admitting, she limps up to Connie, who's with a patient.

"You got a toilet here, lady? Cause I gotta take a crap real bad."

"Ava!" Connie says, admonishing and laughing.

"Do I gotta crap right here?" she says. "Or are you going to let me in? Cause I could, you know, I could crap right here."

Her clothes are old enough, her grey hair loose enough to alarm Connie's patient, who fidgets and gestures when she barges around the counter. "Is she... I mean... Is she supposed to..."

Connie looks up. "It's okay, she works here."

She's forty-five and still pulling these stunts.

"Today's the big day, eh?"

"Today's the day."

"Adrianna come with you?"

"No."

"She coming down later?"

"I doubt they'll let her out for that."

An inquisitive glance.

"She's in jail. Clayoquot, remember?"

Connie shakes her head. "Adrianna? I just can't picture it."

"I can." My mother smiles.

o o o

Dean gets up at four to paddle in from the island. It's peaceful, barely light, sometimes raining, always misty. Tied to his lifejacket pocket is a compass he rarely uses. He believes he can feel directions, that the electrons in his body line up with the earth's magnetic field or something. He's never been lost.

Every two weeks he does this, paddles to the island for a day away from the camp, paddles back in the early dawn. Every two weeks I get a letter. One page on the back of a flyer or press release, never inviting me to come. He thinks I will want more than a hasty pail of lentils in the late evening and a few hours next to his sleeping body. He thinks I will not want to be wakened at four. I will want to spend time with him and he does not have time to spend, not while the summer, and the protest, lasts. His letters tell me about encounters on his morning paddles — seals popping up with watery snorts of air, a swimming bear emerging on shore like an iceberg revealed.

Since the first letter, in which he described his daily routine, he has hardly mentioned people at all. Not the woman he shares a van with (a lesbian, of whom I am jealous nonetheless), not his fellow organizers, not the protesters or loggers or cops or townspeople. He loves them, he says, but there are so many of them, so many. If he wrote about them, it would be like being there and he might as well have stayed. Instead he sends me delicate descriptions of saplings and wildflowers, anemones, clouds and waves.

This morning it is raining lightly. He sees no wildlife. He almost runs into two rafts of driftwood. Cut timber gone astray. His urge is to curse, but he treasures the misty

calmness of his paddle and muscles his mind to peaceful-
ness. A crab boat trundles out of the mist, leaving a slow
deep wake behind it that he bobs in happily. He loves the
feel of the sea moving underneath him. Mother Earth,
Mother Sea. He believes in that shit and with him it fits,
with him it rings true in a way it doesn't with other people. I'm not even tempted to tease him about it.

He points his kayak, so much like a compass needle, towards town and starts across the channel.

He stops at the bakery for one of his few luxuries, cinnamon buns and latté. This is where he writes it, my biweekly
letter, composed in the length of time it takes to drink a coffee. He mails it when he's done, then hitches a ride with the
truck delivering bread to the camp, where he arrives in time
to join the morning circle. He would capitalize this: Morning Circle. In the afternoon he digs a new latrine. He sweats
and puts a green bandana around his head to keep the sweaty
hair off his face.

All day people arrive, in trickles and clumps, vans, cars,
pickups, motorcycles. There's an Evening Circle, too, after
dinner, when it starts again to rain lightly. One woman turns
her face up to the rain, holds out her hands and spins around
in it. Her hair is long, her alpaca sweater beads with rain. He
puts up his arm to call for quiet.

"Anyone here tonight who hasn't done a civil disobedience
workshop yet?" Hands go up. They are just hands, he doesn't
recognize them. "Okay," he says, looking now at the faces
belonging to the hands, "we're glad to have you here, but —"

One of the faces stops him. Mine. His own is unreadable.

"But what?" says the unbearable woman I've driven up with,
she of the alpaca sweater.

He takes a sip from his mug of black camp coffee, still looking at me over the brim of the cup. "But we ask that each
protester attend a full afternoon workshop before joining the
protest. We find it puts people in a better position to follow
through in the actual event. Non-violence is hard, harder than
we want to believe. It takes practice. Not to mention we go

over legal options, consequences you may not have thought of. It's easy to romanticize civil disobedience, particularly when it's something as easy to believe in as saving trees." Unbearable Alpaca grumbles. (*Have you ever*, this woman said to me on the drive up, *felt the heartbeat of a tree?* She claimed to be a performance artist, and pounded the dash. *The scream of the saw, the scream of the tree, the scream of the saw the scream of the tree, how do you know they're any different?* she wailed rhythmically.) His eyes move — reluctantly, I hope — from me to her. "Even if you've done CD before, it's worth it. We need to work from a common plan. One more night's wait isn't going to kill you."

He smiles easily, showing a capped tooth and the places his beardless Scots face will soon develop lines. You'd almost know to look at him he grew up in Northern Ontario, the shy son of a shy logger who died young. As long as I can watch him I'm not bored, but the day gets dark as even summer days will, and the meeting drones on. He's right about the numbers of people. So many, so many.

He hurries up to me when the meeting's over, picks me up in a hug, which I've told him I hate. "Sorry, sorry," he says, putting me down. "Wait right there." His boots crunch away down the gravel road. He comes back with a lantern and his arm around a woman with a sweater like his.

"Karen, this is Adrianna," he says. It's the woman he's shared the van with since his ten-year-old tent rotted through. Either he expects me to socialize or he's got something to tell me, like she isn't a lesbian after all.

"It's a treat to meet you," she says. "Listen, just let me check with Jean and then the van's all yours, okay?"

Takes all these nice people to remind me I'm not.

o o o

My mother is well-liked at the hospital where she works, where she is now a patient. Not uniformly, it's true. The administrators are not fond of her organizing, and some doctors think she is too militant. They think nurses have it pretty good and wanting anything different is selfish and greedy. Some of the other nurses think so too, but my mother is indefatigable. Most people admire this quality.

My indefatigable mother has not eaten in twenty-four hours nor drunk in twelve. She is hungry and crabby and worried and thinking about Ruth, eighteen months dead. "Being a woman'll kill ya," she says to Charmaine, who stops by for a chat between patients. With Ruth, it was her breasts that did it. "So how come there are all those old ladies crowding up the nursing homes, eh?" says Charmaine. "Yeah, but it's not their dicks that kill *them*," says Ava, meaning men, "it's their hearts." "Ooo-ee," says Charmaine, "you've sure hit on something there." Ava thinks so too, she just isn't sure what.

Ruth's second husband went to pieces when he found out she had breast cancer. No use at all. Showed up crying at Ava's house, played TV movie with Ruth, refusing to say the word, proving my rule.

One dying woman on her hands, retreating, "You don't understand, Ava, you don't understand." And one childish man, whimpering, "You understand, don't you, Ava?"

Ava understands perfectly.

She wants to eat an enormous meal and sleep for fourteen hours.

She wants her dead best friend, who understands.

She wants her daughter, who doesn't, yet.

Charmaine leaves, chuckling. Alone, Ava cries.

o o o

"I can't believe you, just showing up like this," Dean says. The van smells steamy and close, I notice. It's not unpleasant.

"Sorry."

"No, it's great, it's fabulous."

"I wanted to be a part of this." I don't say what "this" is. "It's so big," I go on. "I don't want to think ten years down the road, 'I could've been part of that and I chose not to be.' I don't want to regret staying home, doing nothing."

It's almost time to get up, Dean tells me, though it's the middle of the night. We have been rocking the van the last three hours like high-school stoners with no place else to do it.

On the way to the protest, I'm almost falling asleep in the passenger seat when he turns onto a logging road and pulls over. Nobody around. "What, do we have to walk from here?" I ask. He undoes his seatbelt, leans over to undo mine. He grins his risqué grin and nods toward the back of the van where we've each had four orgasms in the last four hours. I find nothing risqué in his proposition; I love it that he does. I want to straddle him in the front seat. I want to do up his seatbelt and pull down his pants — a little whitebread bondage.

I follow him to the foam. Another time.

My mother was in jail for twenty-four hours. Twenty-four hours. I have been here one-hundred and eighty-eight. I have wedded my fate for one-hundred and eighty-eight hours to that of Unbearable Alpaca. What was I thinking?

Unbearable has spent the time trying to put together a guerrilla theatre piece for performance on the legislature steps the day of our release. She has filled the interstices of this enthusiasm with aura readings. Margaret's is sunny and golden. Sunitra's is damask rose and amber. "What total crap," I say at Hour One-Forty-Six-and-a-Half. "Can't you at least try for, say, one iota of originality?"

"I'm just telling you what I see," she says. She looks hard at me, comes closer, squints, closes her eyes, opens them suddenly wide, squints again. She puts her hand out, caressing the air over my shoulder. Her eyebrows rise in surprise. "You don't have an aura," she says. "My point exactly," I say.

Except I'm not sure what my point is anymore.

What is it about jail that makes it easy to keep track of hours and hard to keep track of days? I'm reduced to dividing the number of hours by twenty-four to come up with the number of days. From that I work out what day of the week it is. Then I forget it again.

My mother goes into hospital around Hour One-Fifty-Nine, Day Six, Monday, the day I wake early feeling sick and stub my toe running to the toilet to throw up. As I puke I feel a faint euphoria because I think I know what this means. This is it, my point. To be pregnant in the right place at the right time. Of course my intellect wages battle with this notion. It's too soon for morning sickness. Not only that, it is too fantastic, this repetition of history. It's too fateful; it runs contrary to my beliefs about the randomness of circumstance. Could be just the flu. But. I did go off the pill when Dean went away — sort of a promise to myself to be faithful to him. For the van encounters condoms had to do. And maybe they didn't.

My intellect doesn't have a chance, never did. I'm convinced I can feel the little zygote snuggling into that rich red uterine wall. (Uterine. Cancer.)

I feel better after throwing up. Doesn't feel like the flu.

After some negotiating with the authorities, I am allowed to call my mother at the hospital during the day instead of at night. Her surgery was scheduled for ten a.m. It's now three-thirty (Hour One-Sixty-Six-and-a-Half). After four rings my call is redirected to the switchboard.

"I'm sorry, she's not answering," says the switchboard gal. I get her to put me through to Connie.

"Hi Adi, how's jail?" says Connie.

"Is she out of surgery yet?"

"Hang on, let me check."

The guard sitting in drums her fingers. I start to feel sick again.

"Adi?"

"Yes?"

"She's in the recovery room, surgery successful, no immediate complications…"

I know Connie's speech patterns, I know there's something else coming.

"…except, oh, Adi, I think she's going to lose her ovaries, too. She's a tough lady, though, you should have seen her this morning…" Connie rushes on, trying to fill the space.

I lean forward and throw up between my knees, the phone still stuck to my ear. I manage to tell Connie I'll call back tomorrow and hang up. I definitely have the flu.

I spend the rest of the day and night in a dazed dream punctuated by gradually less frequent purges into a white bucket by my infirmary bed. The next day when I talk to my mother she admits to feeling tired and hollow.

"I wish I'd stayed, Mom, I should have stayed. I should have taken electronic monitoring."

"Still couldn't've been here."

"Oh yeah, that's right. Could've seen you tomorrow, though."

"Anyway, ought means naught," she says.

"What's that?"

"Ought means naught. Something my mother used to say, only she meant it to say it's deeds not words that count. I mean it to say there's no such thing as should."

"Still."

"Still."

"Ought means naught. The Matron would say that. How'd she ever get to be your mother?"

"Same way I got to be yours, I guess."

"What's that supposed to mean?"

"Nothing," she says. "It's not supposed to mean anything." She sighs.

"Mom?"

"When are they going to let you out of there?"

"Another two weeks. Three-hundred and, let me see, two-hundred and forty plus four times twenty-four — three-hundred and thirty-six hours."

She laughs. "I was only in jail for twenty-four hours."

"I know…Mom?"

"I'll be fine."

But she won't. In six months or a year or ten or twenty, my mother will die. One minute she'll be alive. The next she'll be dead. I will have been alive forever.

Dean's voice sings with the others, his breath on my hair. It's like being in church with my grandmother, wanting to sing along, but not wanting to say the words in case they're true — or worse, binding. I find myself humming instead, swaying, holding hands with a hippie-boy on one side and a six-teen-year-old girl on the other. Both of them squeeze my hand as if I need it. The trucks, bright-beamed, eat up the gravel ahead of us, wheeze to a sudden halt. Dean's breath is gone. It's me standing on this road, this loved body blocking it.

You Would Know What To Do

Like a statue of a prime minister — legs apart, shoulders square, eyes in the distance — George stood outside the bank. He was not yet ready to do the thing he meant to do, and standing still for a stretch of time seemed important for some reason. Luckily, it was not too cold for February or he would have had to go right ahead.

As he stood there, a picture was taking shape in his mind, the warmth and clarity of which reduced the street and dull parkette across it to two dimensions and made him forget what chill there was. George found himself doing this often these days, giving equal weight to visions that came from inside the brain and outside it. Memories, one could call them, but the word would never do them justice and was not quite accurate in any case. This was the realm, he was starting to think, of the artist, of the mathematician, the physicist, those who leap into whole new ways of thinking. The world he had formerly inhabited was small, so small, and the worst of it was he had thought it next to infinite.

In the picture, the memory, his wife, Penny, is reading to their children. She did this every Sunday night from the time they were babies until they left home, sitting in her big puffy armchair, her feet up on a small ottoman.

In the picture, the motion picture now, the children are young and she is reading *Peter Pan*. Dorothy, the oldest, is nine or so and sits on the couch doing something with her hands. Knitting, perhaps. And kicking her legs, always kicking her legs. Edmund lies on his back on the floor beside Penny, listening intently and idly running his hands back and forth over the carpet. Alice lies under the piano pretending to be a dog. She pants and scratches herself with her foot and laps water from a bowl Penny lets her keep there. Dorothy and Alice don't always appear to be listening, but every now and then they smile or laugh, or join in on a favourite line. It's a trait they share with their mother, the ability to concentrate on more than one thing at a time.

Alice barks every time the dog in the story is mentioned. She tries for a deep, gruff bark, because the dog is a big dog, but Alice is only six and her deep and gruff is not really either. She gets into a frenzy when Peter lures the children away while the dog is tied up, helpless, in the backyard. Only here can George place himself in the scene. Here he looks up from the *Scientific American* he is reading at the dining room table and roars at her for quiet. Then he takes his magazine to the kitchen. George likes to think that after this departure he puts down the magazine in the kitchen and listens surreptitiously to the rest of the story, a smile of whimsy playing at his lips.

George had remembered that the readings happened, but he hadn't remembered the books they'd read, hadn't remembered that *Peter Pan* was a favourite of Penny's until the children were reminiscing about it after the funeral.

"What would you say, Ed, once a year?" Dorothy half-shouted from the kitchen where she was wrapping up the sandwiches and crudités left over from the reception. "Keeping Saran Wrap in business," George would have said another time.

"At least," Ed said, sprawled in the living room with everyone else.

Alice, slouched in Penny's chair, was looking intently out the window as if trying to identify something outside, a bird, perhaps. George expected her to get up any minute and pluck one of the guidebooks off the shelf. One of the few things the whole family had in common was liking to look things up. Penny and Alice did it for a living — they were librarians, Penny at a public school, Alice at the university.

"Remember how she'd make a big deal out of Tinkerbell dying?" Alice said. George wouldn't have known she was listening, and he felt suddenly like he didn't know his children at all, like they were Penny's, they belonged to Penny, and he was just a sort of difficult pet they had let tag along from time to time. "And we'd have to clap and say we believed in fairies or Tinkerbell would die. Remember, Dad? And you wouldn't clap."

"Wouldn't I?"

"Oh, we kept bugging you," Dorothy said, leaning in the doorway, wiping her hands on Penny's happy face apron. "'Come on, Dad, clap your hands, clap your hands,' but you wouldn't do it, you said something like you *didn't* believe in fairies so it wouldn't be right to clap…"

"And anyway Tinkerbell would never die because she only ever existed in a book in the first place," Edmund said. "Quote, Tinkerbell has life everlasting in print, she doesn't need me to clap for her, unquote."

"Long memory, Ed," Dorothy scoffed.

"I kept a diary."

Alice started quietly to cry.

"I still believe in fairies," Edmund said.

George got up abruptly, taking the last stack of dishes into the kitchen. He could hear Dorothy and Edmund in the living room.

"Jesus, Ed."

"What? It's true."

George leaned into the counter and took deep breaths. Downstairs he could hear the rise and fall of the television. His grandsons, Dorothy's boys, watching videos.

o o o

What George meant to do was rob the bank he stood outside. George McFee, a thin, wide-shouldered man of sixty-nine years, meant to walk into the bank and point the unloaded gun in his pocket at a teller and demand she fill his knapsack with cash. He had no idea how much money he would get, and he wasn't sure to the dime what he'd do with it. Some grand anonymous gesture having to do, in a roundabout way, with Edmund. Something that whenever he thought of it after- wards would tug his lips in a mysterious smile, something that on his deathbed he'd crook his finger to draw them closer and confess in a sly happy whisper. Something that would make a good story.

George was not a desperate man, not in the usual sense of bank robbers, and he was not particularly nervous, but he still needed this time to stand before the deed. Like Penny, that year she took yoga, saying she needed to feel *grounded*. "We're all grounded, that's what gravity is for," he'd said at the time, but now he understood. Penny was dead seven years to the day. That was part of it, too.

The bare treetops made a mat between the city and the sky. A teenaged boy passed in front of him, or was it a girl? He wasn't a teacher anymore; he couldn't tell. George set his eyes on the black web of the treetops. He thought of Birnam Wood and wondered if he'd receive a sign when it was time.

o o o

Penny had been only sixty-one when she was hit by a car while riding her bicycle to work. She rode every day, regardless of the weather. When there was fresh snow, before the streets had been plowed, she rode on the sidewalk in case she slipped.

George's usual birthday gifts to Penny were dull — pleated dresses he should have known wouldn't suit her, kitchen gadg- ets, cookbooks she used only once. So the year mountain bikes came out, he almost choked with excitement. Here was something she'd actually like. Here was something that would surprise her. He spent hours at different shops comparing models, prices and advice, and more hours at the library reading reviews in bicycling magazines.

The Saturday before her birthday he was very close to a decision — it was down to the Sierra or the Rock Hopper. He just had to finish raking the leaves, then he'd pick up the bike and take it to Dorothy's for safekeeping until Friday.

But while he was raking, Penny came pedalling down the street. "Look what I got!" she shouted, ringing the bell on her new mountain bike and grinning to beat the band.

"Oh, Penny!" George said, as disappointed as a boy.

Her face went tight. "Don't rain on my parade for once, George, just don't."

She got off the bike and stomped into the garage, not giving him a chance to tell her what he'd meant. George raked the lawn leafless.

When he came inside, she was on the phone to a friend. Laughing, not sulking or huffing. He decided to go for a run, forgetting she was going out that night to a play he hadn't wanted to see. Not till she was brushing her teeth did George get the opportunity to explain.

"You beat me to the punch," he said. "The bicycle. I wanted so much to buy it for you."

She spat out her toothpaste, took his face in both hands and kissed him on the forehead.

On the morning she was killed, they left the house together into four inches of soft snow and the first clear sky in three weeks — she on her bike, he in the old jogging suit she'd given him one Christmas when jogging was in. She'd bought a matching suit for herself, and matching shoes, but she never took to jogging. She used hers for gardening and bought George new shoes when the old ones wore out.

Penny was riding on the sidewalk as usual when a twenty-six-year-old mechanic with the rising sun in his eyes, late for opening the garage, slid his '76 Duster into her white Norco Stump Jumper as she crossed at a stop sign. Penny flew for the first and last time in her life, thirty feet through the air, headfirst into a parked car. Her neck broke on impact. She did not suffer.

George loved running in the morning, in the park by the river, especially in winter, when he left clouds of breath behind him, when the sun rose clear and yellow over the eddying Speed, and everything, even the shadows, felt clean. He was ashamed of himself for having loved it that morning too, for coming back to the house exhilarated and unknowing. For humming *Bolero* in the shower, for deciding to let the phone ring rather than dripping all over the carpet (at his insistence, they had no answering machine), for going to work as usual, for not knowing this morning was different than any other. As he lay on the couch that night, he ran it all over and over in his head, the run, the shower, his happiness, his oblivion. There was no reason on earth he should have known his wife was being hit by a car, and yet the fact that he hadn't threw his world out of kilter. That was the reason he had to keep running.

Getting ready the next morning, each step seemed insurmountable — putting his legs into his longjohns, lifting his arms over his head to put on his shirt, pulling on the old track suit. When he came to the shoes he kept turning them over, examining the worn sole, the flap at the back where the rubber was delaminating, the stitching across the toe that was starting to come away. Yesterday he hadn't needed new ones. Today he did. Everything had changed.

Where had Penny bought the shoes? How much did they cost? How could Penny not be in the kitchen in her housecoat, blowing on a hot cup of black coffee?

On the feet, he had to tell himself, *shoes on the feet*. He put the right shoe on. The lace was frayed, almost broken through. *If the lace breaks, I won't go*, he thought, closing his eyes and tugging.

A block away from the house, he almost turned back. His heart was racing, he felt shivery with foreboding. Alice had forgotten to pull the screen over the fire as she'd promised the night before, and a coal was just now igniting the floor. Dorothy's boys had made a snowslide that ended on the street where they'd be run over. Dorothy herself had slipped on a bar of soap and was drowning in the tub. He forced himself to keep running.

George had expected to die first. That was the way it happened statistically. The husband first, and then the wife, and later, much later, the children. Edmund beat up in an alley. Alice hit by a truck. Todd daring Kevin to drink Drano. He gave in, he ran home. And there was Alice, looking out the kitchen window, a cup of coffee in her hand. They were fine, they were all fine, it was just Penny, it was just a fluke. Flukes had their place in statistics too. Alice gave him a little wave. He ran on past the house, tears running cold into his ears.

Dorothy was there when he got home. "Jogging? Today? Dad — " Her voice was thick with emotions he couldn't interpret. He didn't bother answering. As he went upstairs he could hear her talking to Alice. "What is he thinking! Jogging! Like it was any other day."

"Yesterday was any other day."

God bless Alice. He ran the bath and sank into the hot water, feeling his chest loosen and his heart contract. He wept until the water went cold.

Every day it was the same. He ran half his route, panic building in his chest until he could not bear it, then raced home to phone his children. He wanted to hear their voices, even on their answering machines. "Hi," he planned to say, "it's your Dad. Just wanted to say — " But he didn't know what he wanted to say, so he listened to their "Hello? Hello?" or to the silence until the second beep sounded, then held the receiver to his chest, depressing the cradle with his finger. He knew he had to stop the day Alice said, "Dad? Is that you?"

George bought a Walkman to run with. He cleaned out the basement. He painted the living room. He wouldn't let

Dorothy and Alice get rid of Penny's clothes. Eventually he went back to work.

The first night that Dorothy and Alice left him on his own he played all the glorious big music Penny had hated, played it so loud it shook the windows. Afterwards, he stood for a long time before noticing the cold of the windowpane under his fingers and against his cheek. Before noticing the silence.

"You would know what to do, wouldn't you?" he said out loud. "You would call your friends, the whole big noisy gang of them. They'd be over here night and day, they'd wrap you up like a big cozy blanket. One of them would take you to Florida for a month, and in Florida you'd forget because it's not a place you'd ever been with me. There'd be nothing around to remind you. It would be warm, that'd make you forget, too."

He felt suddenly that she was outside the house. Not in person, but her spirit. Her spirit was outside the house like a vast cloud snugged up to the brick and glass and shingle and foundation and extending outwards and downwards like an aura. He stood right beside the front door with his head cocked, as if he could hear it. He flung the door open. Gone, as he'd known it would be.

In the kitchen he made himself an instant decaf and felt it again. She was out there, she was right *there*, and he would never touch her. He would never touch her again.

"Maybe you'd stay in Florida longer," he said, pitching his voice louder without knowing why, then realizing it was so the chair could hear it, Penny's big chair in the living room. "Maybe you'd decide to move down there. And you'd meet a widower. Fun guy. Bit of a joker. Not like me at all, and for that reason you'd marry him. You'd go on adventure cruises. Costa Rica. Alaska. He'd get you to overcome your fear of flying."

He went into the living room and looked at the chair while he spoke to it. "Eh? Would you do that? Marry him, the guy who's fun at parties? Sure you would. Go ahead. You deserve it."

Dorothy had given him *On Death and Dying*; he recognized the stages he was going through. It didn't matter. He liked talking to the chair. Before Penny's death George had felt closest to Dorothy. Alice's stillness, her soft deep voice with its hint of misanthropy, had put him off. But it was Alice he told about the chair. Dorothy was the one who would sooner or later put him in a home. Sooner if she found out he talked to chairs.

"I can't bring myself to sit in it," he told Alice. "Like something would happen. It would swallow me up, or, I don't know. Silly thing to think."

"I sat in it once," Alice said. "The day of the funeral. I remember the light came in in a peculiar way. Not brighter or less bright, but — thicker somehow. More thick."

After a long summer, George was eager to get back to school, but when he stood in front of his homeroom class the first day, he felt none of the nervousness and enthusiasm of other years. He didn't care if these kids learned which gases are inert and which are volatile or how to make polyester or how the reaction of sugar and yeast combined with wheat gluten and heat makes dough into bread. He didn't care if he never again saw that moment of unveiling in their eyes when one of them got it, really got it, for the first time. Spring — retirement — rose in the distance like a mountain he was approaching on foot. When he finally reached the top, it turned into a plain again. He sold the house, which angered Edmund, saddened Alice, and was applauded by Dorothy. Of course he kept the chair.

When Edmund got sick, he lost something, some edge. George hadn't expected that. He wasn't surprised otherwise, that Edmund had it, that none of them had told him until they'd had no choice. Penny had set the tone for that when she'd lied about Edmund in the first place. Who knows what else she'd kept from him. The girls could have had abortions for all he knew.

That first lie…every time George thought of it he shook his head. It *still* made him mad. He and Penny had been getting ready for bed after taking Edmund out to dinner for his twenty-fourth birthday. She lay in bed reading. And he, cautiously, as he took off his shirt and tie, had wondered aloud about Edmund and girls.

"When was the last time he had a girlfriend?" he asked.

"That we knew about?" Penny said without looking up. "I guess that would be Amy."

"Amy was a long time ago. Do you think…"

"Mm-hm."

George cleared his throat. "Do you think he could be," he cleared his throat again, "homosexual?"

"Oh, I don't think so. I think he's just shy. I think he's still going through that separation stage, you know, when he doesn't want us to know everything about him." She turned the page, never having taken her eyes off it. George thought she was probably right. She generally was about these things.

But the minute George saw Edmund on the news holding another man's hand, he was never more certain of anything than that Penny already knew. Gay Pride Day. George had never heard of such a thing.

"It's an oxymoron," George said to Edmund the next Sunday. George had not told Penny he'd seen Edmund on the news. Instead he suggested they have Edmund over for dinner Sunday. Penny was delighted. She wanted them to have more of a relationship.

"The hell it is," said Edmund.

"It is. Morally speaking, Gay Pride Day is an oxymoron."

"Oh, it's morals now, is it? We've moved on from science?"

They were just warming up. Penny was in the kitchen, crying. Not because of Edmund, because of George.

"I saw you on the news the other day, Ed," George had started. "On the *news*, for God's sake. It's not enough I have a faggot for a son; he has to broadcast it to the world. 'Look, everybody, I take it up the ass.'"

"George!" Penny said.

Edmund dropped his fork and threw up his arms.

"Oh, Ed!" Penny said. "Didn't you see the cameras?"

That was it: the confirmation George had been waiting for.

"Why don't you go read a book, Penny. Why don't you go read a goddamn book." George started mimicking her, pitching his voice high and shrill. "'You know Ed, he's just shy. Why, even if he did have a girlfriend, that doesn't mean he'd tell us about it, now does it, dear?' You make me sick, the two of you."

So Penny cried in the kitchen while her husband and son yelled at each other in the dining room. After the door slammed behind Edmund, George went to the basement to avoid Penny and then sat there, reorganizing his tool bench, hoping she'd come down. When she did, when she apologized, he couldn't keep from crying. They held each other, saying I'm sorry. There wasn't much else they could do.

o o o

George dimly registered that passersby were noticing him, and thought he had better move from the side of the bank to the bus stop, a place where people are expected to stand still in the cold. He stepped back when the bus came, and forward when it left.

George hadn't fooled himself with his Peter Pan scene — at the moment, he was keenly aware he had not secretly listened and smiled while Penny told the story. He hadn't done it because he hadn't understood the point of either the story or the telling. When he pilfered candle stubs as a boy, it was to read *Popular Mechanics*, not *Treasure Island*. Penny blamed his bewilderment with fiction on his deprived, bookless childhood. Deprived it might have been, compared to hers, but it had given him a practical and uncluttered mind, and he was thankful for that. Why would anyone spend hours, years, reading about things that never happened and people who never existed? It was all right for Penny, but George had a whole universe to explain. He didn't have time for fiction.

o o o

After their big blowup, George and Edmund had seen little
of each other. Edmund came at Christmas and Thanksgiving,
talked volubly to everyone else, asked George a few polite
questions about his work, answered George's few polite questions and then left early. Penny, on the other hand, saw him
once a week for lunch. She was their unspoken go-between,
their interpreter. George thought she was making some head-
way. He no longer felt nauseated by the thought of two men
together, although he tried not to think of it at all; he accepted
that maybe Ed was not sick, just different. And then Penny
had died.

He didn't know where to go next. He didn't know what to
do with Ed's comment about believing in fairies. He didn't
know what to do about Ed, so he didn't do much of anything,
except worry.

And still he got used to it. He just hadn't realized how until
Alice called him with the news.

"We thought you should know. Ed has AIDS." Beautiful
blunt Alice. He imagined Ed and Dorothy fussing behind her,
Who's going to tell Dad? What are we going to say? And Alice
just picking up the phone.

George had been reading up on AIDS. It fascinated him.
A brand new disease. Its very existence was fascinating. And
the kind of disease it was — one that let all other diseases have
their way with the body. If anyone had thought it up, it would
be brilliant. For years George had predicted new diseases to
take the place of former population checks like polio and scar-
let fever and cholera. That even they had not been entirely
stamped out sustained his belief in a world seeking ecological
balance. The battle was still Man against Nature, but unlike
his bush-clearing forebears, George was rooting for both sides.
Here was AIDS: advantage, Nature. Here was Man staging a
comeback, scrambling for a cure.

"Where is he?" George asked Alice.

"Right here, we're at the hospital. You want to talk to him?"

Alice was off the line before he had a chance to ask how bad it was.

"Hi, Dad."

"How are you feeling?"

"Ah, well, you know. Not so good."

"I'm sorry to hear that."

There was a long pause.

"I was hoping you'd tell me before it got to this," George said.

"You knew?"

"I've been expecting it."

"Right. Of course. I was bound to get it. Listen, Dad, I'm going to hang up now, okay?"

George went and stood behind Penny's chair. He put his hands on its back. He knelt down and put his arms along its arms. His son was going to die. He *had* been expecting it, because if he didn't it would take him by surprise, and he didn't ever want to be taken by surprise again. From now on, he wanted to do the surprising.

"You'd be one of those women I see on the news, wouldn't you?" he whispered to the chair. "Yes, you would. Out there with your placards, shaking your fist. I never knew what you were on about." He was quiet for a minute. "You must have hated me sometimes."

The next day he donated ten thousand dollars banked from the sale of his house to AIDS research.

Ed was only in hospital three days that first time. He always seemed to be sleeping or dozing when George visited, and George wondered if that was real or put on so they wouldn't have to talk. George didn't want to talk, anyway; he just wanted to care for his son. He made a list of things to do and get for Ed's apartment — bath rails, toilet rail, bedpan, foam mattress pad, hemorrhoid cushion. Alice told him he was being premature.

On his way out on the second day, George passed a man he recognized but couldn't place. Usually he was quick to identify the adult incarnations of his students, and the fact that he'd missed this one kept him puzzling all evening. It wasn't until he was falling asleep that he realized it was the other man he'd seen on TV, the one holding Ed's hand.

The next day George saw the two of them holding hands again — or rather René holding Ed's hand between both of his. It looked different this time. A bit shocking, but not offensive. Nice, even. As soon as Ed saw George, he drew his hand away.

"I've heard a lot about you," René said when Ed introduced them.

"Yes," said George. "Yes." He cleared his throat. "You went to Mexico together."

"Beautiful place. Great trip." René recrossed his legs and flattened a pant seam. "The doctor says Eddie should be out tomorrow."

"Yes, I thought I'd buy some groceries."

René coughed. "Oh, really. That's nice."

George left quickly. Ed was uncomfortable with both of them there. More accurately, Ed was uncomfortable with him.

George decided he had to do now what Penny had wanted him to do six years ago. He had to get to know his son. He had to see him regularly, and he was pleased with himself for thinking of a way he could combine this with something else he wanted to do — start Ed on a macrobiotic diet. Preliminary studies seemed to show it made a difference in the life span of patients with full-blown AIDS as well as in the HIV-positive population. George decided he would cook for Ed.

He got the key to Ed's apartment from Alice so he could drop the first batch of groceries off and see what staples he might need to get. She didn't say a word about the possibility of René being there.

"Uh…hello," René called out from the living room as George let himself in. George wanted to disappear. He turned to leave, then heard René behind him and turned back.

"No one told me… I didn't realize…" He lifted up Penny's net bags full of food. "Groceries."

René slapped his forehead. "I thought you meant for yourself. I'm thinking, 'Grocery shopping, how nice for him, but how exactly does this relate to Ed?'"

"Well, I'll just…" George gestured he'd leave the bags there.

"No, no, no, you take it home. We have lots of groceries."

"But it's macrobiotic. I spent an hour at the health-food store."

René cocked his head, smiling. "Well all right then, what have you got?"

They developed a sort of friendship, René and George, based on their discussions of Edmund's conditions, current research, experimental drugs, diets, mental health. René was also a scientist, a chemist. He ran a lab at the university.

He made George nervous at first. He did not look effeminate, but his voice and gestures regularly veered off into a language George had only seen in parody. He was not shy about it and gave no sign that he noticed George's discomfort, but he must have, because early on he said, "You have no sense of camp whatsoever, do you George?"

"René!" said Edmund.

"Of course you don't. You're Eddie's father. Never mind, we'll let you make us dinner anyway."

Edmund looked apoplectic. René leaned confidentially over to George. "I adore making him twitch."

George laughed. He realized how much he and Edmund tippy-toed around each other, trying not to give offense. René breaking their unspoken rules was a relief. He found himself telling René — and by extension, Ed — things he would never have told before, like how he was starting to see things that weren't there, and how he felt like Penny lived on in her chair. How he'd appreciated her, but maybe in the wrong way, maybe for the wrong things, and how much that possibility pained him. Ed didn't contradict him or reassure him, but he looked him in the eyes for the first time in ages, and George felt a lump in his throat.

Alice was right about George being premature with the sick-room paraphernalia. Ed got healthy again. Not completely — he still had night sweats and diarrhea — but enough to work. Working made him happy.

George thought the distance between him and his son was closing. The nights he cooked for Ed and René were the high-light of his week. He spent the days leading up to it planning the menu, and whole afternoons hunting down unusual in-gredients. He went to cooking classes at the health-food store. The moments after they took their first few bites became moments of high drama: Will they stop to exclaim over the exquisite taste? Will they savour the taste wordlessly on their tongue? Or will they shovel it in like it was any other dinner?

Their routine was this: George arrived early, around five, and started cooking while Ed, depending on how he felt, ei-ther kept working or watched TV. René arrived at six, took a shower, then helped George with the salad while Ed read them choice bits from the newspaper. "Grey Panther caught," read Ed. "The Florida bank robber nicknamed 'the Grey Panther' was apprehended today while attempting to flee a St. Petersburg bank on a moped. Charles Panowski, 75, is in custody on six charges of armed robbery."

"A moped?" René asked.

"Apparently."

"My God, that's too beautiful."

"Wonder what he did with the money."

"Built a private shuffleboard court."

"Renewed his lawn bowling membership."

"Bought seven pairs of white shoes, one for every day of the week."

After dinner, Ed would always offer to do the dishes and George and René would always refuse. This was when they talked treatment. AZT was the big topic these days. The drug had just been approved in the U.S. after determined lobby-ing on the part of AIDS organizations and direct action by groups like ACT UP. George had reservations about ACT UP, but he admired their brashness and vigour.

After several weeks of discussion, George took the idea to Ed one night after dinner.

"You and René think I should go on AZT," Ed repeated back to him.

"Yes."

"Uh-huh, yeah, and what about my bone marrow?"

"You can stop taking it if you're losing bone marrow."

"Who's going to pay for it?"

"I am."

"That's what I thought." Edmund spun his chair away from George and stared at his computer screen for a minute. He spun back. "No," he said.

"No?"

"No."

"Why not?"

"I don't want your money."

"But…"

"I don't want your money, I don't want you making decisions for me, I don't want you making me dinner every week, I don't want to eat macrobiotics, I don't want this perfectly planned little healthy life. You and René, I swear, you look like you're having fun sometimes there in the kitchen with all your little debates, 'Have you read this article? Have you read that? What do you think about ddI? What do you think about epoetin alfa?' I've been trying to appreciate it, what you're doing — for Mom's sake if for nothing else — but you know what I think in the end? I think it drives you nuts that this is something you can't control. And you can't. You can't control it."

"Maybe AZT can."

"What am I talking to, a wall? I'm dying. You can't stop that."

"Not me, personally, maybe…"

"Listen, Dad. Nice try, okay? You've done your little bit, you've shown you cared, now maybe it's time we go back to the way things really are. I mean, why pretend we like each other? We never have before. Let's be honest here."

George walked away from Ed's feeling like his heart was in his shoes, and his shoes didn't want to go to the apartment he now lived in; they wanted to go home to the place where once upon a time he had counted himself the head of a happy family, a confident man in a modest but important job, providing his three children with an honest, disciplined example of how to be a good person.

He turned down his old street with a sense of rightness. He thought he would stand in front of the house for a while and trace its outline with his eyes, run through its rooms in his head, but as he got close to it he saw the blue flicker of light from a television in the living room and kept walking. The house had no memory — it housed whom it housed and no more.

At home, he sat in Penny's armchair for the first time. An embrace. A bountiful, forgiving embrace. He fell asleep there. And dreamed. In his dream he was a Member of Parliament with offices in a rich stately chamber that he couldn't get out of because the door was barricaded by a group of militant feminists. Then he discovered if he lay on his stomach and licked the floor, the room became an elevator of sorts, descending into the bowels of the Parliament Buildings, a series of dank tunnels from which he could escape only by shutting his eyes and running as fast as he could.

When he woke up, he knew exactly what he was going to do.

o o o

George put his hands in the pockets of his blue trench coat. It wasn't suspicious, the trench coat. Men his age wore trench coats as a matter of course. He fingered the old army pistol in his pocket. Nothing about him was suspicious. It struck him as funny that any number of people could be walking around with pistols in their pockets and no one would know unless they drew them. He blew on his hands and rubbed them together.

Edmund really was dying. He'd never taken back what he'd said to George, but he didn't object when a month or so later George phoned to say he wanted to start making dinner for him again. As he got sicker, Edmund stopped caring who paid for what. René took a leave of absence from his job. George paid for the AZT, and when Ed and René's savings had run out, he paid for the rent. He wouldn't let René cash his RRSPs.

By now George was part of the team: he, René, Alice, and half a dozen of Ed's friends, who took turns visiting, amusing, lifting, driving, comforting, teasing, soothing. They were marvellous people. They loved his son. He almost thought they might love him, too.

In the evenings they started a course of reading Penny's favourite children's books. It felt absolutely right for George to sit in the next room with his journals, listening in. The few times that Ed took a turn reading, it sent shivers up George's spine. He read in exactly Penny's lifts and turns. It was a gift, bringing her back like that, a double gift: Penny's intonation in a voice like his own.

One night after Ed was asleep, George went into his room, took the book from the bedside table and read until he was finished. It was about another world, where animals talked, evil was evil and anyone could be a hero. It was the book Edmund was named for. George took the series home and read them all, sitting in Penny's chair, formulating his plan — simple is best; as simple as possible. Maybe he'd get enough money to start an AIDS hospice for the Guelph area.

The sign he'd been waiting for still had not come. For a moment he'd thought it had, a flicker of light out of the corner of his eye, but it was just the street signal, white walker striding, red hand flashing, over and over.

His feet were cold inside his brand-new running shoes. The shoes were red and white, like the street signal, purchased from a suitably anonymous discount store the week before. He would ditch the trench coat and the shoes down by the river where he had stashed his regular shoes, and then emerge from the bushes, a regular jogger on his regular route. He knew from this morning that the path by the river had been packed down by hundreds of jogging shoes like his own. He wouldn't leave a trail.

He pulled down his tuque and walked into the bank.

Malcolm Loves Cathy

Malcolm put his hand out the window, spreading his fingers and weaving it through the hard air, trying to find one of those soft pockets to rest in, like warm spots in a lake. A stone spit up by the truck in front of them made a tiny dent in the heel of his hand.

"Ow," he said, and pulled in his hand. Cathy didn't seem to notice. Her arm was out the window, too, her hand resting on the sideview mirror as she drove, and she was singing along with Neil Young on the car stereo. His car stereo. Cathy didn't have a car.

Malcolm and Cathy were on their way to Lansing to be married. It was the Friday of a long weekend either side of the border — Victoria Day in Canada, Memorial Day in the States. No one called it Victoria Day anymore, it was just "the May 24th weekend," or worse, "May two-four weekend." Malcolm himself felt vaguely Victorian for not liking the change. So a case of beer meant more to people than a queen dead for ninety-odd years; what was wrong with that? The wedding was on Sunday.

"What's Memorial Day memorialize?" he asked Cathy.

"I don't know. Dead guys." Cathy went back to singing. Malcolm studied her face, the fineness of her nostrils, the strength of her cheeks, red-brown already from the first month of the ball season. Malcolm loved to watch Cathy play, the way she rolled onto the balls of her feet as the pitcher wound up, perfectly ready each time to launch herself at that line drive that came maybe one in twenty hits. The way a stream of inane encouragements issued from her mouth between plays, "Let's go Hummer, chuck 'em in there, buddy, like you can now, like you can, look sharp out there, you Arrows…" until she'd quiet down for the pitch, the hit, the play, then start it all over again. Malcolm drank coffee in the stands with the other wives and never got bored of it.

Malcolm loved Cathy, and that was the worst of it, this marriage thing. It would have been so much easier if he didn't.

"Why are we doing this?" he asked.

Cathy turned up the music. "What?" she said.

"I said, why are we doing this," Malcolm shouted.

"What?" she said again, turning up the music even louder, laughing. The joke had started with his first car, a '79 Ford station wagon, which had been the golden goose of new and ominous sounds — not for it a simple chitty-chitty, bang-bang. "What's that noise?" Cathy would ask when a new gunka-gunka or queek surfaced, and Malcolm would turn up the music and say "What?" It was one of those jokes they kept doing so long after it stopped being funny that eventually it was funny again. Like his brother, Cathy could make Malcolm laugh no matter how mad he was. He hated it, and this time he did not laugh. He thought with relief that maybe the joke had finally had it, until he became aware that his face was relaxing from a half-smile.

Hey, hey, my, my, Cathy was singing along with Neil, *Rock and roll will never die.*

Malcolm had wanted a city hall wedding. That they might do it any other way had never occurred to him until Cathy called her mother one Sunday morning. A sound like the women on the other end of Wilma's phone conversations on *The Flintstones* drew him drop-jawed into the hall. It was Bunny, squealing down the phone line all the way from

Michigan. Cathy held the phone away from her ear and rolled her eyes. Malcolm's own mother was British and serious — and, fortunately, back in England after her divorce, living with *her* mother. He had not thought Bunny possible. But there she was, audibly delirious with excitement that her lesbian daughter was making a marriage of convenience.

"It's not what you think, Mom," Cathy said. "It's just so I have a guarantee I can stay after I finish school. I haven't converted or anything."

Malcolm put the kettle on and went back to the paper. When he heard Cathy saying no, they hadn't set a date yet, he got up, turned on the radio and closed the door.

It had been his idea, getting married. Problem: Cathy wanted to stay in Canada. Solution: a certificate of marriage. Simple. They already lived together. Enough people assumed they were a couple that it had more than once created difficulties getting dates. Covering for the immigration people would be a snap. Cathy couldn't get married to any of her lovers even if she wanted to, and Malcolm didn't believe in marriage. A short ceremony, a piece of paper and Cathy could stay as long as she wanted. Easy.

The phone call gave weight where no weight ought to be given. Why Cathy had even told her mother before they'd done it and it was over with, Malcolm did not know. He didn't plan to tell his mother at all.

Brenda, his friend first, before she became Cathy's lover, came into the kitchen in Cathy's pyjamas and kissed him on the head. The initial strangeness of having her so often at his house, but not to see him, had worn off. She made a point of asking him to do things without Cathy, movies and plays and picnics on the Island, and he liked that. "Bunny?" she asked, nodding her head towards the hall.

"Bunny," Malcolm replied.

Brenda poured water from the boiling kettle into his teapot and folded a paper towel into the Melita one-cup coffee maker. "You don't have to go through with it," she said. "She could find a job like other Americans and just get them to assure the government she's the only possible candidate for it."

"I suppose," he said.

They looked up expectantly when they heard the receiver fall back into place. Cathy appeared in the doorway. "Bunny wants a church wedding," she said. They all laughed.

Malcolm was a mystery to himself. It seemed to him that he had free will and it also seemed that he exercised it, yet more often than not he would look back and only be able to see himself as a cork bobbing along on one huge, angry and ferocious wave that, from the cork's point of view, was actually the whole universe, but that, as he travelled out of cork-body to stand human on the shore, became just another petulant whitecap. *Cathy's right*, Malcolm thought, *a brain like this, I should have been a painter not a law student…Law student. As if it were a profession in itself.*

When Cathy had come to see the "room in shared house to rent," they had ended up talking about numbers. Cathy claimed numbers were abstract concepts; they just existed, independent of their names — one, two and so on — and of their numerals. Malcolm, on the other hand, thought of numbers as a series of dots, roughly in the shape of the numeral they were represented by. A thought that had no shape was no thought at all as far as Malcolm was concerned. He didn't believe Cathy saw nothing whatsoever when he proffered numbers to her, one after the other. He didn't believe that Cathy could, as she claimed, have thoughts without either words or visuals. And no, babies didn't think. Without language, how could they? Which was when Cathy had said, "With a mind like that, you should be a painter, not a lawyer." To which he had replied, "I can't paint."

There was something that kept him at law school, something more than the feeling he got from his small crowd of left-leaning types that to drop out would be a gross moral failure. He wanted to *know*, he wanted to *argue*, he wanted to *convince*. The less he had those things in his personal life, the more he wanted them from his professional life. He could argue with Cathy, but he couldn't convince her.

Now that he thought of it, that first meeting with Cathy had had a bobbing feeling to it, too — gentler than the stormy wash to the precipice they were on now, but random and inevitable just the same. What Malcolm was trying to pin-point was how his idea — getting married — had become something completely outside of his imaginings: a wedding. It was a grand joke to Cathy, and maybe that was the whole answer.

"Think of all the loot we'll score," she had said. "Fifty-fifty, down the middle. You get first dibs, of course."

Malcolm didn't want first dibs.

Primed with contempt for Cathy's mother, Malcolm was taken aback to recognize Cathy under Bunny's middle-aged tennis-lipstick lips and streaked hair as she ran out the door to greet them. She had, in fact, just returned from playing tennis and was surprised to see them pull into the driveway so soon. If she'd only known, she would have — oh, but never mind. She hugged Cathy and kissed her on the cheek. Jock would be home from the office soon; she didn't know *where* John was, probably in some garage somewhere, "jamming." She said it with quotation marks. "I always picture a big kitchen, with canning jars." She laughed.

"And you're Malcolm," she said, pausing for the first time, looking him up and down. Malcolm felt crumpled in his jeans and T-shirt. Defiantly crumpled, proud to be crumpled.

"You must be — " He stopped himself because he felt funny about calling someone he had never met Bunny.

"Bunny. Of course I am. Well. Come on inside, Malcolm, we've got a lot of catching up to do. All of it. I want to hear all about you. Your mother's in England? Too bad she can't make it, it must be very disappointing — "

Bunny swept Malcolm up the walk. He caught Cathy's eye,

a plea, but she shrugged and got their bags out of the car. Bunny led Malcolm to the kitchen, where she was making iced tea. She interrupted herself to tell Cathy to put their bags in the guest room. Cathy's bedroom had been converted to a study.

Malcolm continued to be astonished at Bunny's hypocrisy. She gave not one indication that she knew this wedding was a sham, she was every bit the prospective mother-in-law, yet she must have known that he knew she knew what was really going on. He felt like he'd been dropped into a slightly surreal soap opera, like if he caught his own face in a mirror it would be square-jawed, high-cheeked and framed by virile, backward-flowing, black hair with a single lock that fell boyishly and seductively over his broad high forehead. He drank his iced tea and answered Bunny's questions.

It was a relief when Jock did get home. He looked like his name, tall and grey-templed, the aging collegiate athlete. He was jovial and manly with Malcolm and not much different with Cathy. Cathy had seen his car coming from the kitchen window and dropped the lettuce she was washing to go to the door. They exchanged a hearty hug, two ruddy cheeks grazing. The pure and beautiful delight they took in greeting one another lasted only a moment, but Malcolm felt like he was witnessing the birth of a colt, or a thunderstorm or some other miracle of nature.

"How can you stand to let your father think you're really getting married?" Malcolm asked Cathy as they undressed that night. "How can you play this game?"

"I hate myself every minute," Cathy said, smiling.

"The way you ran to the door, it was like — " Would it be an insult to say, Like you were a little girl?

Cathy waited for him to finish his sentence. "Like what?" she said when he didn't.

"I don't know. It just surprised me. You, like, love him."

Cathy was still for a moment. She was different here, in her parents' house. Almost imperceptibly so, but Malcolm knew her. In fact, most of the time he thought he knew her better than she knew herself. There was some skin she had pulled on as they parked the car in the driveway that she thought protected her, but really all it did was leave the part underneath more vulnerable than ever.

"So?" She pulled her sweatshirt and T-shirt off in one piece and dumped it on the floor. She was remarkably comfortable with her own nakedness. Malcolm had turned his back on the room as he dropped his jeans and put on fresh boxer shorts.

"So, how can you do this to him?"

Cathy pulled off her pants and underwear and stepped into her own boxer shorts, flashier than Malcolm's — white with big red polka-dots. She wore them for ball practice, too. "Sad to say, I'm with Bunny on this one. It's what he wants. It's what they both want, and look how easy it is to give it to them. What does it matter to us? Really. Besides, it's kind of a thrill to put one over on everyone, don't you think?"

"It makes me nervous. I keep thinking I'm going to slip up."

"You're doing great, Mal. Anyway, they see what they want to see."

Malcolm wanted to keep talking. There was so much he wanted to know. The wedding had seemed small enough when he'd agreed to it, a weekend out of his life. Three days and then everything would go back to normal, but now it loomed huge and portentous ahead of him, and damn if he wasn't starting to have doubts just like any other bridegroom. Cathy put on a different T-shirt and climbed into bed beside him, giving him something else to think about. I am sleeping with my best friend, he told himself, I am sleeping with my best friend. It was working until she rolled over and put an arm across his chest. She looked into his eyes.

"Thanks for doing this, Mal," she said and kissed him on the cheek. "Goodnight, sleep well."

Malcolm didn't. He started thinking. Thinking about love, and whether that was what he truly felt for Cathy. He wasn't lovesick and pining, that much was clear, and it hadn't happened in a whoosh like a toppling building, either. No, he'd never *fallen* in love with Cathy. He had just gradually started to prefer her to anyone else. Malcolm sank into the quagmire his mind always encountered when he tried to pursue this line of thought — the love-line. He loved her as a friend, but he also desired her sexually, but he wasn't jealous of her lovers and he had been able to have at least one decent relationship of his own at the same time, even though it had ended poorly. Up to his knees in muck. Was romantic love just a wish-fulfillment myth? Was it a palliative adjunct to the drive to procreate, and if it was, what did that say about same-sex love? Was it merely a social imperative, the great love stories of the collective unconscious forever haunting the individual consciousness? Malcolm hated his brain for doing this to him. Muck, muck, muck.

He tried to free-associate so he could fall asleep — base-balls turning into doves that flew off into a calm blue evening sky that inverted into a lake with reflected trees, ripples emanating from a thrown stone. Eventually it worked.

Malcolm hated the whole idea of golf, but he somehow found himself teeing off with Jock at nine o'clock the next morning. The man thing, that's what he was supposed to be doing, and he wasn't at all sure he knew how.

"I want you to know, I'm terrible at golf," he said to Jock. "I've only played once, and I think I at least doubled par on every hole." It had been with Cynthia, a former girlfriend, who had dumped him that same afternoon. He'd had a vague feeling ever since that golf was not merely a game but some kind of test.

"Everybody's got to start somewhere," Jock said, handing him a driver.

His first ball miraculously landed in the middle of the fairway. Jock nodded approvingly. "Not bad, not bad," he said, then sent his own ball in a perfect arc to the green. They played in comparative silence for the first three holes. Malcolm was

pleased with himself. He'd managed just two over par on each
hole. Even real golfers did that sometimes. Then Jock started
talking.

"It might surprise you," Jock said, "but I don't have a problem at all with young people living together before they get
married. In fact, I think it's a good idea. You should try these
things out before you commit to someone, that's what I say.
Bunny and I, now we didn't live together, but we did try things
out, if you know what I mean." Jock grinned and Malcolm
smiled back uncertainly.

"What I don't understand," Jock continued after Malcolm
dribbled his ball a hundred feet further down the fourth fairway, "is why Cathy never brought you down to see us before.
You're not like other boys she's dated, but you're nothing to
be ashamed of, are you?" He said it in his jovial tone, so
Malcolm assumed he meant no offence, but it seemed like an
odd thing to say. Malcolm had to stop himself before releas-
ing the automatic "No, sir" that rose through his throat. Just
as well, since Jock said it for him.

"No sir, you're not. A young lawyer, steady, keen, ready to
take on the world, that's what I see in you. A bit idealistic,
maybe, but you're supposed to be idealistic when you're young,
plenty of time to be realistic later. No, sir, nothing wrong with
you at all. So I ask myself, Why didn't Cathy ever bring this
boy home before she decided to marry him? And you know
what?" Malcolm didn't. "I don't have an answer for that question. Maybe you do."

Malcolm and Cathy had prepared for this sort of thing.

"Well, there are a lot of reasons, really. One thing about both
of us being in school is we have to choose how we spend our
free time pretty carefully since we don't have much of it. And
neither of us is very traditional. We like to have our independence. We like to be able to do things apart as well as together,
and for myself — no offence to you or anything — but I've
never really liked the idea of in-laws. That's the honest truth.
I feel like, I'm marrying Cathy. I don't have to marry her family, and she doesn't have to marry mine."

All true, but Malcolm's stomach was crawling with deceit. Jock looked off down the course for a minute, then put his hand on Malcolm's shoulder sincerely and said, "I respect that." He lifted his hand and brought it down again. "I do. I respect your honesty."

Cathy took Malcolm on a tour of her childhood haunts in the afternoon. They climbed on top of the sagging baseball cage at her old public school — grade school, she called it — and lay on their backs, feeling the comfortable bounce of chain-link underneath them. Malcolm was wondering how to tell her that he didn't want to do it anymore. *Cathy*, he should have been able to say, *I'm not sure I can go through with this. A verbal lie is one thing, but this is a physical lie, a lie we have to act out, a monumental, perpetual lie.*

But he couldn't think of a good way out of it, either, unless they eloped, and that would be pretty foolish since the whole point was to provide Bunny and Jock with a spectacle. Even saying he didn't want to get married at all meant more lies because it wasn't his place to tell Jock the truth.

Brenda had said all along it was a bad idea. For days after Cathy had convinced Malcolm to have a wedding in Lansing, Brenda went around sighing, shaking her head and saying, "O what a tangled web we weave," as if to herself.

"You sure won Jock over," Cathy said. "What did you say to him out there?"

Malcolm moaned. "What?" said Cathy. She wore the beginnings of a smile, the kind people have when they expect what the other person is about to say will be funny.

"I told him you hadn't brought me to meet them because I felt strongly that our relationship was with each other, not with each other's families."

"What did he say?"

"He said he respected me."

Cathy laughed. "That's great."

Malcolm propped himself on his elbows. "No, Cathy, it's not great. It's lousy. He thinks he respects me, but if he knew the truth, he'd despise me. We're not lovers, we're never going to be. This whole thing is a farce and it's cruel. I hate it."

"You really want my father's good opinion?"

Malcolm brought the heels of his hands down on the baseball cage in frustration and sat up in the same motion. "You're so fucking oblivious. God." He looked at her then. She looked genuinely surprised — hurt too — but he could have sworn that at the very moment he felt a twinge of remorse for hurting her, she had been about to say, Oblivious to what?

"So what are you saying?" she said slowly. "Are you saying you want to call it off?"

"Maybe," he said.

"Well," she said, "it wouldn't be the first time a wedding was called off at the last minute." She rolled over onto her stomach and stared through the chain-link for a while. Then she lifted her head and asked him, "What do you want to do? Jilt me at the altar? That'd be kinda fun, too."

There it was, her credo — everything is laughable, all the time. Malcolm had to admit, it did have a certain charm.

They had drinks together out on the patio before the rehearsal. The four of them, Bunny and Jock, Malcolm and Cathy. Cathy's younger brother John had put in a brief appearance before disappearing again, as he'd done the rest of the weekend. He would show up for meals, sit through them mostly in silence, pulling at his frayed jeans, barely looking at anyone else, and then disappear afterwards. In Malcolm's family it was a crime to be as non-participatory as John, but the MacNeils didn't seem to notice.

Malcolm was worried that Jock would ask why Malcolm's family wasn't coming to his wedding, but Bunny must have provided some excuse that kept him from asking. Malcolm wondered what it was, whether she had created some great family tragedy that mustn't be mentioned, an alcoholic father

and institutionalized brother or something. Which wouldn't
be far off the mark.

"Isn't it lovely that the weather's cooperating," Bunny said.

"Perfect day for golf," Jock said. "Eh, Malcolm?"

"Perfect," Malcolm said. He took a sip of his scotch and
rolled it around on his tongue. Jock assumed a brotherhood
between them that Malcolm actually found himself liking. He
entertained a vision of the same scene fifteen years down the
road, he and Cathy joining Bunny and Jock on a golf holiday, say, having drinks on some verandah in Florida or Palm
Springs. Now that he didn't have to go through with it, he
could let himself imagine these things.

"How's the ball team shaping up this year, Cathy?" Jock
asked. He didn't give her time to answer, but turned to Malcolm.
"Bunny thinks Cathy's too old for softball. She thinks when
girls get to a certain age they should play more genteel games,
tennis, or badminton, but I say you play the game you love
as long as you can, girl or no girl."

"Oh, Jock," Bunny said.

"I'm with you a hundred per cent," Malcolm said.

"Mind you, you keep an eye out. Some of those girls have
unnatural desires, if you know what I mean. You don't want
some bull dagger coming on to your wife." Jock laughed.
Cathy stared at her empty glass, and for a moment Malcolm
did the same, caught in implicit collusion with the man whose
brotherhood he'd been enjoying only seconds before. He
coughed.

"I'm sure Cathy could handle herself if the situation ever
arose," he said. It wasn't quite what he meant.

Jack laughed again, harder than before. "You've got a point,
there. Cathy's not what you'd call a shrinking violet, is she?"

"I mean, it's not like lesbians are any worse than men for
coming on to women — straight women, I mean. In fact,
they're probably a whole lot better."

Jock raised his eyebrows. "Is that so," he said.

"Freshen your drink, Malcolm?" Bunny asked, getting up.
She looked scared.

"Thanks," he said. "Let me help you." He took Cathy's glass as well as his own and followed Bunny.

"We're kind of in a building phase this year," he could hear Cathy say to Jock. "A lot of rookies who could be really good with a couple seasons under their belts."

Malcolm poured a finger of scotch for himself as Bunny mixed a gin and tonic. He couldn't think of a thing to say.

"I suppose you think this is all very foolish," she said, not looking at him. "But Jock would have a fit if he knew, a heart attack, I don't know. The way he dotes on her, following in his footsteps, sports and engineering and all — he'd just have a fit. John's not, well, he's not the — " She started to cry lightly. Malcolm put a hand on her arm. John's not the what? Oh no. Not the son he wanted? John's gay, too? Did Cathy know this?

"You heard him out there," Bunny sniffed and wiped her eyes, recovering. "I don't know if he'd talk to her ever again. I just thought if you were going to get married anyway, how much extra trouble would it be to put the doubt out of everyone's mind. 'Everyone.' I mean our friends, I guess, Cathy's godmother, her grandparents — you'll meet them tonight, Jock's parents, they're very nice. Anyone who might tell Jock." She'd been talking quickly, and now she took a long sip of her drink. "This world," she went on more slowly. "Doesn't it sometimes seem so — " Here she drew her elbows close into her sides. "So tiny? Like a little bubble that you want to burst, but you can't, because if you burst it, it wouldn't exist anymore?"

She was interrupted by the doorbell. Brenda and one of Cathy's ex-lovers, Judy, trying to look straight in their nice clothes for the rehearsal dinner, Judy's eyes laughing about the hoax in which, at the moment, Malcolm could only see tragedy. It was then he decided to go through with it.

Bunny and Jock made a handsome couple as they greeted their friends entering the church: the right disparity in size, the right amount of tan in their cheeks, the right shape of wrinkles about their eyes. Malcolm wondered if that was the reason

they'd got married — that it had just been the thing to do —
the football-playing engineer, the pretty, vivacious debutante.
There was an absence of passion between them that stood in
stark contrast to his own parents, in whose fierce battles had
been the twist of love wrung like a dirty towel. Malcolm didn't
want that twist for himself, but there was something about
Bunny and Jock that seemed unreal. All-American, he kept
thinking, and he didn't know quite how else to put it. Maybe
there was something he wasn't seeing.

If it had been a real wedding, his parents would be there
too, and he would be worrying about how everyone would
get along, hoping that his parents didn't start on some political argument with Bunny and Jock or make disparaging re-
marks about George Bush and the Gulf war, which Jock
heartily supported. He would be worrying that his father
would drink too much and make a scene, that his mother
would argue the validity of the vows even as they were being
made. If it were a real wedding, he reminded himself, there
wouldn't be a wedding. Malcolm shook his head. It was easy
to get caught up in it all, easy to forget the speech he used to
give when questioned if he'd ever get married — that wed-
dings were fossilized rituals that didn't reflect the natural com-
plexity of a union between two people anymore, if in fact they
had ever done.

Malcolm was grateful for Bunny's arm as he walked up the
aisle through the sea of turned and smiling faces. He put his
right hand over hers where it was drawn through his arm.

"Thank you," she whispered as he dropped her off at the
front pew. She started to cry, but she was smiling too. He felt
strong and confident in his ability to protect her.

Brenda came to stand beside him as Judy fanned out to the
other side of the aisle. Brenda had only agreed to come to the
wedding when Malcolm said he wanted her to be his best
woman. Bunny and Jock had thought it a bit strange, but it
turned out to be another thing Jock respected — Malcolm's
courage to buck tradition and follow his own course.

And John, letting go of Judy's arm and following Brenda,

looked straight at Malcolm for the first time since they'd met, reminding Malcolm he'd never asked Cathy about him. He was skinny and pale, with a fine nose and narrow eyes. He raised one eyebrow, but not meanly. Light skepticism, that was the look.

Then they all turned to watch Cathy coming down the aisle. Brenda whispered in Malcolm's ear, "This is weird. This is really weird." Cathy wore a knee-length white dress with small black polka dots on it instead of a wedding dress, but she still looked like a bride. If he'd been there as a stranger, as someone else's date, Malcolm thought he'd be fooled. He was almost fooled as it was — only the dress, with its tasteful dots, reminded him of the bolder dots she normally sported, on her boxer shorts, which he knew for a fact she was wearing under the dress, under the slip, over the nylons that sagged at the crotch and needed something to stop them sagging to the knees.

Cathy released her father's arm half a dozen steps before Malcolm stepped forward and proffered his. Also Brenda's idea. "If you're going to get married to a man," she had said, "the least you can do is refuse to be passed from one man to another, even if it doesn't mean anything to you."

Cathy smiled, a little wanly it seemed to Malcolm, as she took his hand. Maybe it was starting to sink in, what it was she was doing. The boy-scout strength he'd imbibed from Bunny's gratitude seeped away. He felt like himself again, crumpled underneath the shiny double-breasted suit Cathy had picked out for him. Crumpled, but not defiant anymore, just his perpetually uncertain self, confident that his reasons had made sense at a particular time and place, but still wondering how the heck they'd all conspired to get him here.

And then it was time to kiss her. He put his fingers behind her head, feeling the roundness of her skull. A smooth bend of head to hers, lips unstilted against lips, and for a fleeting second he thought it became her kiss too, and then it was over. Her Lipsyl was left on his lips, and he ran his tongue over it, wanting it to have a taste, but there was none, only a waxy blankness.

Atmospherics

The Broad, Chill Troposphere

One of those damp December days that are the same temperature as March but feel much colder, Susan waited on the porch for Jan and Marla. She should have known they would be late. Now she was stuck. If she went upstairs to her apartment, she'd worry about the guy who lived in the basement stealing her stuff off the porch. If she took it with her, they'd show up and she'd have to lug it right down again. Or she'd be waiting inside and her mother would telephone and she'd have to answer because she would feel too guilty standing there listening. Then her mother would make her feel even more guilty for choosing not to go home to Cobourg to spend Christmas with her family, for not being able to take one evening out of the whole year away from her friends. She would be standing there, flummoxed, unable to get off the phone, and Jan and Marla would be waiting for her, getting more and more pissed off, it would all be a big mess, and she might even end up giving in and telling her mother All right, all right, I'll come for Christmas dinner. So she hugged her chest and jumped up and down to stay warm.

Up north there was snow. She was eager to be in it. Cold made sense when there was snow. Paired with snow, cold made Susan more aware of her body, how much work it did to stay warm, what a beautiful machine it was, giving her this warm pocket of space to live in, in the midst of the broad, chill troposphere. And the fact that another life could live inside the warm space of her body, that was incredible too.

Susan did a little sort of Russian dance and laughed at herself. Stupid to be yearning for more cold when she was already shivering. But she missed real winters, the winters of her childhood with their fine, unbroken snowy stretches. Winters now were petulant and bitter, like the brothers of kings.

Just when Susan was starting to get really impatient, Jan's patchy orange Tercel appeared. The cool kids are here, Susan thought as they got out of the car in their second-hand leather jackets, falling-off jeans and big black boots. Jan wore a watchman's cap, edges rolled not folded, angled to show the cropped dark sides and shock of platinum top of her spiky brushcut. Marla's hair — orange this week — made the Tercel seem dim by comparison.

"Sorry we're late," said Marla. "It took forever to get the stupid car rack on."

"Oh, like you were right on time with the groceries," Jan said. They immediately turned in to each other like squabbling children, like Susan as a person didn't exist, like she was a piece of luggage they were loading up.

"I had a client in crisis," said Marla. "What am I supposed to do, kick him out? Sorry, I'm going up north for a fun holiday, I don't have time for this 'I got no money, my best friend just OD'd' stuff."

"Other way."

"What?"

"Skis go the other way."

"You have to have a say in every minor detail?"

"It's not minor, it's aerodynamic."

There was a dullness to their bickering like the low sky turning dark above them. Great, thought Susan, I get to be in a car with this.

But in the car Marla turned up the stereo, preventing both argument and conversation. Susan felt, in the back seat there, like the fly featured in the comic strip Jan drew — not important enough to hide anything from, not interesting enough to talk to. They hadn't even asked her how she was.

She shouldn't have been surprised. Since getting involved with Marla almost a year ago, Jan's ratio of calls received to calls returned had dropped to about three-to-one. When she did return that third call, she complained about having too little time and begged off whatever it was Susan was calling about. Okay, so she had two jobs, a still-new relationship and hockey on Sunday nights. But the love of Susan's life had just dumped her; she needed her friends to make that extra effort to haul her out of the dumpster every now and again. She did not need to feel more pathetic than she already did, and not hearing from Jan for days after leaving woeful messages made her feel supremely pathetic. So Susan called other people instead, like Seana and Calli and Jimmy. Did Jan even notice? Not likely.

Somewhere in the ten minutes it took to make their way through Kitchener to the Bloomingdale Road at the edge of Waterloo, the day turned from afternoon to night. Christmas lights went on at one house at the exact moment they passed. A little while later, a streetlight burned out in the same way. You turn some people on, you turn others off, Susan thought. Marla, for example. Susan had a feeling Marla didn't like her, that she thought Susan was too normal. Too turtleneck-and-sweater. Only one earring in each ear, how normal could you get? She had a feeling that normalness angered Marla somehow.

She looked out the window at the passing farmhouses, noticing they all had lights on only in one ground-floor room. Kitchens. It was that time of day. In all those kitchens, bunch after bunch of not at all normal, in fact absolutely distinct, unknowable people sat eating their dinners.

Susan wanted to tell Jan what she was thinking about Marla and the farmers, to hear Jan's thoughts back. But Jan's hands were like two fists together at the top of the steering wheel, and of course Susan couldn't talk about Marla with Marla right there. I'm happy again, Susan wanted to tell Jan. Don't you want to know why?

Some things became more important when told to others, other things less. Why was that?

Jumping up and down to keep warm there on her porch, she'd been ready to put Jan's negligence aside, to harbour no ill feelings, to act like their friendship had never faltered. All she'd needed was to be asked how she was. Instead there'd been bickering and Marla's music, a dolorous blend of bass beat and medieval-sounding vocals. Susan felt like they were on their way to a vigil instead of a holiday. It started to rain.

"We need donuts," Marla said as they pulled into Fergus. "That's our problem, a distinct lack of donuts."

Afterwards, Marla put on Jane Siberry and passed around the Timbits. Their silence seemed more companionable, but probably only because Susan liked the music and could therefore feel that they were all listening together. It was happy music, she was happy — so what if Jan and Marla weren't for whatever petty reason. She started singing along. *Marco Polo is coming tonight, and he's bringing me things that I like…* Marla joined in. *Things that I like, things that I really really like.* Jan continued to grip the steering wheel in her two fists.

Around the town of Arthur, the rain changed to snow, making with the dark a swirly monochrome kaleidoscope in the headlights. Out the side window, the landscape was suddenly visible: fields, woodlots, hollows, fences, poplar-laned driveways. A cedar swamp. What if she were out there, Susan thought, on snowshoes, stopping to hear the snow settle.

Out the front of the car was a white pebbly moving wall. Behind it every now and then a dim outline of the dark road wavered, then disappeared.

Side view: snow lets you see.

Front view: snow blinds you.

There was a metaphor in that, but Susan wasn't sure what it was — something to do with shining a light on something already bright.

The thing she had wanted to tell Jan now seemed like it

would only be real if told. She sighed and looked out the window again, remembering how snow felt through the moccasins she used to wear snowshoeing: soft, forgiving, luxurious. But stern at the same time, because you knew it was cold, and your feet knew it was cold, too, only they didn't feel it, they were perfectly warm in their layers of leather and wool. Feet warm against snow, cold and soft: that combination changed everything.

What ever happened to those moccasins? Most likely Molly took them. Molly thought she had a right to anything she deeply liked. Actual ownership was irrelevant.

"So I started inseminating last night," Susan said.

"What?!" Jan said. She and Marla looked at one another.

"I started inseminating last night."

Jan laughed an odd bark of a laugh. "You could be pregnant, right now?"

"Well, probably not, but it's possible. I'm hoping."

"Oh, man, that's too funny."

Susan frowned. "I don't get it."

"The Virgin Susan," Marla said, letting it sit in the air for a second. "The Virgin Betty. The Virgin Madge." She turned back towards Susan. "It is immaculate conception, isn't it? You're not fucking anyone?"

"Christ, Marla!"

"I'm curious."

"If you want to define immaculate that way. The sperm's human."

"The reason Marla asks is that she is fucking someone."

"Was."

"And she's pregnant."

"Am," said Marla, shrugging and picking at the frayed knee of her jeans.

Of course. Marla knew how to do it right — just go have sex with a man, any man, instead of all this rigmarole, signing agreements, waiting for tests, planning, planning, planning. Just go out and fuck someone. Marla wasn't cautious. Marla spurned caution. Marla spurned people like Susan.

"Pretty stupid, eh?" said Marla. Maybe she didn't spurn caution.

"Yep," said Jan.

"I wasn't asking you."

Susan didn't know what to say. Jan was about to explode, she could feel it. Anything could set her off. And then Jan exploding would set off the bomb that was Marla. Ka-boom. The Tercel would detonate, it would become a fireball, roaring down the snowy highway. Susan kept her mouth shut.

No wonder they'd been fighting. No wonder Jan gripped the steering wheel like she wanted to wrench it off. Didn't it figure, though, that what started out to be about her turned out to be about them. Everything they did had to be bigger, more urgent, more important.

Here's Sulky Sue, her mother's voice sang in her head, *what shall we do?*

"I don't know why we even came," said Jan. "All those fuckin' stories of hope."

The tires squeaked on the hard-packed snow of Sheelagh's driveway. Up on the hill in its shelter of trees, the house was off a Christmas card, smoke out of the chimney, yellow light out the front window, garland on the front door. And Sheelagh, clomping onto the big side porch in her boots, shouting "Hello. Shalom. You made it," dogs romping around her, was like a younger, dykier version of some hardy New England farm grandma in a made-for-TV movie.

Susan got out of the car feeling like she'd been shut up in a room with milk going sour. She shook herself out and expelled a big breath, watching it form a cloud that hung in the air.

A Car-Interior-Shaped Cloud

There was Sheelagh on the porch. Same as ever, Jan thought.
Workpants, down vest, homemade wool cap, big smile. There
she was, Felice-less and smiling. Brave to smile like that when
the woman you thought you'd always be with had left you and
everyone knew it.

God, it was good to see her. She hugged everyone, even
Marla, who she'd met all of once. Jan remembered one time
they'd all played that "If this person were an X" game, and it
was totally unanimous: if Sheelagh were an animal, she'd be a
labrador retriever. Not just a dog. A labrador retriever. Okay,
so Jan had mocked those doggy qualities from time to time.
Right now they were the epitome of human beauty.

Jan's mood shrank. From the car-interior-shaped cloud it
had been on the drive up it became a thin overcoat, and then
in the boot room it morphed again into Mr. Rogers' evil twin's
cardigan. In the kitchen it fell off her hands like mittens on
strings and hung there out the bottom of her sleeves.

More good people, more hugs. It was predictable, a little
sickening, it was so nice. Calli with her pelvis hugs, Seana with
her fag-doing-continental thing, kissing the air on either side of
their cheeks, "Mwa, mwa, so good to see you darlings," Loren
imitating both of them behind their backs. God, it was good.

For a minute Jan didn't care what Marla thought about
anything. And then she did again and had to look at her to
see how she was taking it all. Fine, apparently. Maybe a little
uncertain, maybe masking that uncertainty by checking out
the huge pine table and gigantic wood stove (lit and pumping out heat like a good stove should), but she was not mind-
ing it. Possibly even liking it. "What's my problem, anyway?"
Jan thought, and then wondered what she meant.

She showed Marla the house so she wouldn't have to think
about it. "God," said Marla when she saw the living room,
"it looks like a Ralph Lauren ad." True. Stone fireplace, deep
colours, pine, plaids. Jan had never made the connection before. Now she always would. Thanks, Marla.

The whole time she took Marla on a tour through the stone basement, root cellar, ping-pong room and sauna she had helped Felice build, Jan had this funny expectant feeling. She thought it had to do with Marla until they went upstairs and she heard Sheelagh's voice coming from the kitchen. Felice, that's what she'd been waiting for, for Felice to come down from insulating the attic, or in from the cow-barn, or up from fixing the sump pump. But Felice was gone. The cows were gone. The house was finished and Felice was gone. How did Sheelagh come home to that every day?

"Where'd they get the money for all this?" Marla asked as they took their bags up to the back bedroom. "Not from farming."

Jan shrugged and said something about Sheelagh making a whack at engineering. Marla didn't like hearing about people like Felice, with family money. Thankfully she was onto something new — the huge iron bed.

"Wow," she said, flinging herself onto it. "This beats my futon all to heck."

Marla's futon. Is that where the big Franz-fuck took place? The sperm-fest? The big C? Coital conception? A week ago, she would have said that out loud instead of just in her head. So what if it sounded snarky and jealous? What was with her? She never used to be so insecure.

Marla patted the bed. "Come here," she said. Unsure she wanted to, Jan obliged. She rested her neck on Marla's arm while Marla stroked her hair. What are you thinking? Jan wanted to ask, though she never had and she never would. She remembered Marla once saying, "When someone asks 'What are you thinking,' they usually want you to say, 'I'm thinking how gorgeous you are,' or 'I'm thinking about how great sex just was,' or 'I'm thinking about the existence of God.' They don't want to hear, like, 'I'm wondering if I should change my hair appointment from Wednesday to Thursday.'"

Marla's hand running through her hair felt good. According to Marla, that should be enough — a physical thing that feels good. She believed that the body said more than we thought it did, that we needed to trust it more, we needed to know when to shut up.

But there was also the matter of interpretation. A hand running through hair might feel good, but it had ambiguous meaning. It might mean the owner of the hand was expressing great love and tenderness for the owner of the hair. Or that Hand knew Hair was feeling bad, and though Hand herself didn't feel bad, she wanted to offer comfort. Or that Hand knew she was leaving Hair, and, anticipating the grief Hair would feel, was stroking as a way of pre-saying sorry. Or it could be pure absentmindedness. Habit.

Jan had been Hand; now she was Hair. She liked being Hand better, although as Hair you got to feel more self-righteous. As Hand you were caught up in this bind of being impatient with Hair's sorrow while knowing she had every right to it and therefore forcing yourself to be patient. Jan thought about Susan, who had been her first Hair. Who had been Hair ever since, come to think of it. How pathetically and lovably understanding she had been. How sad, how needy. God, and she had just gone through that all over again. Poor Susan.

Jan sighed. Marla had to say something soon. Must be trying to think about what and how. Something simple like "I love you"? Or more complicated like "I love you but"?

"Don't you wonder, though," Marla said, "about people who put so much into having everything just so?"

"What!?"

"Look at that detailing around the light fixture. How long do you think that would take someone?"

Jan sat up. "I'm going to see if that chili's ready."

The others had moved to the living room. Susan was in the kitchen, cutting herself a slice of bread. She cut another piece when she saw Jan.

"It's good to be here, eh?" said Jan.

"I thought you didn't want to come." Susan took her chili into the living room.

The fuzzy thick mood of the evil twin's cardigan was back. Jan listened to laughter bulge and subside on the other side of the door. They were having fun. She was supposed to have fun, too. How exactly did that work again? You talked to your friends and they were funny and you had fun. Impossible.

But she went in anyway. Loren smiled at her from her spot by the fire, but Susan, miffed for whatever reason, didn't look up. On the floor in front of them, Seana was demonstrating yoga positions that Sheelagh attempted to follow — an old lab trying to learn a new trick. Jan smiled despite herself.

On the couch, Calli slid up to Jan and squeezed her leg. "So how's it going?" she asked in a sideways sort of voice. Marla's feet, in two pairs of saggy work socks, appeared at the top of the stairs and proceeded to slide together off the edge of each step like a kid's. Slide, drop. Slide, drop.

"Um, I don't know, okay, I guess," Jan answered Calli.

"Just okay?"

The rest of Marla followed her feet. Her boxy torn jeans, her orange T-shirt and little bright-green cardigan. Her chain and padlock necklace. Her bright-orange dyed hair. Her Laurie Anderson dimples. God, she was perfect.

"No, it's going fuckin' great, how's it with you?"

Calli laughed instead of being offended. Just as well. "No word on syndication, eh?"

That's what she was on about. Syndication. The strip. Not Marla, not Marla and Franz, not non-monogamy, thank god. Jan was in no state to mount another defense against Calli's assaults on non-traditional relationships. In the space of ten years, they'd probably had the same number of lovers; Jan had just had them at the same time instead of one after another. Until Marla.

"No, it's paper by paper at this point."

"Slog, slog, eh?"

Jan shrugged and got Calli talking about herself. Not hard to do. Not hard to take either. She was a good storyteller, and being a drama teacher, she had stories to tell. The latest was about two of her students who had been keeping a notebook recording what each of their teachers, including Calli, wore each day, and matching them up based on their various fashion faux pas. They had Calli paired with a skinny, brown-gabardine-wearing math teacher on the basis of her size and what they called her four-hundred-year-old shoes.

Marla joined them on the couch.

"The thing is," Calli was saying, "I remember doing that, assessing my teacher's fashion sense. I was so righteous about it, too, like I had every right to say 'Pageboys on the horse-faced should be OUTLAWED,' and now it's me, I'm the teacher, I'm the scrutinized. I actually felt hurt, too, for all of two seconds. The worst of it is, now I have to do something about it."

"You're a teacher?" Marla asked Calli. "What do you teach?"

Jan winced inwardly. She'd already told Marla that Calli was a drama teacher. Now Calli would think Jan never talked about these people she professed to love and had neglected, when she actually talked about them a lot. Marla just didn't listen. Sure, if you asked her midstream, "What did I just say?" she'd be able to pull it out of her butt, but ask her the next day and she wouldn't have a clue.

Neglect. That was what Susan was pissed about. Well, why not?

Marla and Calli were off and running about theatre, about Calli's radio work, her directing, her hatred of advertising, the size-ism of casting directors, what it's like to work with teenagers, what it was like to be a teenager, about Marla's theatre co-op and the show they took to the Edmonton Fringe. Susan jumped in on the debate about whether Kitchener-Waterloo could sustain a small, alternative theatre company when it was halfway between Toronto and Stratford and was not known as a theatregoing town. Seana jumped in on the other side. Torontonians now, she and Calli thought it was professional suicide for Marla's company to stay in KW, implying, of course, that it was professional suicide for anyone not to move to Toronto.

How animated they all were, the firelight burnishing their faces, their hands waving in the air, their lips moving in strings of shapes that made sounds everyone recognized and reacted to with their own lip-shapes and sounds. They liked each other, it was clear. They didn't need her.

Jan went to bed early with a lumpy feeling in her stomach that wasn't the chili.

That she had fallen asleep, her thought groggily went as she felt Marla's weight on the bed, was a good sign. She must not be as obsessively wrapped up in waiting for evidence of Marla's affection as she'd thought. She grunted and rolled away.

"I like your friend Susan," Marla said, propped up on one elbow. "I can see why you love her." Then she kissed Jan on the ear and rolled to her own side of the bed.

Jan regretted having rolled away. She wanted to be able to feel Marla's body getting warm under the covers. Touch she didn't need, just that they be able to feel each other's heat. But she couldn't move closer herself or she would appear needy and contradictory, given her earlier rolling away. It had to be Marla. If Marla loved Jan, she would position herself so that their shoulders almost touched.

Jan lay there waiting, listening to Marla's breath turn steady, and after that to the night sounds of the cracking, groaning house.

Before being properly awake the next morning, Jan knew from the particular quiet of the house that it was empty. The covers lay heavy and warm on her, and she had the same feeling she used to have as a child waking up the day a fever had broken. Free. Snug. Happy. She half-expected her mother to come in with consommé and crackers and a new Peanuts book to read.

Shouting and laughter from outside brought her more awake. Marla. Marla was laughing. Jan went to the window and through the scrubby trees between the house and the barn she saw flashes of colour — Susan teaching Marla to ski.

Why hadn't anyone woken her up?

By the time Jan got herself dressed and out the door, they were gone, off on the trail into the woodlot. Fuck. Temperature must have dropped almost ten degrees since the day before, too. Her fingers went numb and clumsy fumbling with the rubber straps on the ski rack. Fuckin' stupid things. Stupid rack, stupid skis, fuck, ow. She was crying when she got them off. The sudden warmth of the kitchen where she brought the skis to wax them made her cry harder.

"Jeez, don't go skiing, if you feel that way about it."

"Fuck, Loren, you scared me."

"Sorry." She grinned. "Seriously, if you want to, you know, talk or whatever…" That was big of Loren, sort of, but Jan wanted to ski. All out, as hard as she could.

The cold air hurt her lungs. There was something right about that. She caught up to a happy-looking and fresh-cheeked Susan and Marla.

"Lookin' a little snowy, there, Em," she said to Marla.

"Yeah, but I'm skiing, check it out." And she skied a little way for Jan.

"You're totally skiing, you're a natural," Susan said.

"Good teacher, don't you know," said Marla.

"I'm impressed," said Jan. She was thinking Marla had a foetus inside her. How weird that was, seeing her looking like normal, and she wasn't, she was different. Like Sheelagh looking the same without Felice. Aliens. Body-snatchers. She skied on.

It had always been Sheelagh and Felice's tradition: on the shortest day of the year, you had to tell stories of hope, stories to get you through the winter. Since moving to the farm, they'd been less particular about the actual day. Christmas Eve was close enough. For Jan, the idea of doing it this year without Felice was unsettling, wrong. But how could she say that to Sheelagh? She couldn't.

Jan had drawn her story of hope back when she was feeling more hopeful. Last week. Before Marla had told her her news. It was upstairs, a special edition of her comic strip, with copies for everyone.

The strip featured an old woman, Elsie, who not only talked to a fly named Ounce, but because of the frequency range of her hearing aid, was able to hear Ounce talk to her. Her tenants thought she was nuts, mumbling to herself all the time, but they loved her because she seemed to understand them all so well, she seemed to instinctively know what they were going through. In fact, she was getting intelligence from Ounce, who buzzed in and out of their apartments, grazing on garbage and gossip with equal relish.

In the story of hope, Elsie loses her hearing aid, Ounce goes missing (caught, it turns out, in one despondent and potentially dangerous tenant's cobwebs), and Elsie's tenants worry that she really is going bonkers this time since she's wandering the hallways of the building, peering up at the ceiling and into garbage cans. Through faith, compassion and luck, though, everything turns out okay. Ounce is saved, Elsie finds her hearing aid and the despondent tenant's life turns around.

Jan wondered if Felice was thinking of them and missing them and asking herself if she'd done the right thing. Jan looked at the faces around the room. Were they missing her too, or could they just let her go like that, just let her be gone?

"Well," Sheelagh said. "Guess I'll get the ball rolling. My story of hope also happens to be the story of how Felice left me. That's the way it goes, eh?"

Oh, Sheelagh. So doggy. So hurt and pretending not to be.

"Maybe you remember me talking about our neighbours down the concession. Maurice and Liz. Liz and Maurice. Spelled 'Maurice,' pronounced 'Morris.' They're both true locals, their families have lived in Simcoe County for generations. And, I don't know, maybe because of that, they look older than they are. He's one of those guys who adopts his style at eighteen and has it for life, like those guys from the fifties who are in their fifties now, still wearing greased-back hair. Only when Maurice was eighteen it was the seventies, so he's the guy still wearing sideburns. Somehow, to me, the sideburns don't look seventies, they look Victorian, like muttonchop whiskers.

"Maurice and Liz. They get dressed up to go to church every week, 'cause that's what you do here, eh? You go to church, and you dress up 'cause it's not often you get a chance to show off your nice clothes, it's not like you wear them to the office every day. Except if you're an outsider, like me.

"Anyhow, that's how we first meet them. They're dressed up for church, and they stop in with a pie for us, 'cause we're the new neighbours, and that's also just what you do. To us, it all seems out of *Anne of Green Gables* or something, but to them it's just totally normal.

"So there's Maurice in his grey suit, and Liz in a rose-coloured skirt and sweater. They can't stay for long, just wanted to drop off the pie and say hello and let us know about the church picnic next Sunday, and hope we settle in okay, and if there's anything we need. This is all Liz talking. Maurice doesn't say a word until the end when he asks if we're sisters. And Felice, no hesitation, no nothing, says, 'No, we're lovers.' Gulp. 'Oh,' he says. 'You look like sisters.' Liz blushes and says, 'Well, enjoy the pie, we better be on our way, no hurry to return the dish.'

"Of course, we're panicking — okay, it's me, I'm panicking, Felice is merely unsettled — I'm panicking, thinking, Oh my god, what's going to happen now? They're going to poison our well, they're going to round up a vigilante group, or, or a prayer group, they're going to come pray under our window, god, who knows, right? I'm starting to freak Felice out, too. She's starting to think maybe she shouldn't have told them, and I have to tell her, No, it's okay, it's what we agreed on, we were going to be out, we weren't going to hide anything. We just didn't expect to come out so soon, so suddenly, to the first people we met, our neighbours on their way to church.

"But it turns out okay. We eat the pie. We return the dish — with much trepidation — filled with a spinach-ricotta pie that Liz kinda looks at warily, but she invites us in for tea, gives us a few tips on putting in the garden. Somehow we get onto euchre, and from there we get on to playing it once a week, and from there we get into big, enjoyable, political debates with Maurice. Liz, on the whole, tends to agree with us, which starts to be a bit of a problem between them.

"This goes on for a couple of years, the euchre-playing, the discussions, neighbour things, borrowing and lending, looking after kids and animals, debating when and what to plant, when and what to spray or not spray, all that.

"And then for a variety of reasons, kids hitting their teens, for one, things get worse between Liz and Maurice. Liz starts visiting Felice almost daily, talking about their fights, their fundamental disagreement about how to raise children. I'm aware that the two of them are becoming close, that they're getting to be really good friends, but if I'm jealous it's because Felice has a good friend out here and I don't yet. I have pals and acquaintances, but not friends. I have no idea they're actually more than friends.

"Afterwards I try to pin it down, the exact day they become lovers. The day they made jam? The day Felice couldn't sleep because she'd put her back out? The day Liz took her into town to see a chiropractor?"

Jan had been at her drawing board, as oblivious as Sheelagh, when Marla was fucking Franz. It was hard not to feel duped, looking back on that night. There you were loving them like always, and there they were, boffing somebody else. Knowing intellectually that boffing somebody else didn't necessarily mean they weren't loving you as much as ever at that moment didn't help.

"But I can't pin it down. I can't find a day where Felice starts acting differently. How can she have had an affair for almost a year without me knowing? Am I really that clueless? I'm as blindsided as Maurice when they run off to Barrie together.

"Around here, you have to say 'run off,' 'ran off.' Eloise Shaw ran off with Tracy Gilman's bachelor uncle. Liz Stout ran off with one of those women out on the fifth line. Felice, as you know, told me ahead of time, but Liz just left Maurice a note. He comes in from the fields one day, and she and the kids are just gone.

"So he comes on over here, banging on the door, yelling my name, and I'm thinking, Uh-oh, here it comes. He's gone psycho. Felice takes his wife, and he's snapped, he can't stand it, we corrupted her with our bulldyke feminist ideas, it's our fault, and he's here to, I don't know, beat me up or yell at me or shoot me. So I wait for him to go away. Only he doesn't, which to me only confirms what I'm scared of, that he's on some vindictive mission. But I figure I'm going to have to deal with this somehow, so I sneak out to the barn and then come back as if I'd been there the whole time and hadn't heard him. I pretend to see his truck for the first time, and I come around the front. And there he is, sitting on the front porch, crying. No shotgun, just a big muttonchopped guy in a checked shirt sobbing into his hands. So I go up to him and put my hand on his shoulder, and he turns and grabs me around the waist with his face on my belly and cries until he's done. I make him some coffee, I give him some leftovers, and we don't really talk about it much then, though we do later, and when he leaves he says, 'Thanks. I just needed a friend and you're the only person who would understand.' Coulda knocked me over with a feather."

Sheelagh had tears in her eyes when she finished and there was a long pause.

"Listen to that wind," Susan said.

Jan hadn't noticed it till then. She looked around the room at the heads cocked to one side and felt they all must be hearing it the same way, like a mystery. She wanted the moment to last and last, and then she wanted to hug Sheelagh and let her know she wasn't alone, even though she was.

"It's a beautiful story," said Marla, "but I'm not seeing how exactly it's hopeful. That the local rednecks no longer go after lesbians with shotguns?"

"You really know how to ruin a good moment, don't you, Marla," Jan said.

For once Marla didn't reply. She looked down at her hands and pressed her fingertips together.

Jan went into the kitchen and leaned against the counter. Her jaw was sore from clenching it. She put on her boots and coat and hat and went outside. The wind made the small flakes of snow sting against her face. She squinted her eyes and walked down to the road, feeling the darkness, the wind and the snow as neutral forces. Hope was a human construct made to deal with precisely these things, coldness and darkness and the unknowable wind. It was futile. Pathetic. Laughable. Her little story about Elsie and the fly was a weak exercise in sentimentality. People killed flies and put old people into homes. That's what they did. Thinking it happened otherwise was delusional.

When she got to the road there was nowhere to go but on into the darkness. She stood there for a long time before turning back up to the house. Marla was out on the porch having a smoke, shivering in her thin suede jacket. Susan stood by her with an armload of wood. Were they talking about her? And which would be worse — if they were or if they weren't? Susan laughed at something Marla said, then went in.

Marla folded one arm across her chest and shifted from one foot to another. "Hey, you," she said to Jan as she walked up. She shuffled. "I'm sorry I spoiled the moment for you."

"Forget about it. Just touchy, that's all." Jan ached with hope that she would get over feeling how she felt, that Marla still loved her, that they'd come out the other side stronger. God, they might come out the other side with a kid.

Faith. That's what made Sheelagh's story beautiful, not hope.

Crystallizing Like That

The way Sheelagh clapped her hands together and said, "All right, who's next?" reminded Marla of a counsellor at a day camp. It was kind of sweet. In a vaguely annoying way.

Marla was stumped on her story of hope. When she'd first

seen the invitation on Jan's fridge, she'd thought coming up with a story of hope would be a good exercise. It wasn't usually what she went in for, hope. Despair she could do, angst, anger, vindictiveness, envy, irony — even joy she could do more easily than hope. But she liked a challenge. She started thinking maybe a series of monologues, all the emotions she could think of, in alphabetical order. Except there were so many. It'd be a lifetime project. What the hell, think big, she'd thought.

And then she'd forgotten about it. Now she'd have to improvise. Improvisation wasn't her strong suit.

Around the room, everyone was doing the non-pedal equivalent of shuffling their feet. Seana swirling the wine in her glass, Susan poking the fire, Jan and Loren thumb-wrestling with each other. Calli settled more deeply into the couch, adjusting pillows, as if she was in fact itching to tell her story but didn't want to appear eager. Oblivious, Sheelagh pulled six straws from the broom and evened them up in her hand.

Marla closed her eyes as Sheelagh proffered her neat array. "Long is my mantra," she said, intoning the word "long" before opening her eyes and pulling a straw. Phew.

Susan got the short one. "Okay," she said. "So." She stopped. "Okay." She slapped her hands on her knees. "Right. Here we go.

"I've always, always, always thought that I would have kids. Always, ever since I was little myself. And it wasn't just that assumption, that, um, what's the word? imperative — like, you're a girl, therefore you will marry, therefore you will have children. It was more than that. For me, anyway. It came from inside, it was part of my idea of who I was.

"I'm not talking just one kid, either, I had this picture of myself with four or five. Very hippie-dippy, all the kids in bright-coloured, natural fibre clothes, playing with homemade wooden toys while I'm making lentil soup and waiting for the whole-grain bread dough to rise. The first time I heard 'Ladies of the Canyon' when I was like eight, I thought, That's me, the one with cats and babies round her feet."

Oh, good lord, Marla thought. Like that's a happy picture. Talk to my mother about having lots of kids. Seven in ten years. Christ, I'd like to see you try it. Then she took it back. She wouldn't wish that on anyone. Susan could have her little fantasy, what the hell.

Marla had a sudden picture of Susan at eight, just outgrowing her baby fat, wearing bell-bottoms, with daisies in her long sandy hair. She'd be asking her dolls, "How do you feel about that?" and singing "Let the Sun Shine In."

When Marla was eight, she and Trina, the sister closest to her age, had played a version of House: House of the Vampire. The general action consisted of Mama and Papa Vampire lounging decadently in their coffins while they sent the baby vampires — their younger siblings — out to collect blood from the population at large. Ha. She smiled. Then stopped smiling. She was pregnant and Susan wasn't. Fuck, that was backwards.

"So what was strange, when I came out," Susan continued, "was to notice how the external assumptions immediately changed. Now it's, You're a lesbian, therefore you won't have children. And I was kind of divided, like, Hmm, maybe I was just really well-programmed before, and Jeez, I guess I don't have to have kids. But I still kind of want to. I still, you know, stop on the street to admire a new baby.

"Okay. So a couple of years go by, and I decide it's time to come out to my mother. 'Mom, I'm a lesbian,' I say, and she does the usual thing — cries, asks if I'm sure it's not a phase, tells me there are nice men in the world, you just have to look for them, all that stuff, right? And then after she's settled down a bit, and she's really being pretty decent, she wipes a tear away and says, 'I'm just so sad for you, dear; you'll never know the joys of having children.' And that's when, whammo, I know for certain I am going to know the joys of having children. It's one of those moments where your life crystallizes, you know? It all becomes clear — I've always wanted children, I've always wanted them for good reasons, at least I think they're good reasons, and I'm not going to let being a lesbian, or other people's ideas of being a lesbian, stop me."

Marla wished her life would crystallize like that.

"So great, okay, now I'm going to have kids, but how? And with who? I don't have a girlfriend, I don't know very many men."

Susan looked at Marla here, then quickly looked away. What the heck did that mean? Real lesbians don't know men? But no, she had too apologetic a tone for that. Just one of those times when you look at the person you're thinking about.

"My little 'Ladies of the Canyon' picture never had a clear outline of the other person involved in this adventure, but there always was one. I didn't want to do it alone then and I want to even less now that I have a slightly better idea how much work is involved. Besides, I've just finished school, I'm back at my summer job at the shelter that doesn't pay very well, and I'm still pretty young.

"So along comes Molly. Well. I'm off my feet: this is it, this is the love of my life, this is the woman, the one, ooo, baby! — sorry, Jan — and practically from our first date we've talked about having children, how we both want it.

"Now it's only a matter of financial security. And sperm. Both of which will come. It's partly why I take the Human Resources job at Mutual — boy, did I ever feel like I was selling out — but security, you can't ask for better security than Mutual. And then Molly got the Education Coordinator job with the AIDS Committee, ACKWAA.

"Okay, we've got security nailed. Now it's down to sperm. Who are we going to hit up for sperm, and what role do we want him to have in this whole thing."

Oh, god, sperm, thought Marla. I let that stuff into my body. How stupid could I be? Very stupid. Extremely stupid. As stupid as Gillie Ferris, as stupid as Kelly Rowan, as Gina Froese, Oana Schmidt, Alison McDowell. She went through the list of girls from her high school who'd dropped out to have babies. Or not have babies: her sister Trina, her friend Rebecca.

"We've already decided not to go the sperm bank route —

too anonymous, too expensive." Susan waved her arm in the air dismissively.

How easy for her. Deciding yea or nay, deciding to wait until she had enough money, confident that day would come. What about people who didn't have money? What about people who didn't have a choice?

"Enter Jimmy," Susan was saying. "Fundraising directer at ACKWAA, all-around swell guy. Wants kids, would like a role in the child's life, but would be willing to sign something agreeing that major decisions will be made by Molly and me. Respectful, funny, handsome, HIV-negative and willing to abstain from sex for six months just to be sure not to give it to the baby. That's commitment.

"All right, so I've got commitment from Jimmy, at least in principle, but meantime, Molly is dragging her feet. Basically, I think, she was scared of the responsibility, which I understand, you know, I mean, it's big, right? What pissed me off was that she wouldn't admit it. She just kept saying she wasn't ready yet.

"Then we're up here for the solstice weekend two summers ago, remember? When Kelly was here with her kids? I'd been saying, maybe you need to spend time with children, maybe you need to see what it's like, so you can decide: do you want to do this or not? So I'm all thrilled when she spends the whole weekend hanging out with Kelly and Jay-Jay and Mitch. And I'm even more thrilled when she says it totally made a difference, it confirmed she did want to have kids and she'd just been scared before, but now she's ready. We get home, we call Jimmy, we start waiting out the six months.

"I am so excited and impatient and happy that it hurts. You know?

"After a couple of months, though, I notice that Molly doesn't seem to be right there with me anymore. Her enthusiasm is forced, she kinda puts on this face when we talk about it, like an actor trying to show what the character is supposed to be feeling."

A bad actor, Marla thought.

Susan went on, "I keep challenging her about this until she admits she's putting on a face. She says she feels stifled. She says she feels forced to stay in her job, which is getting more and more high-pressured. She says she feels stuck, pinned down, caged in, and she can't do it anymore. She needs out. She's sorry, she still loves me, but we don't want the same things, she got carried away with my enthusiasm, it never really was something she wanted. And she moves out.

"She stays with Sheelagh and Felice for a month. And then... and then, she moves in with Kelly in Toronto. Yeah, never something she really wanted. Two kids, a dog and a cockatiel. Right.

"Well, you all remember what sort of state I was in after that. I felt, like, this high. I lost everything — the love of my life, my kids, my future, my idea of myself. For like half a year I did hardly anything except go to work and lie in the bathtub. Good thing it was a nice bathtub. There I'd lie, watching the water run out, thinking, My hopes are down the drain. There they go, down the drain. Bye-bye, little hopes. Bye-bye.

"So anyway, like six months ago, I'm lying in the bath once again, and the phone rings. Of course I let the answering machine pick it up, since I don't want to talk to anybody — I'm mostly over it, but I'm still wallowing a little — and it's Calli, saying she just thought I might want to know so I can gloat a little that Kelly dumped Molly.

"Gloat? Moi? Ha-ha-haa. You bet.

"So I pull the plug on the tub to phone Calli back and get the juicy details, and these big glubbing bubbles come up. I mean big ones, way bigger than usual! Glub, glub, glub, they went. That's weird, I'm thinking. And then I think, Of course, of course, they were never gone altogether, they were just clinging to the sides of the drainpipe all that time The crazy little devils were down there with the dead skin cells and rotting hair just biding their time — my hopes! Coming back up the drain! 'I don't need Molly,' I think. The world doesn't revolve around her.

"First thing I did I called Jimmy and asked him if he still

wanted to do it, if he was willing to do the whole test thing again. Yes, absolutely, he said. I was even willing to trust him — he's a trustworthy guy, and working for the AIDS Committee, he knows about safe sex — but he insisted on the full six months and a new test, so I guess we know what that means.

"Last week the test results came back: negative again. And I'm keeping a close watch on my mucous, which happens to be right the very day before we come up here, so I call Jimmy, and he comes over with a little Nalgene jar to do his business into, and that's it. I inseminate."

"Whoa," said Marla, as Sheelagh, and then everyone else began applauding.

Jan was smiling at Susan, full of affection. She was beautiful. Marla didn't know if she'd ever seen her look that precise way before. The introspective sorrowed look she'd adopted lately wasn't entirely gone, but it was mixed up with this happy look, this particular kind of happy look. Happiness for somebody, that's what it was. Marla filed it into her mental stock of actable emotions, under H: happiness for a friend's happiness.

Marla sure wasn't making Jan happy these days. She wanted to comfort her, but there was something odd about being the one to comfort your lover when you're the reason she's upset in the first place. Better that her friends should comfort her for that. With them she could get mad and say things she didn't mean and it would be all right. Marla hoped Jan would have a chance to do that during these few days.

While the others gossiped about Molly and Kelly and people she didn't know, Marla thought about what she was going to do. If she was going to have an abortion — she was, wasn't she? — she'd have to go to Toronto for it. There was no way she was going to go to KW Hospital. They made you feel like shit there. She knew that from sitting in that waiting room with Trina, and then with Rebecca. No way was she going to sit there, bawling her eyes out, cursing herself and then trying to keep it all in when a nurse walked by. She remembered how she'd felt then, when it was somebody else. Worried about them. Sorry for them. Heartsore. But also stronger than them. Smarter than them.

Up until a week ago, that might have been her story of hope, that she'd got away from the hick town she'd grown up in without getting waylaid by babies or boyfriends or booze. Determined and lucky, that's all she'd been, not smarter, not better. She couldn't believe she'd never realized it till now. How arrogant can you get to think you're better than a whole town?

Driving on Clouds

Susan was on a high after telling her story. She was going to have a baby. She was going to be able to nuzzle its skin and feed it with the bounty of her own body. And all of these women would be around to love it.

"Hey," said Loren. "We can have a baby shower. I've never been to a baby shower where I didn't totally feel like I had NON-BREEDER written on my forehead."

What a relief to be over Molly. She was able to hear, as Seana was relating right now, that Molly was going through a hard spell and feel compassion for her instead of fury. She could imagine patching things up, being friends. It wouldn't be like with Jan — or what it had been like with Jan — but a friendship could still exist.

Marla got up and went out, presumably for a smoke, which reminded Susan again that she was pregnant. Funny how easy it seemed to be to forget.

It must have been strange, Susan thought, for Marla to listen to that whole long rigmarole about longing to be pregnant when she actually was and didn't want to be. It must have been hard. As hard, perhaps, as for Susan to hear that Marla meant to have an abortion. It wasn't that Susan wanted her not to, or that she thought she shouldn't. But she felt a surge every time she thought of Marla aborting. How could a person let that potential go? How could you negate the magic of conception? Wouldn't it tear you up not to know how it would have turned out?

Probably Marla felt those things too, which would make it all the harder for her to go through with it. Susan had been wrong about Marla. The old Marla, the person Susan had thought she was, would have been able to have an abortion without batting an eyelid and would have made morbid jokes about it afterwards. The real Marla…well, she might make jokes too, but she wouldn't mean it.

The real Marla probably wanted company out there on the porch while she smoked — the company of Susan, who knew what she was going through and who wasn't Jan, the person who blamed her for it.

But Jan headed her off as she made for the kitchen. "That was beautiful," she said. "You'll make a great mother." She gave her a hug and Susan smelled the particular Jan smell of the grey sweater she always wore. The smell and the touch reminded her slow brain that this was what their relationship really consisted of, this easy intimacy, not the standoffishness of the last year. She hugged her back. Jan began to cry. Susan didn't let go.

When they noticed Jan crying, Calli and Seana made inquiring glances at one another and then at Susan. She gave them a sort of facial shrug, and they filed into the kitchen after Sheelagh and Loren.

"Hey!" Susan heard Calli say. "Where's Marla going?"

Susan and Jan broke apart and looked out the front window. Headlights were receding down the driveway. Jan ran for the front door, forgetting it was decorative, not functional; it didn't open. She and Susan ran through the kitchen and out onto the side porch. The others peered out the open door after them. The lights were backing onto the fifth line.

Jan and Susan looked at each other and then at the road, dark again.

"Did she say where she was going?"

"For smokes?"

"She has lots," Jan said.

"Something else?"

"There's not much that's open around here on Christmas Eve," Sheelagh said.

"There's the Mac's Milk in town."

"Somehow it doesn't feel like she's just gone to the store," Susan said.

"Come back inside," Sheelagh said.

Jan came in and slumped on a chair at the table. "Oh, man."

"She must be going to the store. Where else would she be going?"

"She wouldn't just leave like that, would she?"

"Oh, man," Jan said again.

"She might," said Susan.

"I guess we'll just have to wait and see," said Sheelagh.

"Damn," Jan said, jerking her head forward with the word. "Damn." She covered her face with her hands, then stretched her elbows flat on the table and rested her head on her fingers. Susan sat beside her with a hand on her back. Everyone else looked at the two of them in an awkward, curious silence.

"There's something going on here we don't know about," Seana said.

"Jan?" Sheelagh asked.

Jan shook her head without moving.

"Do you want me to tell them?" Susan asked.

"No." Jan still didn't move. They waited. Finally, she lifted her head. She opened her mouth. Closed it. Sighed. "The short answer is, Marla had an affair with some guy, and now she's pregnant."

"Oh, my," said Sheelagh.

Affair is a little strong for sleeping together once, Susan thought, but she let it go. "I don't think my little story made her feel any better," she said.

"No, no, it's me," Jan said. "I've been…Well, I don't know what I've been. Not very understanding."

"Why would you be?" Seana asked. "She just had an affair."

"With a man," Loren said. There was a marked silence. "Well, sorry, but it would make a difference to me."

Jan put her head down again.

"Maybe she'll be back," said Sheelagh.

They waited an hour, then two, and Marla wasn't back. If she was going home, she'd be there by now. Susan stood by while Jan phoned and got no answer. "Hi, it's me," she said to the machine. "Where are you?" She paused. "I just want to know you're okay." She paused again. "I love you," she said, and hung up. She left a message on her own machine just in case Marla would go there. She phoned every half-hour till one o'clock, between stories of hope. They'd offered to postpone them, but Jan said she needed stories of hope, so they went on.

The next day — Christmas, Susan suddenly remembered while they were discussing what to do — there was still no answer at any of the places Jan called. Loren offered to lend them her truck. "*You guys*," she'd said. "Why don't you guys take my truck?" Everyone, including Jan, assumed Susan would go too. Susan liked that.

It was even colder than the day before, and windy. Susan was feeling less like she wanted to be out in it and more like she wanted to be in by the fire — but only after they'd found Marla and brought her back.

Amazing how quickly things change. Two days, and she cared about Marla. She could see that Marla cared about her, too. She even thought maybe Marla had been flirting with her a little, in an innocent, nothing-will-come-of-it way. Susan had let herself be flattered. It had been a long time since anyone had shown that kind of interest in her, at least so she'd noticed. And Marla was cute, there was no doubt about that.

The seats in the truck were stiff with the cold and crunched when they sat on them. Everyone watched to see if the truck would start. "Like a charm," Loren said. Susan scraped ice off the inside of the windshield with a credit card while Jan used the scraper on the outside. Teamwork, a sense of purpose; Susan felt great.

Their ride down was as conversationless as the ride up, but utterly different in quality. A thin wash of snow blew across the highway, giving the illusion that they were driving on clouds. They passed through towns in which different combinations of people in their good clothes hurried from cars into churches — families with small children, older women taking each other's arms, teenage boys awkwardly wearing ski jackets over their suits.

Susan found it interesting that Jan was worried and not mad. If Molly had done that, driven off in Susan's car without a word, without saying where she was going or when she'd be back, Susan would have been furious. Susan was surprised, given the bickering Jan and Marla who had picked her up, but something had happened to them when they got to Sheelagh's. They'd turned away from each other in a move opposite to the way they'd turned in when they picked her up. Susan had counted it some kind of truce.

The snow ended just south of where it had started on the way up, but the cold remained.

Jan and Marla didn't live together. In some ways it made them seem more adult, like they had their separate lives, independent, beholden to nobody; in another way it seemed young, like they hadn't grown up yet. Marla's apartment was in the attic of a house made of yellow brick. It was cozier than she'd expected of Marla, though what exactly she had been expecting she wasn't sure. Everything in black, maybe, with odd gothic adornments like candlesticks made of bones. Instead there were bright colours, orange walls with yellow trim in the kitchen, a royal blue with orange trim in the living room.

Jan scouted for signs of Marla's having been there. There was no ring of snow meltwater on the boot-mat. ("Way to go, Sherlock," Susan said.) None of the clothes she'd been wearing were in the laundry basket. The tub and shower were clean and dry. The messages, all from Jan, had not been listened to. The milk in the fridge expired the next day. December 26. Susan again registered that it was Christmas. "Remind me to phone my mother," she said to Jan. "Oh, god, me too," Jan said.

They checked Jan's place. Not there either. Susan had a brainwave: maybe Marla had an address book back at her apartment. They found it in the bag Marla had left at Sheelagh's. Luckily, they had brought it with them.

Jan began phoning people Marla might have gone to stay with. She frowned and cleared her throat before the first call. "Franz?" she said into the phone, then waited. "Franz? Is Marla there?" She looked tired and pale and on the verge of tears. "No, she shouldn't, it's just... Uh, Jan. Her friend. I don't know, I thought she might... Oh, yeah, that's right, up north. Okay, thanks." She hung up, sniffed and wiped her eyes. "Thank god that's out of the way," she said to Susan. "Okay, down to business." She started dialling numbers.

Way to go, Jan, Susan thought. He'd be last on my list.

Person after person trumpeted "Merry Christmas!" through the receiver, and Susan thought about her family at home. Her nieces would be totally wound up by now, tearing around the house with their new toys. And their grandfather would be yelling at them to slow down in his house, so Susan's sister and her husband would take them outside to play. Maybe they'd go skating if there was ice, and there would be. Her mother and her aunt would be gossiping in the kitchen about their brother, who would be telling stories — lies, his sisters thought — about his travels to her father, who would barely pretend to listen. There would be sure to be at least one big fight, and many small ones. Next year she would be able to appreciate it in some twisted way because she'd missed it this year.

"Where do Marla's parents live?" Susan asked.

"Her mother's in Tavistock."

"Where is that?"

"Not far. South of New Hamburg."

"You think she might have gone there?"

"She hasn't talked to her mother in about two years."

Jan grabbed Marla's address book and flipped through it. "There's no Tavistock addresses in here."

"We can go there and look for a phone booth."

But they didn't need to. As the houses started becoming a town, Jan spotted her Tercel in front of a ranch house with aluminum siding and a single string of Christmas lights along the eaves.

They pulled into the driveway. Jan turned off the headlights, but not the truck. She breathed heavily with relief. Susan watched, waiting for her to turn the ignition off, waiting for her to be ready. But she put the truck in reverse, turned the headlights back on and started to back out of the driveway.

"What are you doing?" Susan said. "We can't just drive away." Jan backed onto the road. She put the truck in forward. "Pull over."

Jan drew forward on the shoulder and stopped, resting her wrists on the top of the steering wheel. She waited, looking at Susan, who turned to look at the house. Someone was peering out the window at them. Susan put her hand on the door handle.

"She left for a reason," Jan said. "Whatever it was."

"Yeah, but…" We've come all this way, Susan was thinking. She should know we came all this way. Susan wanted Jan and Marla to stay together now. She wanted to be the level-headed friend who saw clearly how the lovers were each doing the precise thing to alienate the other most while thinking they were doing the noble, honourable, loving thing. She wanted to be the wise, avuncular character who engineered a happy reunion.

But she didn't see anything clearly, not the person in the window, not the emotions behind Jan's composed, waiting face, not the murky workings of her own mumbling heart. Jan put the truck in gear and pulled onto the road. The curtain at the window dropped.

Susan lunged for the horn, punching out the hokey old greeting — honk-honk-a-honk-honk, honk-honk — before Jan good-naturedly batted her hand away. The curtain lifted again and Susan waved at the cloudy figure behind the glass. On went the coloured lights in the dark afternoon.

The Glare of Something Bigger

A week ago, I was the instrument of another man's death. It's a weighty thing to wake up to each morning. Not for the first time I wished I were Mennonite. Mennonites never go faster than they ought to. The top speed of those horse-drawn carts has to be what, about ten miles an hour?

I was on my way home from skiing, another thing Mennonites don't do, at least as far as I know. An office thing — I don't normally ski either, but I'm a good sport — Golf Day, Ski Day, I show up, I play a terrible nine holes, I stem-christie across the easy hills, the ones with the green circles and welcoming names like "Piece of Cake." The proverbial tortoise. I took all of Aesop's fables to heart. Yet here I am, the tortoise, with blood on his hands. What am I to make of this? What am I to think but that some seed of necessity, nestling in my gut for who knows how long, finally germinated in this "accident," this death, this thing that had to be?

It gets dark early this time of year. Also, it rains a lot. So driving home in the rain and the dark was not an unusual combination, and it was one that I took into account by driving slower than the speed limit. I was alone and glad of it. Group events can make solo travelling problematic — you have to invent uncertain plans, and like Conrad, I, too, feel the taint of mortality in a lie.

The two people closest to me conspired to make me feel

guilty for not riding to Ski Day with a carload of fresh-cheeked companions. It wasn't through actual conversation that they did this — in fact, they probably didn't remember that the year always rolls around to Ski Day eventually — but I don't have to have them in front of me to know what they're saying. My wife, Gail, occupied my head with complaints of my unsociability, my perverse desire to shut people out around me. My niece piped up, appalled at the frivolous waste of our dwindling supplies of fossil fuel occasioned by irresponsible single drivers. A Honda Civic is not exactly a gas-guzzler, I countered. The best thing about conversations in your head is you usually get the last word. Defying the two of them compounded my pleasure. I stretched my arms and cracked my knuckles.

I sang to Jurgen Gothe's selections on CBC Stereo as I drove. In between songs I talked to Jurgen. He so often sounds like he wants an answer, prattling away to his cats over the radio. He has a cheery façade of contentedness, but I can tell he would really prefer human companionship. I should know. I have cats, too.

I turned off the radio when Jurgen ended. Three cars behind me were tailgating one another. The closest one was tailgating me. Very dangerous in the dark, in the rain. If I let them pass, I would have the road to myself again. Tailgaters never give up, they just keep getting more and more frustrated until they take chances passing that they wouldn't normally take. This is what I have learned from letting other people drive. I knew of a place just a little further along where I could pull over safely, a lookout point over the sound, around the next bend. I would have to do it quickly. You can't trust drivers like that to even notice your turn signal, much less slow down enough to let you turn off safely.

I came around the bend, putting on my signal part way around. As anticipated, the cars behind showed no sign of slowing down. Then just as I was pulling over, a transport truck came round the bend the other way. The sudden flash of its lights in my eyes blinded me, like the trick the other boys in my cabin played on me the year I went to summer camp. They'd wait until I was asleep on my bottom bunk, then two of them would stand in front of my head with two big flashlights, while the others shook the bed and yelled "Trucks!"

I didn't see the parked car until there was no time to stop before hitting it. I couldn't swerve back onto the highway. The tailgaters were roaring past me, the pent-up energy of their slow descent exploding under their edgy feet.

The guardrail should have stopped both of us. Instead it happened like curling. My car stopped on impact. His skittered out of bounds, busting right through the guardrail out into the air. I thought it was an abandoned car. I thought whoever the owner was must have had a breakdown and got a ride into town with someone else. I could see the interior of the car. There was no one in it. But just as it went over the edge I saw a shadow that I couldn't be sure was the right front headrest.

I called the operator. I didn't know if you could call 911 from a cellular phone. If it had turned out that there was no one in the car, I certainly would have felt foolish, for even as I was reporting what had happened I felt I was making it all more important than it really was. I don't remember the whole conversation, but I do remember with great clarity saying, "I pushed a man off a cliff. I've never done anything like it before."

It took a long time for them to come. I got out of the car. The edge he had gone over was not quite sheer. He must have bounced on the way down, hitting the mountain, taking air, hitting the mountain, taking air, like plucking petals off a daisy, always hoping you'll end on the right one.

They whisked me into an ambulance. I tried to tell them I wanted to stay. "You're in shock," they told me, and they said it as though that absolved them from having to listen to anything I said. But they didn't know there was any doubt someone had been in that car, they couldn't anticipate my embarassment if there was no one, they couldn't know my bond with the man if there was.

It was a nurse at the hospital who found out for me. She

had a friend who worked at 911. She was frazzled, I don't know why she did it. Nurses are not like other people. Something happens when they adopt the white that lifts them toward the heavens. You wouldn't know them at the checkout counter, leafing through the tabloids, yanking chocolate bars out of their children's hands, but put them in a hospital or give them a heart attack on the street and they transform like non-violent superheroes.

"He's dead," she said. "The car was totalled. He probably died right away. He must've been sleeping — he was in his sleeping bag."

"Early to be sleeping," I said.

"People do odd things at odd times," she said. She looked like she wanted to sit down. It was an examining room. There was no place to sit. "I wonder if he woke up," she said. She looked me in the eye, then. I don't think it was an accusation.

My chest was sore from the seatbelt. None of my ribs were broken, and I just had a few minor head wounds where the glass from the windshield had flown back at me when my skis went through it. They sent me home in a cab. The cats swirled around my feet like ground mist, pleased to have me home. I fell asleep on the couch, reading my VISA bill.

Leif Olson. A Scandinavian name, but he was originally from Australia. Not many people you know personally get genuine obituaries in the newspaper — written by newspaper staff, I mean, not paid for by the family. Leif was no ordinary citizen. I knew that when I killed him. I just didn't know *how* he was special until I saw the item:

DAREDEVIL DIES IN ROADSIDE ACCIDENT
Daredevil and adventurer Leif Olson, 38, died Friday on Highway 99 south of Britannia Beach when the car in which he was sleeping, parked in a pull-out, was struck by another vehicle. The impact of the collision sent Olson's car through the guardrail

and over the precipice. Rescue workers had to be lowered 150 metres on safety lines where they pried Olson's body from the wrecked vehicle. The other driver sustained minor injuries. RCMP officials say the guardrail must have been weakened from an earlier unreported collision. They are still investigating.

Olson is perhaps best known for his daredevil exploits during Expo 86 when he "dropped in" on the opening ceremonies with a parachute reading "Expo-se Greed." Olson often combined stunts with political messages. In a previous interview, Olson called himself a "freelance activist," refusing to align himself with particular groups. "I do it for the buzz," he said. "If I can get people to think at the same time, then it's a double buzz, that's all." Olson was also known as a speed skier, clocking up to 160 km/h, and as the mountaineer who twice scaled K2, the second time making his descent largely by hang-glider.

Olson left his native Australia at age seventeen by stowing away on a freighter. He came to Canada in 1976. He is survived by his wife, Adele, and daughter, Ingrid.

It was in Monday's paper. I had spent the weekend trying to decide whether or not Leif had saved my life by losing his own. Would I have hit the guardrail myself if he hadn't been in the way? The RCMP officer who came to the house on Saturday thought I would have. But I had planned it. I knew how long I had to come to a stop. I knew my speed coming off the highway. I knew I might skid in the rain. I would not have hit the guardrail. I should not have hit Leif's car hard enough to send him over. Something else was at work here other than pure physics; some force of the universe, some paralyzing intensity channelled through the lights of a transport truck, winging through those open windows to the soul, my eyes, rabbity in the glare of something bigger in the world. I am not inclined to flights of fancy — I knew I was on the lip of a genuine revelation, waiting for a breath of wind, or a Honda Civic, for that matter, to push me over the edge.

His number was right there in the phone book. I called it. A woman's voice answered.

"Adele?" I said. "This is Ter — "

"Hang on, I'll get her," the voice said.

I started again. "Adele? This is Terence — uh, Terry — Godwin. I read about Leif in the paper — "

Adele sighed. "I thought we'd called everyone already," she said. "There's no funeral. He wanted a wake, complete with the body sitting up when the door opens." She laughed, or rather, breath escaped from her in the form of laughter. "With this body, I don't think it'll be possible. Anyway, Friday we're having it. At the floater, here. Seven o'clock till whenever."

So easy. The slim little lie I had prepared slumped like an empty glove. I had wanted to say that Lief and I had met skiing. Almost the truth, and vague enough not to excite further questioning. I almost tacked it onto the end of the conversation just to be rid of it, but caught myself in time. Explanations provided without being solicited always sound false. I picked up from Adele's directions that "floater" meant houseboat. It fit.

Gail called me the evening of the wake. How do these things get around? Gail lives in Toronto now, where she always claimed I should live. "The West Coast is no place for people like you," she would say. "You'd fit right in in Toronto. Right alongside my parents." I never knew exactly what she meant. I rather liked her parents. We still exchange Christmas cards. I had sometimes wondered if the West Coast really was for me, but when I imagined alternatives, it was the prairies I settled on, not Toronto. Gravity isn't as important on the prairies as it is here — there just aren't the things to fall off of. In Toronto there's the CN Tower.

But if I was meant to live on the prairies, why was I born in Victoria?

"I just heard about the accident from Mei-Ling," she said. "Are you all right?"

Mei-Ling is my niece. My sister went to China as a missionary with her husband. At the time it didn't seem unusual. Our father was an Anglican priest who was keen on missionaries and kept bringing them in to the church to give slide shows. My sister went to China as a missionary and the apple of my father's eye. She came back with Mei-Ling, but without either her husband or Mei-Ling's father or any shred of religion, for that matter, and settled in Tofino on Welfare. Mei-Ling had had enough of Tofino by age fourteen. She lived with Gail and me for four years. She still comes by to use the washing machine and she had been surprised this week to find me at home.

"I'm fine," I said to Gail. "As a matter of fact, I'm just on my way out to a party."

"Are you sure that's wise? You might — "

"What? Have to talk to people? I might — have fun? I know all your lines, Gail. I'm not in the mood for them."

She didn't say anything for a second. "God, I'm not that bad, am I? Never mind, don't answer that. Mei-Ling said —"

"Mei-Ling said what?"

"She just said you were acting a little strange, 'even for Uncle Patio,' I think were her exact words." Mei-Ling, due to a childhood confusion between "Terence" and "terrace," calls me Uncle Patio. "She thought you were still in shock."

"Well, I'm not. I'm fine, and I'm going out, if it's all right with you."

"Okay, all right. If you say you're fine, I believe you, you're fine. I just — if you want someone to talk to, call me, okay?"

I knew what to wear to funerals, but wakes? I scouted my closet for something appropriate, thinking about Gail and Mei-Ling. I didn't know they were still in touch. It bothered me to think of the two of them discussing me, comparing notes, putting meaning into particular things I'd said without giving them a second thought. Like when Mei-Ling was here, I asked her if she knew about traditions surrounding the saving of a life. Was it that the person who saved your life was responsible for the rest of your life, since they had delayed your meeting with death, kept you from your proper end, so to speak? Or was it that you, as the saved person, had to dog their footsteps until you could return the favour? Either way, you're paired for life. Either way there's a bond of responsibility there. It didn't make that much difference that Leif had died, except that one option expired with him. I didn't say this last bit to Mei-Ling. I just asked her about traditions, but it did occur to me: if I couldn't save Leif's life, I could *be* his life. I just wasn't sure how well I could do it.

I put on a sports jacket with a white cotton shirt. I could take off the tie if no one else was wearing one. I looked at my watch — seven o'clock, I was going to be late. I must have sat on the edge of the bed in my undershirt longer than it had seemed.

I thought the rental car would be sluggish. I was surprised just how zippy it was. It was smooth, too — you could be going eighty in a sixty zone before you even noticed. I made good time to the houseboat. I'd been a little worried that I wouldn't want to drive at all, but it wasn't a problem. I felt better driving than ever. More confident of the power under my foot to make those last-minute passes, more confident of the brake to keep me in control. Already I've assimilated something of Leif's essence, I thought, smiling. Leif lives on in me. I found a rock-and-roll station on the radio and tried to make plans. I could not think to surpass Leif's feats, or even parallel them, at least not right away. I had to think of something I could do with the skills I currently have. A tricky proposition. The only athletic thing I do well is swim. Not dive, swim. Swimming is not a big thrill sport. That's what I used to like about it, that it's slow and steady, that it doesn't lend itself to grandstanding. Not until I approached the problem from the political angle did I start to make progress. I pulled off my tie and loosened my collar.

The houseboat was crowded with people. They were spilling out the door onto the deck. Mostly about my age, Leif's age, little groups of men and women in their late thirties — they looked a lot like Gail's friends. Some of the men had ponytails. I stood for a moment in the dark by a hedge on the riverbank, watching. It could have been a cocktail party.

A boy and a girl, both wearing camouflage pants, burst out of the hedge beside me. The boy had a black armband on.

"Security check," the girl said, holding up her hand to me in a stopping motion. She was maybe eleven years old. The boy trained a stick on me like a gun.

"Name?" she said.

"Terence Godwin." I was too surprised not to answer.

"Relation to deceased?"

I hesitated for a microsecond. She didn't notice. "Buddy," I said. It was a word I had formerly only used in concert with "system." I was surprised it slipped out so easily.

"How come I've never seen you before?"

My god, he had a daughter. A commando daughter, evidently. Maybe it was a response to grief, this aggression. Everyone had their own ways to cope. Her eyes were narrow, her face was expressionless, her revolutionary impersonation perfect — the regimented passion, the profound seriousness. How would it feel to have your hero father die while you were a child? While he was still a hero? Maybe this was it. I was twenty when my father died, old enough to feel relief every bit as big as the emptiness I carted around in my chest. Sometimes I was surprised by my image in the mirror, how small my chest was compared to how it felt. I expected it to be big and boxy, maybe just a bit deformed, but there it was, smooth and tight and thin as ever.

"Before your time, Ingrid," I said, not treating her lightly, not making her grief a thing of pity, but of respect.

The girl looked at the boy and motioned towards me. "Counter-revolutionary?" she asked him. He nodded.

"Ingrid's only four, doughboy. Whaddaya say to that?" She allowed herself a corner smile. She was good at this.

Trapped. By children. It's true, before they ambushed me, I'd thought for an instant about getting back in the rental car and driving home, maybe calling Gail even. But that kind of cowardice was unfair to Leif. I couldn't let them stop me.

I walked purposefully past the girl, not looking at her, not according her any visual importance. She lost her cool, she responded like a child. She followed me, yelling "Counter-revolutionary, counter-revolutionary," until one of the pony-tailed men intervened, taking her arm, telling her he'd had enough and he meant it.

"She practically grows up at peace rallies and this is what I get," he said, shaking his head and smiling.

I smiled back, duplicitous.

"He's a security risk," the girl insisted. "He thought I was Ingrid."

"I only knew Leif for a short time — " But I felt very close to him. I wanted to finish my sentence, but the man waved me off. Don't mind her, the wave said, she's going through a phase.

"We're all friends here, Diana," her father said. "We don't need security."

The girl ran off again, back up the ramp to the hedge. Perhaps she would also feel relief when her father died. Perhaps everyone did. I stood there awkwardly for a moment. The man pulled a beer from a cooler filled with ice beside him and handed it to me.

"I guess I'm a little late," I said. "Has there been — a ceremony or anything?"

The man shook his head. "There was some talk of doing something spectacular with his ashes, but I think Adele wants to keep them."

I asked him where Adele was. He thought inside somewhere, but he hadn't seen her for a while. She was taking it pretty well, he said, almost as though she'd expected it, as though she'd always been prepared for this. I nodded. She'd have to, wouldn't she, with the life he led? I realized I had a certain freedom in that regard. Only an ex-wife who called once in a while, and a niece who borrowed my laundry facilities. I felt stronger. I put a hand on the man's shoulder. It seemed like the appropriate close to our few minutes of companionable silence with the words of funeral home visits unspoken but present between us.

"Life and death might be more continuous than we think," I said and turned to go inside.

The place was bigger than I'd expected a houseboat to be. Even crowded with people the way it was, it still didn't feel small. I nodded to the people who noticed me as I passed through the hall into the two-storey living room. Music I didn't recognize was playing on the stereo, blues of some description. I helped myself to some bread and cheese from the island that divided the kitchen from the living room. People were clustered in small groups, a man and a woman on the floor leaning against another man and woman on the couch, others sitting at a long pine table, two people sitting on the coffee table. I found a free piece of wall I could lean against next to a burly man with a beard who was staring off into space. He turned to me and slapped my shoulder. "Good ol' Leif," he said. "Whatta way to go."

"Did you know him well?" I asked.

"Know him?" the man was clearly drunk. "Know him? We were like brothers. We did Logan together."

"Pardon me?"

"Logan. Mountain. We climbed it, Leif and me and a couple of other bums."

"Do you know what he was planning for his next stunt?" I asked.

"No. What?"

"I don't know. I thought you'd know."

"Not me," he said. "I haven't seen Leif in, oh, it must be ten years, now."

"Oh," I said. I still hadn't formulated my plan exactly, what I could do to take up where Leif left off. "Have you seen

Adele?" I asked. He shook his head, slowly, like a big dog waking up.

I went to get coffee for my burly friend. A woman stared into the open fridge and started crying. She wasn't Adele either, but she was crying for her and what she must be going through. If Steve ever died, she'd never eat again. I put my hand on her back and closed the fridge door for her, then poured a coffee for her too. She leaned against the counter and hugged the cup with both hands. I brought the other coffee back to the ex-mountain climber and let him talk on about Leif, the good old days, and the financial success but spiritual emptiness involved in computer sales. He seemed to need it. I didn't tell him I worked with computers myself. Systems analysis didn't seem to have anything to do with me anymore.

I could see why Leif would gradually lose touch with a man like this, a former companion-in-arms who had given up pursuit of the grand things in life. Friends like this could drag him down when he needed to be out there shocking the world with the speed and beauty of his daring and the largeness of his heart. It was Leif's largeness of heart that kept me beside his former friend, made me a willing sponge for his pain and loss, not his pain at losing Leif, but his pain at losing the part of himself that was as large as Leif. It was Leif's largeness of heart that took me around the room, drawing the same grief out of everyone in turn — that they were not Leif.

I was trying to find the second washroom up in the loft, but it had a line-up too. I spied a balcony through the open door of the master bedroom. I could always piss in the river, and besides, I wanted to think. No one I had talked to knew what Leif planned to do next. Some people said he had given up political stunts since Ingrid had been born. Others said he was incapable of giving up, it was just his nature to keep making grand statements. I relieved myself, then turned back to the house full of people who needed Leif, who needed me, and saw a woman sitting in the shadows in one of those Adirondack deck chairs. Her legs were drawn up to her chest, and she had a blanket over her knees.

"I didn't know anyone was out here," I said.

"Would it have made a difference?" she said. "In my experience, men won't let anything stop them from peeing."

I shrugged. It might have made a difference to me earlier, but not tonight.

"How well did you know Leif?" I asked. Gail would be astonished if she could see me tonight, I thought, striking up conversations with people I don't even know, hell, coming to a party where the only person I know is dead.

"Pretty well," she said.

"I didn't know him that well, but I feel like I do, you know what I mean? I feel like I know him better than I know myself. What I'm trying to find out is what he had planned next, and no one seems to know."

"What he had planned next?" she asked.

"Yeah. Like four-wheeling over a golf course on native land with a loudspeaker blaring something about aboriginal rights, or climbing trees about to be razed by MacMillan Bloedel, or bungee-jumping off the Lions Gate Bridge while unfurling a banner about the cruelty of keeping whales captive at the aquarium, or — "

"He liked going to the aquarium," she said. "He didn't mind that the whales were in captivity. *I* minded that. He just loved to watch them swim."

"Oh," I said, looking at the floor. "Maybe there's something else I could — " I looked up. She was shaking her head.

"You know what he was planning? He was planning to get a full-time job. He was planning to rest on his laurels. He was planning — " She stopped talking because she had started to cry. I felt like I was in that car, hitting the mountain, taking air, hitting the mountain.

"Adele?" I said, making it a question. I was pretty sure it was her, but I'd already jumped to conclusions about Ingrid, I didn't want to make the same mistake twice. Not that it really mattered anymore. She lifted her eyes to the name, wiping them on the blanket.

"If his car was broken down," I asked, "why didn't he just

hitchhike into town? It wasn't late. Why did he go to sleep instead?"

It occurred to me that my question might identify me. Who else but the driver of the car who pushed him over would ask that question, and ask it with an intense need to know that almost made it rhetorical in the end, like a child's angry why why why?

She didn't meet my eyes, and I thought for a while she wasn't going to answer, but she did. "He hated letting other people drive. He didn't trust anyone to drive as carefully as he did. Drove me crazy." She shook her head with the memory of it.

Drove my wife crazy, too, I thought. I turned and leaned over the railing. The river churned gentle eddies below me. I felt hollow and light, like if I fell in the water I wouldn't even penetrate the surface. I would stick like an insect in the surface tension, unable to fly, not allowed to drown. I turned back to Adele. She was staring across the river, as if no one stood where I did, almost directly in her line of view. As if from this moment on she would always be alone. I wanted her to cry again, to show me she had a personality that felt grief and could be comforted, so I could put my hands on her shoulders and draw her indoors to the people who loved her. I wanted to leave her with her friends' warm hands stroking her damp hair and steal softly out like some anonymous benefactor in a Dickens novel. I stepped forward. I reached for her shoulder, but she pulled the blanket up tighter, and my hand found the doorhandle instead.

Pool-Hopping

The first night of the heat wave, Clive and Julie used a chair to prop open the refrigerator door; on the chair they set a fan. Periodically, while sipping wine and playing double solitaire, they probed the coolish stream of air with their noses, trying to isolate individual scents in the fridge's bouquet. Broccoli. Barbecued chicken. A hint of cut peach. Later they made love with slick urgency.

Now, four nights later, the milk has gone bad, the fridge stinks, and Julie cools herself as much as she can by lying on the concrete balcony of the apartment. She tries to convince Clive, who wants her to come in and sleep, to go pool-hopping with her.

Clive's bare feet — his sweat machines, Julie calls them on good days, but not today — make warm little pools of the concrete underneath them.

"Sure, I'll go swimming with you," Clive says.

"No, no, no. Not the apartment pool," Julie says. She tries to explain to Clive about pool-hopping.

"You rich kids," he says.

"No, it wasn't like that," she says. "Dad was rich. We weren't."

Julie has been, that morning, to the morgue.

o o o

Julie's brother James had hated the world and loved his friends. "It's like, death is this lifelong dare, and only the chickenshits make it all the way through to the end."

James and Julie had lived with their mother on the edge of the pool zone.

o o o

"Think about it as an aerial photo," Julie tells Clive. "Like the ones in Grade Nine geography showing the boundary between the Canadian Shield and the Great Lakes-St. Lawrence Lowlands. To the north, rocks and lake-filled striations; to the south, fields cut neatly into squares by dirt roads one mile apart."

Clive shifts his weight to the other foot and folds his arms across his chest. Julie waves her arms in the air as she continues. "To the north, pools: oblong, round, kidney-shaped; to the south, little twenty-foot squares of grass cut with chain-link fence. Same thing."

o o o

The July heat wave, 1979. Anthony, James' best friend since public school, brought over a Disney wading pool that he'd taken from his next-door neighbours' kids to James and Julie's house.

"The little vermin were in and out of it all day, screaming. I thought Goofy deserved better." Anthony's mother was paying him to build a fence, a task he drew out as long as possible to put off file-clerking at his father's office. He spent a large portion of each day playing with the kids.

The wading pool proved inadequate. By the end of the night the water in it didn't feel much different from the air, and besides, it was too cramped with all four of them in it.

o o o

"James, me, Anthony, Dougall," Julie says, and Clive sighs and sits on the lawn chair.

"Who's Dougall?"

"Friend of ours from high school. Black, brilliant, beautiful. All the b-words. Speaking of which, could you get me a beer?"

Clive holds his breath as he opens the fridge door. He should clean it out, but that would mean he'd have to take the garbage out to the chute in the hall, and he doesn't like the chute, the convenience of it, its out-of-sight-out-of-mind mentality. He follows the route of the garbage in his mind, imagines the plop and split of the bag landing on a pyramid of others, and wonders how long it all sits there in the basement before being taken away, and where, for that matter, it sits while it waits. Now that he's thought of it, he will have to find out. The things that take you by surprise when you move in with someone. He rolls a beer against each cheek as he goes back out to the balcony.

"I think James was a little in love with him, too."

Dougall. Right. Clive undoes her beer with his bare hand and winces. Usually he'd use his shirt, but he's not wearing one. Too hot, even at eleven-thirty at night, even on the eighth floor. He undoes the second with his shorts.

"Too?" he asks, but Julie is answering only what she wants to.

"A suicide counsellor friend of mine once told me the ones who talk about it never do it." She's back on James now. She takes a slug of beer, then pulls up her shirt and balances the bottle on her stomach.

"Never say never," Clive says, stupidly, and looks out over the city as Julie laughs. The beer bottle bobs on her stomach. He lifts it onto the concrete.

o o o

Anthony ferried the wading pool back and forth, but they didn't immerse themselves again, only set the front legs of the lawn chairs inside it and dangled their feet.

Anthony was always playing an instrument — his thighs, the floor, an elastic from his lunch for lack of anything better. Now he was onto Julie's long-discarded ukulele, and after actually making it sound like a real instrument, he was taking his violin bow to it.

"Listen," he said. "A cello on helium."

James extemporized. "Helium. Helios. The sun. Beats madly down. Beat. Beat. Heat. Heat. Madly down on the turning earth, venting its fury on the ruined girth of the fruitless earth — "

Julie and Dougall played chess on the folding table set in the middle of the pool. Around their ankles floated the bishops and pawns and rooks they'd taken from one another. Full contact chess, they called it. Julie thought she was in love with Dougall, but she wasn't sure.

o o o

Aha, thinks Clive, question answered. "Chess? Pretentious bunch, weren't you? James, Anthony, Dougall." He says the names with what he imagines is an Upper Canada College accent, emphasizing the lack of diminutives. He's trying to keep things light, trying to follow Julie's lead. He doesn't know what she needs. He's trying not to be impatient.

"Pretentious? Of course we were pretentious, we were teenagers." Julie lifts her head off the concrete to take a swill of beer. "For a while we used the last parts of our names. Ames, Lee, Thony, Gall. Gall was the only one that stuck. The puns. 'You've got a lot of Gall, haven't you?'" Julie laughs. "Gallbladder. Gall stones. Oh, The Gall!" Clive slumps back into his lawn chair. Other people's nostalgia, he thinks. Then feels unkind. Her brother is dead — a Parkdale rooming house John Doe with a phone number in his pocket and a noose around his neck.

"Why don't you come to bed, Julie?"

"You go ahead, Ive. I'm going to stay out here. Unless, of course, you've changed your mind about pool-hopping."

Clive stays where he is.

o o o

Dougall had been the only one of them reluctant to pool-hop.

"Look, Gall," said James, "it's one in the morning. There are all these pools out there sitting empty, just waiting to be frolicked in, and here we are, choking in the heat. It's a simple equation. From each according to his means — and we have but meagre means; and to each, according to his need — our need is great." James thought he was on a roll.

"Think you're maybe twisting the rhetoric a little there, James?"

"Okay, how about this? Waterways as free passage. There can be no trespass on or in bodies of water. And truly — " James paused here to belch quietly. "What man can say he owns water? Or fire? Or air?" Of course they'd been drinking all night.

"Or earth?"

"Exactly," said James. Dougall smirked.

"Oh. Well, the revolution'll change all that, you mark my words."

"What's it going to hurt anybody if we take a dip in their pool?" Julie said.

"Why not go to your dad's?" Anthony said to James.

"What? I don't believe I heard you right, Anthony. Did you say — "

"Oh, fuck. Never mind, I didn't say a thing."

"No, I didn't think you did."

"All right, all right, if we're going, let's go," said Dougall.

The first pool: small, rectangular, almost square, tucked away out of sight of the house behind the garage. They crawled through three backyards to get there, running tree to tree, dropping to their stomachs, hopping fences. Like never before, Julie felt they were one. It was the getting there that unified them.

They had not said a word, not a whisper, since they'd cut into the first backyard; even at the pool they did not break silence but stripped, each of them, completely, and slipped into the water. The night was overcast and bright, the city's lights reflecting off the clouds that kept in the heat. Julie bobbed up, held her breath, sank down and pushed off from the wall. Three bodies on her left did the same, James' chest a light grey, Dougall's black, Anthony's dark grey. In the daytime, James was so pale as to verge on pasty. Anthony's skin was olive, and Dougall's dark brown. Now there were no colours, only shades. Julie swam a length underwater, and another, and still it wasn't enough. After the third pulling length the heat was gone and she came up by the wall, feeling calm and strong and beautiful. The water on her vulva and up the crack of her ass felt good.

Anthony held onto the far end and spouted water from his mouth. James leaned against the wall beside her. He smiled at her and let himself slide underwater, blowing out so he would sink to the bottom, and stayed there. To scare her. It worked, even though she knew he could hold his breath as long as she could, even though she'd done it with him more than once to scare their father's new wife when she was still new. Forget it, James, you're not sucking me in again.

She sculled out to rest beside Dougall, who lay on his back, floating. Did she love him or not? Dougall was the considering one among them, the one who annoyingly liked to look at every angle of a problem before making a decision, which made their chess games very long. A born scientist, James often told Julie, just as he, James, was a born poet, and Anthony, despite his quips about the little vermin next door, was a born father. "And what was I born to do?" Julie asked finally. "You?" he answered slowly. "You? I would say you were a born lawyer." This was not a compliment. Their father was a lawyer. James prided himself on his unflinching honesty, but when Julie tried to tell him what she really thought of his poetry, he pouted and called her a philistine. *He can dish it out, but he sure can't spoon it in*, their mother always said.

o o o

Clive laughs, of course. He can't help it. Julie is now a lawyer.

"Don't be so damn predictable, Clive," Julie says.

"You make him sound like an asshole, but you know, I think I might have liked your brother."

"Do I?" Julie says, disarmed. "It's not my intention. I mean, we're twins. If he is one thing and I am another, it's only two aspects of the same thing."

Was, Clive thinks. *Was* one thing.

o o o

The pool: Dougall's hand brushed hers as they wafted the water to stay afloat, then returned and grasped her wrist only a little awkwardly. She turned her hand palm up to meet his and they floated, looking at the sky. A mind as blank as the clouds she wanted, and almost had, but James was still on the bottom.

She dropped Dougall's hand. The water felt cool where the warmth of his palm had been. She wanted it back. She wanted to put her arm across his chest and tow him in like in a rescue, her chest against his back, her legs strong in the water, but James came up and Dougall was already swimming away. He got out and walked to his clothes, towelled himself off with his shirt. Everything he did was beautiful. She was in love with him.

o o o

"But you married Anthony," Clive says.
   "Don't interrupt."
   "But — "
   " — Ah!"
   Clive reclines on his lawn chair, puts his hands behind his head and determines to say no more until Julie either weeps or shows signs of moving inside.

o o o

In love with his body, with his quiet steady soul. She wished, fiercely, that she could draw. She wanted this scene on paper, she wanted to linger over it with a soft pencil, over the light curve of muscle either side of Dougall's spine, the brief flat triangle above and between the muscles on his ass, the water catching glints of light on his dark skin. Even James was beautiful, the skin taut and smooth over his narrow chest, the dark flop of his penis between his defiantly open legs.
   She could not draw any more than James could write poetry. Artists' souls without any talent. She swam another three lengths and used the ladder in the deep end to get out. It was James and Anthony who watched her walk to her clothes.
   By the time they got home they were sweating again, but it was a sweat that would dry smooth under a single cotton sheet. Her body would feel cool and clean at dawn.
   Of course it would sweat right up again as soon as she rose, wetting the band of her Dici bra by the time she got to the bus stop, making her back stick to the bus seat, her legs stick to the subway seat and everything stickable stick to the streetcar seat all the way to the CNE and her stinking sauna of a job making fries and hotdogs and filling up the machines with coke syrup at the CHUM Summer Midway.
   On a day so hot that the idea of touching another body was almost unthinkable, Julie thought about Dougall, imagined

the two of them revelling in the slick of sweat between them, imagined them in and out of the pool, laughing and tasting chlorine and salt in their kisses.

Julie got home around nine, just as the sun was thinking about going down, not that that would make a big difference in temperature, what with the smog containment field and the cement sidewalks, the blacktop streets, the brick houses and pebble shingles emitting the radiation absorbed during the day. She came around the back and found James lying in the wading pool, arguing with Anthony, on a lawn chair today with his guitar. They were trying again to write songs together, but James kept wanting to write the music as well as the lyrics.

"Quelle belle vue. Est-ce que tu vois le lac?" Julie said. It was the opening line from one of their Grade Nine French *dialogues*, which were so ludicrous they were still funny three years later.

"You're interrupting the creative flow," James said.

"Oui, il y a des castors là-bas," Dougall called from the kitchen window.

"Who's calling who a castor?" Anthony yelled.

Inside, Dougall was staring into the fridge. He looked up when she came in, and for a moment it seemed they would never have anything to say to one another, though they had talked endlessly in the past. Then Julie said, as she must, "Vite, vite, où est mon appareil?" and the moment was over.

"Oh, que je suis bête! Je l'ai laissé à l'hôtel," Dougall said, smacking his forehead. Julie was suddenly aware of how much she smelled of french fries.

"Uh, I'm going to go take a shower," she said.

"Jacques, regard la foule là-bas," Dougall said.

The ravine run: three pools along one side of the ravine, two on the other. Anthony, comically, dangerously loudly, plunged into the first, shorts, shoes, glasses and all, without breaking stride. He wore a spaz strap on his glasses, which, with his height and his short kinky hair, did not make him look spazzy, but made him look less like Kareem Abdul-Jabar than he imagined. Dougall and Julie took the time to kick off their shoes before slipping in, quietly, after him. Two lengths was the rule for the ravine run, and Anthony was out, dripping and laughing, by the time the purist James disengaged his long bony foot from the liner of his track shorts and lowered himself into the pool. Julie saw a light come on in the house while they waited for him, but no one emerged yelling or waving their fists. James scooped his shoes and shorts at a run, and the four of them faded into the bushes, hopped the illegally low fence and went on at a trot along the footpath on the marge of yard and cliff-edge, the squelch of Anthony's wet shoes punctuating each step.

It was at the first pool on the far side that they nearly got caught. The pool was closer to the house than most and took up more of the comparatively small yard, but the house had air conditioning, which meant the windows were shut and the engine made a loud whirr to mask the small noise of their strokes.

Julie, Anthony and Dougall crept from their reconnaisance position between the cedar hedge and the six-foot cedar fence, keeping low, continuing to scout for danger before slipping into the water. Then James came at a run and hit the water with a roaring cannonball that wet the deck tiles on three sides. Three heads came up to look at the house.

Sure enough, the porch light went on. Julie cleared the pool full-speed. She looked back as she chucked her shoes over the fence. The sliding door opened, and a man in pyjamas stepped out onto the deck.

"Hey!" he yelled. "Hey, what do you think you're doing?" He threw his cigarette into the bushes and ran down towards them.

Julie hoisted herself up on the fence and flipped her legs over. Before she dropped on the other side, she saw that although Dougall and Anthony were not far behind her, James had just made his turn and meant to finish his two lengths.

He would not make pool's end before the angry householder, whose flapping slippers had just reached the pool deck. James, her James, would be trapped and naked. And he would laugh — at her concern for him as much as at the householder's outrage. So much to hate about someone you love. He was a child.

"Come on, man," Anthony wailed. "Don't fuck around." But James did not hurry or change his course.

"Jane," bellowed the man. "Jane, call the police."

The thin ridge of the fence bit into Julie's hands. Her arms were starting to shake from supporting her weight on them. She'd have to drop or flip a leg back over. A light went on in one of the upstairs windows. Julie dropped.

"Bob?" came a woman's voice. "Bob, what's going on out there?"

She was answered by a shout of surprise and a thud. The man had fallen. "Fuck, fuck, fuck," he said.

Dougall dropped beside Julie. They waited, listening.

"Oh, man, are you okay?" Anthony said. His shoes squelched towards the fallen man.

They could hear James getting out of the pool. "That was refreshing," he said loudly. He was worse than a child, he was a cruel child. Julie hated him even as she knew herself capable of equal cruelty, though it would always take a different form.

"Are you okay?" Anthony said again. The man groaned.

"Little shits. No fucking respect — "

"No, but are you hurt?" Anthony insisted.

"Don't you laugh at me, punk. Don't you dare laugh at me."

Anthony did laugh, in astonishment. "I'm not, I swear."

"Leave him, Anthony." This was James.

"Bob? I called the police. Bob?"

"Jane?"

"Fuck it," Anthony said. His squelching shoes ran towards the fence. Julie took off down the path, Dougall following. She could hear Anthony's shoes land and then follow, and the sound made her laugh, though nothing else was funny. She cut down a path into the ravine, grabbing onto branches and trees to keep her balance.

"Where are you going?" James called out from the top of the cliff. They stopped.

"Where do you think?" Julie said as quietly as she could and still be heard.

"We're not finished yet."

"I am. I'm finished."

"Half-miler."

"Fuckhead. You're the one that ruined it."

"Ruined it! I made it better. I made it real."

"Oh, grow up, James." Dougall usually stayed out of their arguments. Even James was surprised into silence, a long silence. By the end of it Julie got the sense that James had turned it into a dare.

"Put your shorts on, for god's sake," Dougall said finally, and turned down the hill. Julie went after him.

o o o

Julie is silent for so long that Clive opens his eyes and sits up. Julie stares at the sky. He gets off his lawn chair, pushes it out of the way and lies down beside her.

"Look, they're going so fast it's like the building is moving," she says.

It's true, the grey clouds are scooting across the sky.

"What happened after that?" Clive asks after a while.

"Dougall and I made out in the park," Julie says.

"And James finished the ravine run?"

"With Anthony. Good ol' loyal Anthony."

"And?"

"After Thanksgiving, James quit school and went out west. Only came back for the wedding and then stayed drunk pretty much the whole time. I thought I knew why. His best friend, his twin sister. He wasn't the main thing anymore. But I thought we'd got over that."

Another long silence.

"I didn't even know he was here, Clive. I didn't even know he was back. How could I not know? We were twins, and it's been so hot." Clive doesn't follow the logic of this until she says, "How could he have endured the heat without calling me?"

Clive doesn't know, and doesn't say either that James didn't endure the heat, that the heat is still not over.

Julie and Clive lie out on the deck all night. In the morning, he puts her to bed, angling the fan to blow cool arcs on her sleeping body.

Virginia

Half an hour ago the counter had been a gleaming, faux-gran-ite expanse that gave Megan a small shiver — after the drain-ing-board-sized counter of their apartment, what a luxury, eight feet, eight whole feet of counter space. (Part of the shiver, a fraction of it, came from the thought of the two men who had designed this kitchen and built it, believing they'd be cooking in it for years to come. One of them was dead now. Megan felt like a vulture, living in their house. She'd get over it.)

How quickly luxuries start to seem like necessities. Now the counter was as crammed as the old one after dinner for eight. Megan had dumped everything on the counter, thinking that once it was visible she'd have a clearer idea of where it ought to go, but she was still undecided. Should the wine glasses go above the sink or above the fridge? What about the colander and the cheese grater — should they go with the bowls or with the pots, or should they maybe hang somewhere instead? Should the cutlery go beside the stove or beside the dishwasher? My god, they had a dishwasher. Never mind, they wouldn't use it. Maybe after dinner parties. On Energy Saver mode.

Megan surveyed the overwhelming stack of kitchenwares and decided to work on the pantry instead. Baking supplies on the back wall, the Mason jars of dried beans and rice on the left, food processor and mixer on shelf nearest door, canned goods on the right. As she shelved cans, she noticed how tired her arms were from the move. A tin of chick peas felt like a five-pound weight.

A sudden boom like an electric bass made Megan drop a can. It cracked across her kneecap.

"Sorry," Ann yelled from the living room.

Those were their priorities: Megan, food; Ann, audio-visual.

Megan was glad to be doing something on her own after the last few days' squabbles over how to pack boxes, how to load the van, which end of the couch should go first through the door. She was glad their friends had left and she didn't have to communicate anymore; she just had to take things out of boxes and put them on shelves.

Joan Armatrading played on the stereo. Ann came into the pantry and wrapped herself around Megan, who was still crouched at the lowest shelf.

"Enough," Ann said.

Megan kept unloading cans. Ann prodded her in the ribs. "I want to finish this," said Megan.

Ann kissed Megan's neck and ran her hands up the inside of her thighs.

Megan sat for a moment, wondering how exactly she felt, whether she wanted to be aroused or whether she wanted Ann to leave her alone.

"Isn't it great?" Ann whispered fiercely. Megan could feel the little hairs on her neck lifting. "Isn't it just unbe-fuckin-lievably great!?" She meant the house and the two of them, that it was theirs. It was.

Megan turned around and pulled Ann on top of her. "I knew this would be the first album you'd put on," she said. Ann grinned and kissed her slowly, and Megan was taken aback for the eight-hundredth time by the softness of her lips.

When the phone rang, they didn't pick it up.

Patty called again the next morning. "I thought I'd go down about, oh, two o'clock. I think that's when visiting hours start for the afternoon. They don't operate till tomorrow. Do you want to come with me?"

"I have no idea what you're talking about," said Megan.

"Didn't you get my message?"

"No."

"Oh." Long pause. "Aunt Ginnie fell. Broke her hip. She's at the Wellesley." If you cared, her sister's tone said, you'd know, you'd have listened to your messages.

"How?" Megan asked. "What happened?"

o o o

Ignominious to come into hospital in a bathing suit when you're in the swim of life (groan!), but at my age you feel especially foolish. They unwrap the blankets and the lifeguard's terry robe and what they see is nothing new to them, another body to be fixed. That they hold no shame seeing the white wrinkly thighs, the spotted brown chest sagging out the sides of a suit that's grown too big, makes my own shame monstrous, out of all proportion to the event. In that moment I swear I'll never go to the pool again to slip on some man's spit, slimy on the tiles, to end up here contemplating the insertion of a piece of plastic to do a job my own bones once did admirably on their own.

You hurt yourself and you start to notice how many muscle contractions and nerves and synapses it takes to make the smallest movement, even sliding a pen across a page. No wonder, then, I couldn't put away my diary fast enough when they all trooped in. Megan excited as can be to find me writing in it. "I didn't know you kept a diary, Aunt Ginnie."

"Ever since I was fourteen," I said, "but don't get your hopes up about reading them, my dear. I burn 'em, every year, on my birthday."

"Who said anything about reading them?"

Ah-ah-ah, you can't fool me. I can see it in your eyes, girl. Nigh on time to do it again.

Convenient having your birthday the first of the year. You can start fresh, or you can fool yourself into thinking so. A

new number to give yourself. I'm twenty-one this year, you
can say to yourself. When people ask how old I am, I can say,
I'm twenty-one, that's much better than twenty. And then, I'm
thirty-five this year. Thirty-five, think of it. All of a sudden,
it's My goodness, I'm sixty, of all things, would you believe
it? Eighty-two this time. It doesn't bear thinking about. And
Susan always twenty-nine.

Oh, it hurts. Yes, it does hurt.

I asked Patty to get some things from the apartment. It's
instinct to ask Patty first, I must watch that. Megan seemed
to take it as a comment on her. Which I suppose it is, and
probably unfair now that she's grown up. Never big on chores
at the farm, that one, only liked certain tasks — mowing with
the scythe, painting the shed — the big chores, not dishes and
sweeping. Whatever it was, sweeping or mowing, she'd do it
her own way, whether it was most efficient or not. Easily side-
tracked, Megan. Like Sinead, now. Funny.

Sinead. I wonder if she wanted to come or if she had to be
asked? Never mind. I'm glad she came. She'll turn out to be
responsible too, some day, they usually do. Too bad about the
name, though. I never liked it. The family hasn't been Irish
for a long time, I said to Patty when she was born, why sad-
dle her with a name no one will be able to spell? Now I hear
there's a singer, really Irish, with the same name and a shaved
head. Quite famous, so the spelling's not an issue anymore.
Our Sinead hasn't cut her hair for years. She tells me she doesn't
brush it either — it gets all matted and she likes it that way.

Poor Patty. She only sees the glaring close-up things about
her daughter — the hair, the slouching, the curled lip. She
doesn't see the bright eyes, the shyness, the brave face put on
uncertainty.

Megan's doctor friend, now, Ann. So stiff and nervous and
brusque even for the few minutes she stopped in. You could
feel Megan relax when she went off to her own hospital. And
they've bought a house together. Well, now.

o o o

Aunt Ginnie had lived in the same apartment on St. Clair for as long as Megan could remember. At four, she had spent her first night away from her parents there, but it wasn't till she was six that Megan was able to convince her mother to let her go up on her own. Her mother could watch from the car to see she was safely buzzed in. Everything would be fine.

Getting buzzed in was not the best part, but it was very good. To press a button on the ground and have her great-aunt's hand open the door from five storeys up — yes, it was very good. They'd had a password, she and Ginnie, she couldn't remember it.

The elevator, that had been the best part, a mechanism so antique it could only be called a lift, with a brass gate you had to pull across and clang shut so it echoed up and down the elevator shaft. Then the hum of the machinery, the chug and lurch of take-off before settling into the gentle rise to the fifth floor where Aunt Ginnie waited in the corridor.

On Megan's first solo trip up to Aunt Ginnie's, she had put her hands on the handrails, lifted herself up and jumped off. She was six, she was taking an elevator by herself like it was a matter of course. She couldn't stop jumping. She loved the way the floor met her feet faster than the ground usually did. And then the elevator shuddered and stopped.

Because she had jumped? Her mother had told her not to jump in elevators, but she had taken that to be yet another of her mother's arbitrary rules. Don't fidget. Don't talk too loud. Don't make that noise pushing air through your teeth. Slow down.

Megan pushed the fifth floor button again. Nothing. Then a whine came from high above, and the floor fell. All her weight left her feet and glommed together in her chest before slamming back into her feet and leaving an airy feeling around her heart.

The elevator had dropped only a few feet and would drop no further, but Megan did not know that and stood next-tomotionless for the next half-hour, not daring even to crouch down in the corner.

When Megan told the story to friends, she repeated the first thing she had said to Aunt Ginnie when the firefighters lifted her out: "Don't tell Mom. She'll never let me do anything again." She didn't actually remember saying it, but that was the way she always told the story. What she did remember was the wool of Aunt Ginnie's lapel against her face, scratchy and warm. She didn't tell Ginnie about jumping, and consequently was never entirely disabused of the notion that it had been her fault — and that it could happen again.

"They've put in a new elevator," her mother said matter-of-factly the next time they went to Ginnie's together. "About time." Megan wanted to take the stairs but thought she'd give herself away if she said so. She puzzled her mother by clutching her hand and standing perfectly still on the way up.

Now the building that had loomed above a six-year old was not only brought down to size by adult eyes, but was dwarfed by a gleaming tower next door, as if Ginnie's building had shrunk. It seemed dirtier, too, drab and old-fashioned, like the tenants who lived there, perennials in brown wool suits pulling wire shopping carts.

Ginnie had given her clear instructions about where to find the things she wanted, but Megan walked slowly around the apartment, examining the place in a way she hadn't had the leisure to do before. The whole back wall in the alcove where Ginnie kept her desk was covered with school pictures, rows and rows of girls in kilts and crisp blouses. The early ones, at the top, were Ginnie's home-room classes and had chummy inscriptions, like "To Briny, Form III's Salty Captain, 1938. XOXOXO." Then later, when she became headmistress, "To Miss O'Brien. With affection, Class of '53." And later again, no inscriptions at all. It must have gone out of fashion.

On the left wall were pictures of family, and on the right, friends. The only photo actually on the desk was an old one showing the farmhouse, where Ginnie still holidayed, in the background, and a young woman on a campstool in front of an easel in the foreground. Ginnie's painter friend, the one who had died young, whose paintings dotted the apartment. Megan couldn't remember her name.

She toyed with the handle of the top right desk drawer, pulled it out as far as the pen tray, then pushed it back in. Did Ginnie really burn her diaries? What was in them she didn't want people to know?

She opened the drawer again, all the way. Just pens and paper, envelopes and stamps. She opened the left drawer. An account book, ruler, scissors. It was the same in the other drawers, everything spare and neat. No diary. Megan felt hot and silly, and hurried to collect Ginnie's things.

"She won't be able to go back to her apartment, not right away, anyway," Megan said to Ann that night. They were in the bathroom, Megan on the toilet, Ann washing her face.

"Why don't you just say you want her to stay with us?" Ann said.

"I thought that's what I was doing."

"No, you were skirting around the issue, trying to get me to say it."

"Okay. I want to ask Aunt Ginnie if she would like to stay with us in our big new house. How do you feel about that, Ann?"

o o o

This or a convalescent hospital — well, the choice is clear. And it's not so bad. An opportunity, really, to get to know Megan better. Ann, too, I suppose.

Used to be we did a lot of visiting. Only took a few days to feel comfortable in someone else's house. No more. Even the farm doesn't have the same drop-in-any-time feeling it used to, that happy confusion of comings and goings, the nights we had to pitch the big tent in the dark to accommodate unexpected latecomers.

The flowers were doubtless Megan's touch. She beamed when I said how nice and colourful they were. I couldn't very well say I've never been fond of cut flowers, could I? Give them away, I told the nurses at the hospital, give them away. I can't stand to see the poor things wilt. How much better to find them still in the ground, still attached to their roots. But Susan, too, loved flowers in the house. She'd see a flash of colour on the roadside and we'd have to stop to gather them, whoever was in the car. She'd always take care to leave some for others, though. I remember one time, I was in a fury — I wonder why? — and we passed a stand of irises. She wouldn't let me alone until I turned around and went back. There I was, madly ripping them out of the ground, just to be done with it. The catch in her voice when she said, "Virginia, you've left none for the next people." Oh, I felt like such an oaf next to her. An oaf one minute and a prude the next. The things she could come out with. Yet she was entirely of a piece.

Megan asked about her yesterday. "Tell me again about your painter friend — what was her name? — the one in the picture on your desk." "Susan," I said. "Susan George." What could I say about Susan? How had I talked about her before? "We were great friends," I said. "We were the youngest of the teachers, you see, everyone else was forty or older, and we were in our twenties. I'd been there three years and they were still calling me 'the new history teacher.' She was 'the new art teacher,' and everyone was talking about her. 'Did you see what the new art teacher was wearing? Oh, my!' Bohemian, they thought, because she'd lived in Paris and New York. And she *was* worldly for Toronto, I must say, such a provincial town in those days. But the girls loved her — " My pause there, like leaving a blank, Megan's quick look. I felt suddenly very tired and did not tell her any more.

Ann is up early. Companionable as I've seen her, though still a little stiff, or maybe gruff is a better word. She saw the light on under my door and thought to bring coffee in, offered the paper when she was done with it. Perhaps we will get along.

∘ ∘ ∘

Ginnie was asleep when Megan poked her head in the door at eight o'clock. The newspaper lay across her chest, her mouth was open like a pouch. Megan tried not to feel distaste for it, and failed. The body becomes more obvious as it grows older, she thought, more crude. Megan habitually argued against the duality between body and spirit, but Aunt Ginnie's body, asleep, its mouth open, seemed to hold nothing of the woman Megan knew Ginnie to be. It was a receptacle, and an inadequate one at that. Did you see things differently if you grew old alongside someone? Ann was there in her body always. If Megan watched her too long she would wake up, blinking and uncertain, until she recognized Megan with a grunt and rolled over.

Ginnie's mouth closed, opened again, closed. Megan knocked lightly on the door. Ginnie raised herself slowly to a sitting position.

"Help me up, would you, dear?"

"You don't want to do the exercises first?" Megan said. Leg lifts, ankle turns — she had a list from the physiotherapist.

"Getting out of bed is exercise enough," Ginnie said, swinging her legs over the edge of the bed. Her nightgown bunched up around her hips, revealing her shiny tight shins, the skin on them peeling and translucent like layers of mica, and above, the loose leathery folds of the skin on her thighs. She held her arm out expectantly. Megan hurried to the bed.

"One, two, three, up."

Standing, Ginnie's arm had to reach up to rest on Megan's shoulders. This was new. It had been Ginnie's height, together with her easy, square-shouldered posture, that had given her her presence. Her voice had something to do with it as well, rich as it was, and round. Like her building, or unlike it, Ginnie had actually shrunk.

The ground-floor washroom was an elegant little room. Its pedestal washstand and toilet, if they weren't the original fixtures, were certainly vintage and in near-perfect condition.

Megan imagined the house's previous owners hunting them down on weekends at small-town flea markets and estate sales.

Unfortunately, as they had discovered the night before, the room was too small for Ginnie to manoeuvre in with the walker. It was an awkward production, and no smoother for one day's practice. Ginnie went ahead this time, holding onto the washstand for support, then turned, poised above the toilet. Megan came forward and loosely wrapped both arms around her. Ginnie turned her head away.

"Okay?" Megan said.

Ginnie nodded and tried to hoist her nightgown, a jerky motion that set her off-balance. She teetered and suddenly fell. Megan wasn't braced to take the weight heading away from her and not down. Ginnie landed heavily, knocking into the tank. She let out a startled yelp as the porcelain tank banged against the wall, cracking the lid.

"Are you all right?" Megan asked. No answer. "Aunt Ginnie?"

"I'm *fine*," her aunt said in a determined whisper.

Ginnie wriggled, trying to settle herself onto the toilet properly, her head down, her hands curled into fists. She had not managed to get the nightgown up.

"Are you sure?"

"I'm fine," she repeated in a tight voice. "Fine."

"How are we going to get this nightie up? Do you want me to lift you?"

Ginnie was shaking. "Leave — me — in — peace," she said.

Megan backed out of the bathroom and closed the door behind her. She felt the sting, the bewilderment of being chastised by someone from whom you don't expect it — a friend's mother, a normally kindly neighbour, a driver at a stop light. It lingered in her chest as she went to put the kettle on.

The rain slanted in on the kitchen window, striking it in long gashes. Seeing it earlier that morning, she'd felt good about staying home, she'd felt the warmth of a lit house on a dim day. Now the rain made her feel lonely and a little cold. She did not want to see Ginnie fragile like this, small, prone to losing her balance and worse, to losing her calm. She did not want to make the mistakes she was evidently making, the indelicate references to bathrooms and nighties, the obtrusiveness of her strong, easy body trying to heave Ginnie's awkward, uncertain one to the places it needed to go.

Patty dropped by on her way home from work — her first time in the house, though she'd driven by once. Patty and James lived in North York and had got a good deal on their house when they'd bought it twelve years earlier. She couldn't believe what Megan and Ann had paid for their skinny Victorian three-bedroom, only in the Annex by the skin of its teeth, with its outdated oil furnace and uninsulated attic.

"You'll have icicles galore in the winter," Patty said as she surveyed the inside of the roof from the top of the attic stairs. "All that heat seeping through."

Megan resisted telling Patty that insulating the attic was the first item on their list of home improvements. It was true, it was first on their list, but Megan wanted to try out a new tactic. If she didn't respond defensively every time Patty made her feel defensive, would Patty stop making those comments?

"I like icicles," Megan said.

"That's our Megan," Patty said. "Form over function."

Megan turned to start back down the stairs, but Patty stayed where she was. "How are you managing with Ginnie?" she said.

"Fine."

"Of course, Ginnie's in better shape than Grandad was. Mentally *and* physically."

Megan had been out west bumming around the year Patty took their grandfather in. Patty clearly still held that against her, the way she held living in Calgary and not sending birthday presents against their brother, Graham. *Don't worry, your position as family martyr is secure*, Megan thought, knowing she wasn't being fair.

"How's Ann with it all?" Patty asked.

"Fine. She's doing fine with it all." Actually, Megan had barely seen Ann and didn't know how she was doing.

"It's really good of you to do this, Meg. The way things are around work now, I just couldn't take any time off." Like it was a favour to Patty.

"It's no problem. I wanted to. Really."

"If you want an evening off, I'd be happy to come over — "

"Sinead beat you to it, she already offered."

This was obviously news to Patty. "Has she? Well. Good for her. I'm glad she's taking an interest in family. Good."

Megan found out how Ann was feeling the next night in bed. "You're so twitchy with Ginnie here, it's driving me nuts," Ann said. "You don't kiss me hello, you don't call me Sweetie, you tiptoe around — "

"I know," Megan said, "but she's my aunt. My great-aunt."

"Your great-aunt who you think is a lesbian. Why don't you just come out to her?" Ann was out to everyone in her family — cousins, aunts, uncles, nieces, nephews. One aunt told her she was going to hell, and a sister-in-law didn't want her taking the kids overnight, but they all knew; Ann had made a point of it.

"I don't know. I mean, if I knew one way or the other it'd be easier. If I knew she was straight, no problem. Well, you know, sort of a problem, but I'd get over it. If I knew she was a dyke, no problem."

"Oh, come on. Of course she's a dyke. Headmistress of a girls' school, never marries, buys a farm with another woman, loves to hike, wears sensible shoes, coaches field hockey…"

"I know, I know. It's just, I don't know."

"I don't like being closeted in my own house."

"I know."

"I'm not going to stop kissing you hello."

"I know." Ann was right. It was stupid not to have it out in the open. But what was she going to say? *Ginnie, I'm a lesbian, and I think you are too?* It didn't feel right, any way she put it. Maybe it was cowardice, maybe it was the kind of tacit agreement that being a dyke was a bad thing or at least not something to talk about that Megan loathed in other people and other situations. But it was the way it was.

o o o

She's trying too hard, Megan is. Hovering. "Shoo," I want to say, like I do to the pigeons on my balcony. "Go on with you." Almost did say it, too. Thankfully she does have work to do. She's been enjoying this break from work, I can tell. Personally, I would want to be out of the house more. I've always made a point to get out at least once a day. Something symbolic about it, or maybe it's superstitious. Fear of becoming a shut-in. God, it might happen yet.

Bird bones. And doesn't it figure I'm having dreams about flying, me in a huge flock of grey-haired women lifting from the city into the sky, our porous bones no longer able to keep us earthbound. Bobbing like pumice at the top of the stratosphere. Huh.

Sometimes when I look in the mirror, I realize what's happened. I try to age Susan along with me, never able to get her much past forty-five. It's getting to be so I only remember how she looked from pictures. Hateful. I can see the pictures in my mind, but not her. And now I want the picture from my desk, because if I saw the picture I might be able to take the next step, to see her serious eyes in the firelight during our summers at the farm, to see her bright walk along the halls, nodding and smiling at the girls, laughing at their jokes.

It's Megan has me thinking so much about Susan, with all her questions. I can see that itch in her. She wants me to — lovely expression — spill my guts. If I wanted to write my memoirs, I would, I told her. "Why don't you, Aunt Ginnie?" she said. You're not taking my point, I didn't say.

"How did she die?" she asked today after lunch, just when I've finished digesting and at home I would be putting on my walking shoes to go down to the community centre. It's Friday, so I'd be on my way to Belmont House after that to see

Lise. Someone else who calls me Virginia. I miss it. Ginnie is an aunt's name. Virginia says something more — dignity, respect. Love. Of course, I thought Lise said my whole name because she was French. It was Susan who thought differently. I still don't know whether she was right or not. Perhaps we could have been comfortable together, Lise and I, if I'd taken her up on her offer to move in. More likely we'd have gotten on one another's nerves.

Susan was supposed to come to the farm with me that weekend, we'd a work party planned. But her mother refused to come and kept Susan home with her. In the same way she had brought Susan back to Toronto in the first place, and maybe I should thank her for that. Oh, but those pathetic letters to New York once a week, pleading. Complaining of every ailment under the sun, not to mention the shiftless house-keeper, the prison of her house, the barren society of Toronto after her husband's death. Loneliness, plain and simple. Anyone can fix loneliness, doesn't mean you have to grasp and cling.

Yes, a lonely and selfish old woman, Margot George, not even that old then. She had a cough that weekend — claimed it was TB. She'd *always* had a weak chest, she'd *always* known she'd die of consumption, how *could* Susan want to drag her off to the country on such a wet weekend, why, if she stepped out of doors, the moisture might get into her lungs and never get out.

Too little to do and too many novels was her problem. Susan let her get away with it, pampered her, even.

She lived sixteen years longer than her daughter, and what was it she died of finally? Pneumonia. No one could convince her it wasn't TB, and after a while we stopped trying. She rehearsed her dying words all that last week in a soft faltering voice. *Don't think too harshly of me, Virginia,* she'd say, then let her head fall back against the pillow and close her eyes.

"Susan was hit by a car," is what I said to Megan. "Getting off the streetcar. They didn't go too fast in those days, cars, and there weren't too many of them on the roads — the Depression and all — but there was that one, and it went fast enough." Susan had been hurrying to get to the late pharmacy before it closed. Her mother, waiting at home, thought she'd been abandoned. She thought Susan had run off to the farm after all. To me. She rang me there, screaming bullets into the phone. *I know she's there. You're pitting her against me, against her own mother, her own flesh. You let me talk to her. I don't trust you as far as I can throw you, twisting her to your own ways...* I finally got it out of her Susan had gone to the pharmacy and not come back. Probably the hospital was trying to call her even as we spoke, and there she was, tying up the line. Stupid, stupid woman.

"That must have been awful for you," Megan said. Well, yes. But don't think you know how awful. You don't.

I swear that girl wants my tears. Well, I'm not giving them away now.

o o o

Every day Megan made attempts to bring the conversation around to lesbianism, but no matter how close they got, she could never take that next step and say, You know Ann and I aren't just friends, right? It went past the point of ridiculousness and into some weird psychological barrier. After looking for every opportunity to say something, then debating internally whether this was the opportunity and losing the moment, Megan became ever more tongue-tied.

Ginnie, for her part, kept bringing conversations around to national unity.

After lunch, Megan got a desperate call from one of the board members of the 519 Community Centre, saying, "I know you're taking time off, but Martin has rubella and we need you for quorum. Can you come to tonight's meeting?"

Rubella?

Megan rode her bike to the meeting. The air was crisp. Free, free, she thought, the wind hitting her face, her legs pumping. When she was her usual insanely busy self she thought about how great it would be to just stay home and rake leaves and make bread. A week of it and she was going nuts. She called Sinead to come over and spend the evening with Ginnie.

Megan came home late from her meeting and found Ann still up in the living room, watching a rerun of *Perry Mason*. She turned off the show when Megan came in.

"Not enough Della in this one?" Megan asked, flopping down on the couch.

"There's never enough Della."

"It's not often I find you watching TV."

"Thought I'd take a break from cleaning up puke."

"Puke?"

"Your niece drank the bottle of wine that was in the fridge and then puked all over the bathroom."

"Where is she now?"

"I put her to bed. Fat lot of good she would've been to Ginnie if anything had happened."

"Oh, my god. Ginnie. Is she all right?"

"She's fine. She's asleep. Sinead must've started drinking after she'd gone to bed. It wasn't very pleasant to come home to, let me tell you."

"Oh, Ann, I'm sorry."

"Wasn't you drinking."

"Still, I'm sorry you had to deal with that."

"Yeah, well. It's family, right? You deal with it."

Or not, Megan thought, feeling guilty about still not having said anything to Ginnie. She dialled Patty's number, trying to remember if the phone was on her side of the bed or James'. James'. Score. She told him Sinead had fallen asleep and was spending the night.

Megan woke Sinead up at seven-thirty. "How are you feeling?"

"Sleepy," said Sinead. She sat up. "Oh, my god. Did you tell Mom?"

"Not sick or anything? No headache?"

Sinead shook her head. "Me-gan," she said, demanding an answer to her question.

"No. I didn't tell her."

"Thankyou, thankyou, thankyou."

"Not that I feel good about it." Sinead lay back down.

"Don't go back to sleep," Megan said.

Sinead was fourteen. What would make a fourteen-year-old want to get drunk like that. The opportunity? The bottle of wine in the fridge? Megan didn't know how to bring it up with Sinead, and she questioned again whether she ought to tell Patty. What if Sinead had done this before? What if she was starting to have alcohol problems at fourteen? It happened.

Megan had been sixteen the first time she got really drunk. One of her friends had filled two wineskins and they took them down to a concert at Ontario Place. They got cups from the concession stand and hid in the bushes to squirt wine into them before going to the concert. She couldn't remember who'd been playing. A short-lived band called Zon, maybe. She started throwing up less than halfway through. Her friends took her to the washroom, bent her over the toilet, walked her around until she was ready to take the subway home. She threw up once more, on the platform at Summerhill station. Her friends sat her on the front steps of her house, rang the doorbell and took off. They didn't know what else to do. Luckily it was Patty, home for the summer from university, who came to the door. As Patty dragged her inside, Megan could hear her mother calling, "Who is it, Patty?" "Just Megan," Patty called back. "She forgot her keys again." "Hi, Mom," Megan said. "Hi, dear, hope you had a good time," her mother said. Their father, an early-to-bed, early-to-rise kind of man — not that that saved him from an eventual heart attack — was no doubt asleep. Patty made Megan drink two full glasses of water, put her to bed and never said another word about it.

It's people within the same generation who are supposed

to stick together, Megan thought. Me and Patty and Graham against Mom and Dad. Not me and Sinead against Patty. She realized the sides must have changed some time ago and she'd never noticed. She was still playing by those other rules. When their mother called from Florida, Megan would speak glowingly of her latest visit or dinner with Patty, even if it had been a disaster. And if her mother had anything to say about Graham, Megan did her best to defend him, though she barely knew Graham anymore. While all along, Patty and their mother had probably been gossiping about both Megan and Graham, commiserating on how they had to bear all the burdens of keeping the family together. Though how her mother kept the family together living in Florida half the year, Megan couldn't say.

Ginnie was up already, eating her Grape Nuts and toast, listening to *Metro Morning*. The only things she needed help with now, two-and-a-half weeks after her operation, were stairs. It seemed like a quick recovery to Megan. That's why they used plastic hips, Ann explained. Because they start working right away. It's only the tissue and muscle that need to heal, not the bone.

Megan wanted to tell Ginnie about Sinead, but didn't know how the schoolteacher in her would react. She wondered when it would wear off, the idea that old people are more prudish than young ones, or whether it would always be that way.

"What did you and Sinead do last night," Megan asked.

"Played Scrabble."

"Did you talk at all?"

"Some, I suppose. Why do you ask?"

"I was just wondering how she's doing. In general, whether she's happy, whether she likes school. You know."

Ginnie smiled and waved her hand. "She didn't tell me anything worth passing on. I wouldn't say she's any less happy than most teenagers."

"She drank at least half a bottle of wine last night — probably more — I assume after you went to bed. Ann found her passed out on the couch and put her to bed."

Ginnie looked up sharply. "Well now, that does surprise me," she said. "They start younger and younger all the time, don't they? Drink and sex and drugs too, I suppose. At one time, we expelled girls the minute we found them doing any one of them. It's not so straightforward now, is it?"

"No. It's not."

They sat in silence for a minute.

"I didn't tell Patty," Megan said.

"No, I don't suppose you did," Ginnie said.

Sinead appeared, none the worse for her night, though she did look a mite sheepish.

"Morning," she said, pouring herself a glass of orange juice and putting on some toast.

"Good morning, dear," said Ginnie sunnily. "Another coffee would be nice, Megan."

Ginnie busied herself with the paper until Sinead sat down at the table, then she folded the paper up and peered at her great-great-niece. "One question," Ginnie said in the same cheerful tone. "What on earth were you thinking?"

Sinead went red. She toyed with her juice glass and spoke in a small, small voice. "I wanted to see what it was like. Drinking and everything. Getting drunk."

Megan felt a huge wave of relief. Way to go, Ginnie.

"And?" said Ginnie.

"What was it like?" Sinead asked. "Foggy. Like everything was far away. And spinny. Whoa, *that* was weird. That was when I, oh god, I threw up, didn't I? I'm sorry, I'm sorry, I'm sorry, I'll never do it again." She buried her head in her hands.

"Sinead, Sinead, Sinead," Ginnie said, reaching across the table and touching her on the wrist. "Buck up, it's between us. Eh, Megan?"

"That's right."

The kitchen with the three of them in it felt comfortable, the way family ought to be and rarely was. Maybe it was the looseness of their bonds that made them so easy with one another. They were three generations, but no one was parent or child to anyone else. No one could tell another what to do, or get very angry, or be disappointed, or bear much blame.

"Um, while I have you both here," Megan said, taking a breath, then speaking quickly, "you probably already know, but I wanted to make it official. Ann and I, we're not just friends, we're a couple. We're lesbians."

Megan's heart was pounding. Why'd she have to disrupt that great moment of concord? Stupid. Nonetheless, she keenly watched Ginnie for a reaction, a flinch or a turning away or a softening, a hardening, something. But no. Ginnie sat there cool as a cucumber.

"Old news," Sinead said.

"We do have eyes," Ginnie said.

o o o

So that's what she's been on about this whole time. She wants me to tell her, Yes, yes, I'm one, too, don't we have so much in common, aren't we just the same? Well, we're not. Before Ann there was Martha, and before Martha there was Simone, and before Simone, I don't remember her name, the one with the German Shepherd. For me, there was only Susan, there has always been only Susan. Oh. Dear. What would Susan make of this? She used to tease me about being prim. She used to like to swear around me and propose preposterous things I would never agree to, like wearing men's clothes and posing as a married couple, or photographing me naked in the woods. Would she have wanted more? Would she have wanted to go further than I could go? Can go? If it weren't for the school, if it weren't for my brother, if it weren't for her mother, if it weren't, if it weren't, if it weren't — oh, god, where would we be now?

Damn Megan. I won't share Susan with anyone. I won't make her less, I won't make *us* less. Our love was as pure and deep and fine as the world has known. That's what it was, nothing else.

o o o

Megan came home from dropping off Sinead and assumed Ginnie was resting when she didn't call out hello to the sound of the front door. It was time for their pre-noon walk. Megan gently pushed open the door to Ginnie's room. She wasn't there.

"Aunt Ginnie?" she called. Not in the bathroom, either. "Aunt Ginnie?"

"Up here," Ginnie called back.

Megan took the stairs two at a time. Ginnie was sitting at Megan's desk, looking out the window over her reading glasses.

"I've just been watching this pair of squirrels," Ginnie said. "They're having quite the battle over something or other. Acorns, it must be."

Megan sat on the open pull-out couch where Sinead had slept the night before. "You gave me quite a scare, there," she said. "When I didn't find you downstairs."

"I had planned to be back down by your return. The time seems to have gotten away from me this morning."

"Well. Are you ready to go down now?"

"Yes, I suppose I am." Ginnie put one hand on the back of the chair and one on the desk and pushed herself up. She teetered the slightest bit as she unhooked one cane from where it hung on the chair-back, and Megan stepped forward, her hands already poised to catch a fall.

"I'm all right, I'm all right," Ginnie said, waving Megan aside.

Megan let her go ahead and noticed then the book pushed to the corner of her desk: *Odd Girls and Twilight Lovers*. Subtitled *A History of Lesbian Life in Twentieth-Century America*. She knew she had not left it there, and Sinead had not been in any state to read before bed the night before. Must be Ginnie.

Was Ginnie going to tell her now? Now that Sinead was gone, and she'd had a chance to think about it? Megan was dying to hear the whole story — how Ginnie and Susan had come together and what happened when they did, who else knew about them, who did they have to hide from, what kind of parties did they have, did they have gay friends, what did they do for fun, where did they go dancing, *did* they go dancing? Everything.

Ginnie was already out the door, and Megan hurried to precede her down the stairs.

"Take your time," Megan said because she found Ginnie's progress painfully slow. "No need to rush things."

"How do you think I got up here?" Ginnie asked sharply.

I can wait, Megan thought. I've got lots of time. I can wait.

Ginnie wanted to have a rest before lunch rather than go for a walk. She'd had the equivalent from doing the stairs, she said, and she wanted to swim in the afternoon. Megan found no opportunity to ask her question.

They had to go by Ginnie's apartment to pick up her bathing suit and cap before going to the pool. Megan had suggested flip-flops, too, so Ginnie would have some traction on the tiles. Megan thought she would just run in while her aunt waited in the car, but Ginnie opened the car door to come with her.

"I miss my home, you know," Ginnie said.

"It only makes sense," said Megan. "Well, it won't be too much longer till you're climbing stairs like a Sherpa."

Of course they had to take the elevator, not the stairs. They rode in silence.

"You know, I still haven't told Mom about getting stuck that time," Megan said after they were off.

"Nor have I," Ginnie said. She opened the door to her apartment. "Sometimes," she continued, "you need to have experiences that are yours and no one else's. Sometimes it's better not to share everything."

Ginnie opened the door to the apartment. "Smells stuffy in here," she said. She went to the bathroom to get her things.

The alcove with Ginnie's desk in it was opposite the door. It was natural for Megan to wander over to it while she waited. Natural to look at the picture of Susan, to pick it up and feel the weight of the silver frame in her hands, to look for something hidden or revealed in the shadows of the painter's eyes.

Bugged

Everyone, eventually, is annoying. Everyone. Your dog, your best friend, that student at work who's a genuinely decent person and kinda cute to boot but has to put it all in jeopardy by making a point of having done everything culturally relevant in the late twentieth century, seen every movie (film, she would say), every band (in small venues before they were famous), every lecture (Noam Chomsky, bell hooks, Rigoberta Menchu), you name it. Your parents, god knows, your brothers and sisters, your in-laws — they're all annoying.

Notice I haven't said lover yet.

Think about it, though. Think about all the people you had crushes on, all the people you daydreamed about being with forever. Your grade nine geography teacher, for example, with his splendidly shaped hands, their springy grasslands of hair running down from rolled cuffs on under the elephant-hair bracelet he got when he was in Africa with CUSO (about which he could be counted on to reminisce for entire periods if so encouraged), to the pink marge of his fingernails. Hairy hands! You liked that once, remember? If your daydreams had come true, you might be living with not only A) a man, and B) a hairy man, but C) a hairy man who can't spell simple words, and D) a hairy misspeller whose entire life history seems to consist of one year in Africa, for all that he talks about anything else.

Think about the straight woman who lived down the hall at your university residence, the one with the porcelain skin, the wit to shave legs with and an unfortunate fondness for patchouli oil. You'd be frighteningly addicted to patchouli-ridding showers by now if you'd gotten together with her, except to tell the truth, if you had, she'd have dumped you long since and gone back to men, leaving you to wallow in olfactory nostalgia.

Or the woman on your ball team with the great vocabulary and an entire wall of classical records, the woman who cut off all her T-shirts at the navel to show off her tanned, not-quite-perfect-but-pretty-darn-close-for-forty stomach. Think about that ego now and think about your own, and know that you would have driven each other nuts, and she would have won because it was a competition — it had to be or she wouldn't have played.

They were all charming, weren't they? Yes, absolutely they were, and they weren't the only ones. Think about your exes and how your heart turned into a kettle drum and your clit sang Hallelujah the first time each of them put a careless hand on your shoulder and leaned into your ear to tell you a joke. And how annoying they got just before they dumped you. The unlidded toothpastes, the jealous recriminations, the indifference to your flirtations, the wet spoons in the sugar, their flirtations, their dependence, their independence.

And you can't neglect, while ruminating on the foibles of all these basically fine and honourable people, to think about how annoying you must yourself be at times. Your adamance about wet spoons and toothpaste. Your surliness before noon. Your apparent inability to pass on important phone messages, your tardiness returning your own phone calls, your slapdash housekeeping, your habit of leaving unbloodied panty-liners in your underwear so they go through the wash and little white bits stick to everything else.

Everybody is annoying eventually, so why not your lover too? Okay. There. I said it. Your lover too.

There's the small things, like leaving her towel on the floor or never taking her turn to talk to the landlord. And then there are the other things, the things you think might be bigger, but you don't know if it's just you've been with her longer than anybody else, making them natural, endurable annoyances. For instance, what? Well, for instance, the way she finishes your sentences for you. The way she says how nice you look when you dress up, as if you don't do it often enough for her liking. The way she wants you home at a certain time. The way she makes you feel married. The way she makes you correct yourself and say "I feel married" instead of "You make me feel married."

The way she cranks up the heat in the winter instead of putting on sweaters and saving a good third of the gas bill. It's true she is skinny and chronically cold and she can't help that, but she also hates feeling bundled up. She hates the feeling of a turtleneck around her neck, she hates the weight of sweaters and the static charge of fleece, the cling of long underwear. Even so, she wears flannel pyjamas to bed at night, buttoned up to the top, the bottoms tucked into wool socks. This, while you wear your thinnest boxers and kick off the covers. She wants you to snuggle up to her, and you suspect her of being entirely mercenary, wanting your body heat, so you don't at first, and then you do. "This feels great," she says. It does, and you feel bad for doubting her motives, and then she says, "It's the first time I've been warm all day."

You roll over, away from her. "What? What did I say?" she asks.

"Nothing. I'm hot."

She props herself up on her elbow waiting for you to say more. How does she know there's more? Why can't she just accept things at face value? You're hot, that's all.

"You've been bugging me," you want to say. "Okay, or I've been feeling bugged. For weeks. More than that. Months. Little things. Like, minuscule, ridiculous stupid things. And I don't know if it's related, but I've started thinking about — you know — other people. What they're like. What they'd be like. It's nothing big. It's little, it's just, little, it's there, you know?" And you say it. Rolled over, not looking at her.

"Look at me," she says. A command. "Look at me." You look at her, her brown eyes hot with something that's not anger, or not just anger. "You big gomer," she says, taking your wrists and flipping on top of you. "You think you're the only one?"

There's a bite in her kiss. It releases something in you. Your clit ain't singing gospel now, it's singing pure roadhouse raunch, and your lover, your skinny lover, is so hot she undoes her paisley pyjama top and chucks it in the corner. You sit up and press your lips to her breastbone, turn your head left and right, drinking in the weighty promise of flesh. She pushes your shoulders back onto the bed and holds them there, grazing her nipples all over your face but out of reach of your tongue. She's got you now, and you realize that in ten years — Jesus, ten years — there has not been a single thing she's done in bed or in the kitchen or bathroom or car or anywhere else you've entangled your bodies that has bothered you in the least. Not a single thing.